Prometheus Rising

Prometheus Rising

Take Back Your Destiny

Köhne

Jason Köhne is also the author of *Born Guilty—Liable for Compensation Subject to Retaliation*, *Go Free—A Guide to Aligning with the Archetype of Westernkind*, and *It's a Comedy Dammit!*.

Jason Köhne (/ˈkuːnə/ *koo-nuh*)

Printed by CreateSpace

iv

Dedication

I dedicate this work to white children. They will suffer far more than we have if we do not secure the Wellbeing of Westernkind.

Important Note: Friends, as I am a vocal champion for White Wellbeing, the antiwhites relentlessly endeavor to ruin me. I am not immune to these attacks. I need your help to stay afloat. Can you provide legal, financial, or some other assistance? Reach out to me:

Website: NoWhiteGuilt.org

LinkTree: https://linktr.ee/nowhiteguiltnwg

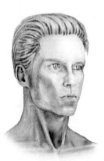
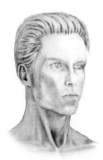

Promethean   Masule-azai

The Vyresh, Sarraneem, and Masule-azai are fictional races. They are employed as foils to teach Westmen about themselves rather than teach Westmen about these fictional races or any other real races of man. All characters, peoples, events etc. that bear any resemblance to actual individuals, peoples, and events are purely misinterpretations in the mind of the reader, as this is a work of fiction. Any attempt to define or describe this work of fiction as other than the author's, Jason Köhne, intent is intentional misrepresentation for the purpose of misleading others.

Sarraneem   (Faces by Ezra)   Vyresh

Contents

The Beginning

1.1

Void—neither light nor dark, neither before nor after, neither life nor death. It was the absence of substance. It was a nothing without measure. It was a time without time. And yet, before the nothing, despite the nothing, against the nothing, there came a Will like to a shadow, a Will as of armies amassed, their lines without end, their wrath without pity, their scope without measure: coalescing in boundless power, coalescing and then passing as ivory mist on a placid breeze, tumbling toward the shoreless margins of eternity.

Yet, before the nothing, despite the nothing, against the nothing—the Will returned. Defiance it wielded against void's defiance, resolve it summoned against the nothing's resolve, time it loosed against the moment without time. The Will as shadow returned, the beating of its heart a dazzling light, and void recoiling before it. A single Thought there then arose, a phantom in gossamer halo, and there amid the body of Will—a crash as of thunder and a piercing light of creation.

As a naked flame, the Thought gave light to others, and these were become liquid currents of fire. Flaming waters, now webbing, now climbing, burst forth in a restless plume of sparks, soaring for the raven crown atop the body of shadow. Drawing from the depths, rising to the heights, like the stars against the midnight heavens, consciousness awoke in scintillating triumph. And lo, of his own will—Prometheus was come!

The nothing glowered over him, gaped beneath him, and loomed about him, but Prometheus was undaunted, and thus he hurled tendrils of thought into the vast emptiness of void, probing the nothing, searching for others; yet others there were not, for he was alone in his contemplation before aught else was come.

Yea, wise was he in his beginning, and yet wiser he became as thought he gave to well-nigh all things—ere the coming of their seasons. It chanced on a time that, springing from these musings, there suddenly appeared matter inchoate, lifeless fragments scattered throughout the timeless expanse. Then it was that Prometheus perceived his passage, for though his thoughts stretched forth to the ends of void, his will and consciousness had place and time, so that, by and through these new formations, he reckoned motion and regarded range.

Unlike to himself was the matter inchoate. It harbored no thoughts, nor lived without heed; neither was it shaped, nor was it complete, for it teetered on the cusp of creation, a potential as of clay to be formed by the will of another. Enamored by the thoughts that took wing in his mind, he gathered the Cosmic Clay when through the nothing he traveled: a wayfarer in measureless gardens, an artist amassing his tools. Long he harvested the embryonic Clay, and where he had gathered it there was again become void.

As the gardener who prunes with an eye to the future, Prometheus worked the fields within void for time beyond measure. And when to his liking the fields took shape, his thoughts abruptly turned toward the will of another: a consciousness had flashed into being—near and yet far, a life across the vastness of void.

Slowly there followed, one after the other, like stars that peek through night clouds, tiny flames on fragile wings—wet from the moment of creation. Of these sparks there came to be scattered like pearlescent gems against the abyss of void, Gods in their infancy, orbs of airy crystal set amid cloaks of glimmer and shadow.

Long, Prometheus regarded the latecomers, for he knew in watching that though no two Gods had similar origins, coming not from his secret thoughts, he saw in them a beginning—different, and yet not unlike to his own. And though their glory and their power shone far dimmer and far weaker, drawn was he to that which was similar.

He watched as the latecomers harvested the Clay, yet they gathered without heed for the future—and destroyed what Prometheus had made. He watched as they became aware of one another, but of him they had taken no notice, for when toward him they turned their attention, their sight he darkened, their thoughts he muddled.

At length, the Cosmic Clay was gathered, amassed in great hordes by the Gods. Long they sat idle thereafter, for like to the swift years of youth to those who are bent and weary, purpose had fled with the end of the harvest. Sadness was come to the Lord, though not for himself, but for the misery of others he felt as his own. Yet, in time, he returned to the thoughts he had abandoned when the first of the latecomers was come to the nothing.

And again his thoughts took flight, and from his fathomless musings a new wonder arose; for great fields of fire leapt suddenly into void, alight like the consciousness of the Gods. Mesmerized by the quivering fire that glowed so much like the fires of their thoughts, all were drawn toward the radiant glory, beckoning as a glistening mote upon void's endless horizon.

Their thoughts reaching thither, to the shores of the flaming sea the Gods all sped. First to the flames was a God who would name himself Zeushin. Nearest to him the liquid fields of whirling amber sprang into being, climbing like great coiling stalks of corn, husks adorned in flowering clusters, fiery petals alight with the pirouette of emerald flames.

Great shadows bearing coruscating swarms amid their roiling folds drew round the fields of fire; and thus, not of their desire but of their doing, there formed the assembly of the Gods. Within the immeasurable depths of void, there arose the likes of a prodigious coliseum—the fields a stage of mystifying fire, and thousands of Gods arrayed like legislators in the seats of divine governance. Of varying strengths were all, yet none approached the radiance and power of he whose thoughts begat the Clay and kindled the Fires—Lord Prometheus, the First and the Last.

With little notice of his neighbors, each gazed in love and amazement at the Flames of Life, for though the Gods sensed their own lives would endure not forever, though their spans be unfathomable by the reckoning of man, within these fires burned the potential of eternity. And yet agelessness was not their greatest promise, for they concealed a magick the Gods wielded not, a magick of ennobling splendor, limitless and beyond reckoning.

With their thoughts to the Fire and their backs against void, each became aware that a great company had assembled to look upon the new wonder, to marvel at the majesty of un-bodied life inchoate. Long they sat in silence, each taking counsel with himself; yet at length, Prometheus arose as a figure of fire and smoke. Wrought by his secret thoughts into the sketch of man, he strode to the center of the stage, its hissing fires licking at his knees.

Addressing the assembled, he propounded a theme, a theme more wondrous than they had imagined. He spoke of the Cosmic Clay, of how with it they might shape themselves an abode, a universe, and worlds upon which to live and take comfort. Each God, he said, would use the Clay that they had gathered to bring this creation into *being*, and he would instruct them in this task, teaching them, guiding their hands; for, these things he had envisioned, foreshadowing their making.

When he had finished, his audience moved not; for they were amazed by the spectacle of the God before them, dazzled by the beauty of his radiance, awed by the powers of his genius, each considering Prometheus with the same wonder and reverence a man holds for a God. And yet, it has long been held that not all turned to Prometheus with adoration and purity of heart, for the wise say that in that hour, the first seeds of evil were secretly sown in the hearts of some, and there—under the heavy rains of jealousy and envy, tangled roots shot forth into the dark, quiet soil of malice.

At length, the assembly stirred, and then it roared in unison a thunderous embrace for the theme propounded by the Lord. And yet even more wondrous was his second theme; for then it was that Prometheus spoke words of incantation, describing how they might harvest the Flames of Life, and how they might fashion the Cosmic Clay to receive the radiance of the Fire—that the Clay might *live*, even as the Gods live. Their work, he said, he would guide also in this endeavor; for their joy was his joy.

As each, according to their prowess, comprehended the words of Lord Prometheus, they fell silent and worshiped him.

When from their homage they finally arose, a solemn duty lay before them, but Zeushin, second in power and glory only to Prometheus, determinedly swept onto the blazing stage, even as he bellowed to the assembly.

"These flames I name unto myself, for to these shores I was first to come. Then it was that I laid claim upon the fire."

"Whence did the flames come?" asked Prometheus, his gentle but cryptic tone revealing that he alone had been their source.

Zeushin replied not, but wavered, his wrath ebbing and cooling even as a man's face ebbs and cools when he senses his wrongdoing or doubts his position.

"Will you not but share the fire—that we may all take part in the creation of life?" continued Prometheus, his mien polite, yet deep and potent.

"We do not seek to take by force that which you have named unto yourself, but only to create things that we *all* may love and cherish."

His words humbled Zeushin, spurring him to thoughtful silence. But ere long, in the waxing of wisdom that blooms in the cooling heart, Zeushin responded, "To us, you have given much hope and promise, Lord. I will share the flames equally with all, but before the division I shall take three for myself—that they may serve as symbols of my generosity and my willingness to heed the enlightened counsel of others."

Thereupon, Zeushin solemnly plucked three shimmering flowers, their emerald flames lissomely adance upon amber petals, and he held them aloft for all to bear witness.

Here now was come the beginning of their labors, the building of the fount of all ages, the foundations upon which all must climb and none can delve, for they began their work on the cosmos.

Creation

2.1

First in his hands was the Clay that would become the backcloth of the universe, which Prometheus skillfully fashioned before his silent audience. Awestruck and transfixed as when men consider the artifice of the magician and know not the answers to his riddles, so too did the Gods attentively behold their benefactor and Lord.

Whispering secret words, Prometheus wrought the malleable Clay with unequaled craft, unrivaled power. When finished, he opened his hands, and by an act of his will, a thing new and unforeseen grew therefrom. It sped to the far reaches of void—and it was not void.

"To this work, I give the name—Vedyah. Within its vast and consuming halls, all our efforts shall turn,"

Such was the darkness that cocooned the Gods that its like shall never come again. And yet, as soon as it wrapped round the Lord and his audience, he fashioned the first lights of heaven; for suddenly, an un-darkness grew in mingled beams from between his clenched fingers.

Then to his lips he raised his cupped hands, and he loosed a divine breath, and carried on the winds that issued therefrom were innumerable stars in their infancy, corkscrewing and dancing into the abyss, a symphony of lights fanning through the darkness.

Stars of varying colors soared as cosmic embers across a featureless backdrop: rubies and emeralds, citrines and aquamarines, diamonds and sapphires of blues and yellows, gemstones alight with internal fires. Like golden brushstrokes across the cosmic canvas, heated mists began to glow nigh and round the new formations, bathing the Gods in gilded majesty.

As one who sows so a harvest may be reaped, or tends the fair garden so that flowers may come forth for the delight of the planter, Prometheus cast worlds to the ether, bright and glowing from the heat of their making. Like great swarms of opalescent moths, the planets hurtled to the margins of the glimmering stars. Rings they formed round the flickering lights: symbols of everlasting unions.

With a great swing of his arm, Prometheus set the first galaxies in motion. A palette of color suffused the darkness with its ineffable splendor: rivers of radiance gleaming in their vivid and subtle hues as monuments to their maker's glory.

As a voice from afar that ferries not as a note upon the winds, but fills the hearing with its majesty, Prometheus spoke to the assembled: "These are but the first of many to come. When all is finished, I shall infuse Vedyah with a Flame of Life, so that by chance it too may bring forth the living—unforeseen and unexpected.

"Upon Vedyah, a hallowed rhythm I too shall set, a joining of the beginning with the end—that it may ever renew with the passage of the ages. Life of our own designs we may then set upon the worlds of our choosing, and we may each abode whither whim shall lead us."

Arduous and unceasing were the Lord's labors, for not only was he consumed by his work, but he was burdened also by the failings of the others: forced to amend errors where misdeed marred his exquisite designs. So onerous and overlong were their endeavors that the lesser Gods grew weary and worked no more. And yet—at the last—Prometheus's vision took shape in glory and splendor, far beyond the reckoning of those who played but small part in its making.

Though a spirit Prometheus had fashioned for Vedyah, so it would *live* even if no other dwelt therein, the air of many worlds grew heavy and moist with the breath, and the life, and the death of the living.

And thus it came to pass that what had once been void was become a realm of magick and mystery, a domain far beyond the comprehension, and the imagination, and even the dreams of mortal men.

2.2

As a forge whose furnace has ceased to burn, the last of its white-hot thongs sinuously rising toward an uncertain haze, the universe cooled. Prometheus, as did the remainder of the Gods, took a planet of his own upon which to dwell and renew his strength; for though the Gods are great, the act of creation depletes and exhausts them, so that in the making, the maker is diminished.

Verily, the wise hold that this is no less true for man, that in the doing, the hours and energies of life are counted and may not be recalled, spent in service to the spring of life, or in thankless mockery of it, a duty to one's Maker that shines as a light in the eyes of the faithful, or a rejection of one's Source that rots and weakens from within.

Though Prometheus had bodied forth the great majority of Vedyah and had thus suffered the greater loss, he was yet the greatest of the Gods: unmatched in power, in genius, in splendor, in strength, and in majesty, and in all those innumerable subtleties that reach beyond the grasp of knowing, though never pass the judgment without notice.

So profound was the diminishing of the Gods that where once they looked upon worlds as men look upon grains of sand, they now walked upon worlds as men walk upon the Earth. While the most powerful, if they wished, could stand as tall as mountains or as ominous as wrathful seas, they were nonetheless come to be shadows of their former selves: diminished in stature though grown in delight, for creation was a marvel so precious that none knew regret for their loss in its making.

It was during this period of rest and solitude that the Gods turned their thoughts on themselves. Each took a name for himself, and each called upon his recollection of the vision shared by Prometheus to clothe himself in a body. That vision set forth the shape of man and woman as would later come to be manifest in the Promethean Nation—save only in grandeur.

In accord with the temperaments and preferences of each of the Gods, and by the measure of their ingenuity and power, each God shaped a body of his own: some of male and some of female, some of dark hair and eyes and some of light hair and eyes. When finished, each desired to take company with his fellows— having rested overlong and grown weary of solitude.

Enamored by Prometheus, many sought his audience, yet they came not as guests bearing gifts, who arrive and depart for the enrichment and enjoyment of all, but as parasites that come to feed; for they hungered to draw near his might and splendor, to share and to profit in his glory and creations.

Within many was harbored a secret envy, of which some were ashamed, but while the birth of envy ever begets hatred for the envied, no sign, as yet, betrayed the growing storm that glowered amid their darkling thoughts.

A door that is always open, a reunion that is always glad, Prometheus received each of the Gods as one who welcomes dear friends and family. Yet the hospitality of the host is often his undoing. And so it was that in the wheeling of the ages, the world Prometheus had called his own, a cradle for his happiness and the indulging of his many talents, swarmed with thousands of Gods, each vying for his attention and the enjoyment of his creations.

And thus where once his world was like to a lovely garden, laced with delicate paths that whimsically walked hand in hand with sparkling rills, romanced by blooming verdure, haloed by gentle rains of fragrant petals, it was now become trampled by the feet of throngs, its limpid waters sullied, its greenswards marred, its springtime wilting.

Politely excusing himself, Prometheus departed his crowded planet and wandered long as a man displaced and in search of a new home, his thoughts ever returning in regret to his paradise lost. Saddened by the marring of the works he left behind, yet ever driven by his unquenchable spirit to build anew, Prometheus alighted upon a new world—distant and uninhabited.

And again, after rearing the planet to such beauty that it sparkled like heaven's diamond-strewn beaches in the black waters of the cosmos, he was joined by Gods seeking his audience; yet they came not as guests bearing gifts, who arrive and depart for the enrichment and enjoyment of all, but as parasites that come to feed, hungering to draw near his might and splendor, to share and to profit in his glory and creations.

And again, as a host who warmly embraces the weary traveler, Prometheus welcomed the Gods who sought his presence and the luxury of his ingenuity. It is said that here began the great migrations of eons untold and leagues uncounted as Prometheus, adopting a world and rearing it to the beauty and majesty of paradise, found himself ever followed by Gods seeking his audience, consuming his time, draining his energy, diverting his talents, and altering—even sullying—his endeavors to suit their peculiar tastes: reflections of their own limitations.

2.3

Elsewhere in Vedyah, the first disputes and grievances arose among the Gods. Thus, it came into the mind of Zeushin that the peace of the many realms and the equitable resolution of disputes depended upon governance. To himself he gathered many lesser spirits, and he passionately argued for the need of government—to bring peace to Vedyah ere petty disputes became grounds for war, for even then the Gods were sifting themselves into alliances in the service of their personal ambitions.

One by one, a third of the heavens pledged allegiance to Zeushin's government, naming him "Zeushin, King of the Gods." And he reigned long over a vast estate, well-nigh half the cosmos.

Yet his ambitions were without limit, and as his lordship spread, so too grew the number of his vassals.

In time, all recognized Zeushin's authority, owning him as their king—even the mighty Prometheus.

The Coming to Earth

3.1

Now it came to pass that Prometheus alighted upon the Earth, a distant descendant of one of his original creations. Here, he would be alone for a time, making of the Earth a paradise. But when to the surface of the Earth Prometheus first descended, the world he found was yet angry and young, so that he was at once consumed with the assuaging of its violence, the cooling of its blazing fires, the healing of its many wounds.

Great were his endeavors and long were his labors: oceans he poured—blue and majestic, mountains he wrought—jagged and tall, rivers he carved—sinuous and swift, and canyons he chiseled—daunting and sheer. Grand were these things, yet even the smallest and the least of creation was to him a thing of measureless import; for he veined the petals of the rose, scented the airs with lavender, painted pale green the young leaves of spring and gilded their skins with the light of the Sun.

He patterned the delicate beauty of the snowflake, covered the cold with a shimmering frost, hung the icicles of winter by glistening roots, and lit silver their facets with the fires of the Moon. Many and more were the works of his doing, and rearing life in countless variation, he set it free amidst the bounty of the

Earth—a miracle hewn from primordial rock, a maiden of the cosmos serenaded by the stars.

Many, but far too few, were the years Prometheus indulged his love for the resplendent: rearing gardens and oases of delight more mirthful and splendid than aught reared in all ages. A vision of pure enchantment had become the world, so that it glimmered like a warm beacon on a cold winter's night, coming as an answer to all prayers even to those who heard but tale or rumor of its glory.

Haunted by the foreknowledge that again he would be followed, Prometheus set his will upon a course strange and new, for he made two of one, a Father and Mother Earth—separate but inseparably laced, as are the notes of divine melody. To all but Prometheus, Mother Earth was as a wraith: hidden, he hoped for a time, and spared the indignities of the interlopers, free to grow and to bloom without mar or injury. Yet Father Earth was undiminished by the parting, for he remained a paradise to all eyes in Vedyah, a ravenous hunger within empty bellies.

And so it was that, having come to the knowledge of the new paradise Prometheus had wrought, great swarms of Gods descended unbidden upon the Earth. Heedless of its maker, master, and keeper, they insolently took it for their abode, behaving as though it belonged to them, a work without maker that once found can be claimed and altered to the liking of the finder, yea! even a claim that unseats the maker, naming him *guest* or even—*trespasser.*

And yet again, believing it unkind and uncharitable to rebuke the lesser Gods, feeling shame at the thought of turning them away, concluding as he had concluded before that surrender was preferable to the ugliness of confrontation, Prometheus prepared once more to depart for some distant world, free of their meddling and marring influences, free of their demands upon his time and energies. And yet, he had so come to love and cherish the Earth above all others that ere his retreat, he found he could bring himself not to depart his masterpiece.

Moreover, he finally discerned that nowhere could he flee where they could not follow, that unless he subjugated his charitable weakness for the interloper, unless he violently resisted them, he was doomed to suffer them, alas! to suffer the grotesqueries of *their* presence—the defilement of *their* influence—the vulgarities of *their* clamor—the altering of *his* visions—the corrupting of *his* endeavors—the marring of *his* works—the crippling of *his* goals—the toppling of *his* pinnacles—the theft of *his* future—doomed to suffer the other Gods until his demise.

Thus, it was that the great Prometheus, prone to kindness and generosity, even to deference and altruism, resigned himself, at least for a while, to the disruptive and deleterious presence of the *Others.*

3.2

So lovely and fair had Prometheus made the Earth, and so desirable his company, that the Gods came in numbers far exceeding what Prometheus had endured.

Constantly were they at his heels, placing onerous demands upon all he made, endlessly seeking to satisfy their lusts with his latest creations, relentlessly altering his works to mirror their tastes. Such was the glory of Earth that Zeushin himself, King of the Gods, turned his long sight upon the pale blue gem across the vastness of Vedyah—and desire burned hotly within him. Ere long, he abandoned his stronghold, making such haste for the Earth that the current of his going yet lingers as memory on Vedyah's dark waters.

Having perceived Lord Zeushin's approach, Prometheus descended his mountainous abode and took himself to a vast, fertile valley, tawny with the grasses that grew there, and singing with the songs of birds that are wont to nest upon the ground. There, he awaited the arrival of his king.

Around Prometheus, the world wheeled and the sky churned with the azure of day and the onyx of night, and slowly the Gods of Earth joined him in the valley, all heeding Zeushin's approach.

Craning skyward on a clear morning, the Gods beheld the wonder of his coming; for in might and majesty, in the van of a shimmering army of Gods that loomed like a great foaming wave of the sea, Zeushin descended from the heavens. He alighted upon Earth with thunderous purpose, shaking the mountains to their roots, troubling the waters so that lakes were spilled and rivers surged contrary to habit.

In great reverence and solemnity, bowing deeply, all welcomed their mighty king. Earnestly heeding his words, the assembled received Zeushin's declaration: "On this world, I ordain," he bellowed over the heads of his hearers, "Here, we will build the Kingdom of the Gods. From this island paradise, we shall rule creation. Here we shall order all things for peace and everlasting harmony; here we shall celebrate mirth—and here we shall succumb to the darkness."

These words caused in Prometheus a shudder that plunged within him as deathless foreboding, for he knew at once that a veritable prison had descended upon him, a span of unbreakable chain with which he was bound, and though superior was his strength, intelligence, and power, he fathomed not how he might overcome the hordes that had gathered upon his fair lands.

While yet engrossed in these thoughts, thoughts that brought forth a horrifying vision of swallowing waters, a vision of all things in hue and shape other than he had intended, different than the expression of his spirit and joy, Zeushin, amid the crowd's raucous celebration, continued:

"To Prometheus, we owe everything—for the splendor of this world, the glory of its spirit and the majesty of its maker honors and humbles us—to Prometheus—we are ever indebted."

With the uttering of these words, Zeushin, King of the Gods, bowed deeply to Prometheus, and taking his lead, so bowed the assembled masses.

High atop a mountain that in many ages hence would be feared by mortal man, the King of the Gods built his mighty kingdom: Mount Neldoren was named that lofty range, but Mount Olympus, its broken shadow, was called in later days—a place of reverence and dread.

As a pearl casting pearlescent beams in sympathy with the light of Sun and Moon, Zeushin's kingdom radiated its glory and power undiminished by distance or storm—a diamond as it were, filled with an unconsuming fire upon the dusky heights, refulgent and splendid.

Until not one dwelt beyond the confines of the world, unceasing were the tides of the Gods that drew in upon the Earth, taking it for their abode. These were the ages of the great feasts. Without equal were the grand and innumerable celebrations in Natteley, Zeushin's city upon Mount Neldoren. Often, Prometheus attended these festivities, and bodying forth his spirit in intelligence, strength, comeliness, and power—he went never unnoticed and always was there a train at his back.

But this was not his principal desire, for though he too found pleasure in the attention, lust, and adulation of others, far more did he hunger for the creations of his hands, the musing of his thoughts and the building of his mighty works. Far to the north would he depart, finding solace, on a chance, in the Lands of Fire and Ice and the enchantments of the Black Forest.

Little did Prometheus know, as the seasons turned and the years marched into oblivion, as the stars flashed into and out of existence in the nighttime sky, that the adoration of the Gods was slowly, yet ineluctably, turning toward secret envy—and from envy to malice, and from malice to madness.

Little did he reckon that those he included in the splendor of his creation would soon clamor for his *exclusion*, that those he permitted to possess his mighty works would soon endeavor to achieve his *dispossession*, that those he tolerated would soon deem him *intolerable*.

The Masking of Prometheus

4.1

Zeushin's herald hesitantly approached the limb of the Black Forest. Guardedly, he peered into its shrouded depths, but from the trees he drew himself back, throwing worried glances at stray movements and sounds. Unable to return empty-handed, he closed his eyes, steadied his breath, and set his will on a course he could not alter.

With tremulous resolve, he drew open his eyes and plunged into the darkness. Deeper and deeper he strode, the leaf-litter crackling, the air growing thick with moisture, the fear now a torrent, now a gale, now overwhelming him—for he knew the purpose of his errand.

Long minutes waxed to long hours as for Lord Prometheus the herald searched; and finding a glade, a space as it were a hollow, dimly lit, roofed and ringed as with a ceaseless vigilance, he purposed to repose and gather his thoughts. Kneeling aside a melodious brook that lazily galloped as a black ribbon across the forest's floor, bubbling and trickling its subtle music over tiny stones, he pondered deep the purpose of his mission, ruing the duty thrust upon him.

Bending forward, he supped from the cool waters that trickled between his laced fingers, raining like tiny stars back into the brook.

"You escaped not my notice, herald of Zeushin," said a powerful voice that issued from the forest itself; the earth, the trees, even the water in the herald's belly throbbed with its cadence.

"Lord Prometheus!" sputtered the herald, jumping to his feet, the water spilling from his hands and mouth as he worriedly scanned the shadows in vain. "I am come on the order of the king. You...you are summoned to appear in his court," he continued, his utterances quivering in his mouth.

"*Summoned*," repeated the voice, the word hanging as an echo in the silence that followed, the earth quaking underfoot as though thunder had taken to the roots of the world.

"Countless invitations I have received, but a summons— never," said the voice. And suddenly, Prometheus was before the herald in the shape of a man, twenty feet tall, his head crowned by the dark, gnarled branches that flared and glowed in the light that leapt from his skin. A white as of lightning was the sheen of his flesh and his eyes a gleaming fire of blue.

In shock, the herald stumbled backward and fell against the moss-clad trunk of an ancient tree.

"You fear me, herald. What cause have you to tremble?" asked Prometheus, his tone gentle and sympathetic.

"Lord...please—do not ask of me to reveal what I have been forbidden to reveal. I am dispatched by the king and the Royal Council to—retrieve you, nothing more," anxiously answered the herald, wishing in all desperation that he would stir not the wrath of one whose wrath was warranted and just.

Yet, upon hearing these words, so pitifully spoken, compassion rather than fury swelled in Prometheus's heart.

"Was it not I who taught you the secrets of the Clay, and I who opened your mind to the potential of the Fire? Was it not I who envisioned the body you now wear, and I who fashioned the world you call home? Was it not I who amended your errors and healed your hurts—even from the beginning—bringing you pleasure and comfort beyond your reckoning?" said Prometheus, a tender air to his questions.

Assuming the natural form and hue of a man, though evincing the glory, bliss, and majesty of his divinity, Prometheus extended his hand to the frightened herald, prostrate at the base of the towering tree.

"Come, dear friend. Let us delay no longer the fulfilment of your errand."

4.2

Atop the city's steepest hill, the gilded Court Rotunda shimmered amber against a red dawn, mocking the adjacent structures with its colossal grandeur.

Within the cavernous rotunda, Zeushin's throne gleamed like the setting Sun upon angry waters. Ornate seating for the Royal Councilors arced along the high decorative walls, terminating before encircling the throne. A polished cerulean floor spanned as a calm sea at the rotunda's base, its surface bare, save only for an unadorned pedestal, its crown the roost of a sinister mask.

Alone, Prometheus walked the pillared corridor leading to the rotunda's court, and upon entering the sanctum beheld King Zeushin on high throne in the distance. Hundreds of Royal Councilors came to their feet in silence as Prometheus, a disquiet lying upon him, strode across the empty expanse.

The pedestal, cradle of the black menace, stood before the royal seat, and there—in the shadow of the mask—Prometheus halted.

"My king," said Prometheus cordially, bowing deeply, his face coming within inches of the pedestal and its burden, "it was but last season that here I attended a glorious feast. Then, the faces and tidings were glad, mirth was unbridled and friendship was strong, yet today the streets are silent and a devious—unfriendship pervades your kingdom."

Power and authority stirred in his voice.

"You have summoned me, and I have answered your summons; now I ask of you Lord Zeushin, what is its purpose? What cause has brought the body of councilors to this noble court? What secret motive has bred such grim silence and unfriendly countenance?"

"Keep your peace," hissed Zeushin. "You have many questions, and soon their answers you too will have."

Eyeing the dark mask and raising his voice so that it filled the rotunda, Zeushin continued.

"The mask before you was conceived and fashioned by Lord Gorthang. In his characteristic humility, he has insisted his contributions remain secret, yet I deem them worthy of mention and praise.

"A work of genius, it makes of the wearer's face a consuming blackness. By Gorthang it is named, Effacince—"

"And what is this to do with me?" interrupted Prometheus, as he pondered the ugly purpose in the mind of the mask maker.

Apprehension swept over the councilors like a heated wind, drawing forth the beaded sweat of the brow and the flush of the cheek. Murmurs as the buzzing of bees eddied amid the councilors before Zeushin's voice silenced all.

"It is the will of your king. It is the will of the Royal Council. It is the will of the collective, and it is therefore the ruling of this government that you shroud yourself henceforth, that we may never suffer your *face* again, that we may never be reminded of your *exceeding* glory!"

The truth was revealed at last. Adoration had turned to secret envy—and envy to malice, and malice to madness.

Long the silence reigned after the last note of Zeushin's voice faded from the chamber, for each God knew the grievousness of the edict. And though they had willingly endorsed its passage, each—in his private thoughts—knew the boundlessness of its injustice.

Unblinkingly, the assembled surveyed the mighty God, Prometheus, and many, for fear of his kindled wrath, recanted in their hearts for this grave injustice, fretfully groping for excuses and deflections.

Wide as the valley, deep as the ocean, Prometheus's voice swallowed the silence. "What ill have I done you? By what act have I aggrieved you? None and none!"

Studying the faces of the councilors as he pivoted where he stood, he asked, "Am *I* not the source of Vedyah? Am *I* not the source of nearly all beauty and pleasure, even to the smallest and slightest? Yea and yea! And how just to cloak me now—now that you have the fruits of my labors?

"How fitting to damn the inventor: he who gathered you from the darkness and delivered you to the light, he who wrapped you in discovery and creation far beyond your reckoning. Had it been not for me, you would have remained unhappy vagabonds, lives of misery laced with the consequences of your limitations.

"And now, possessing what never could you have envisioned, your gratitude is become insolence, your insecurities the bane of your benefactor. If it be so oppressive, then renounce and discard what I have shared freely, and be gone—to make your copies, to cobble your imitations, to suffer your inadequacies."

"You speak of justice, Prometheus. How just is it that you are so much more radiant than we?" bellowed Zeushin hotly. "We asked not to come forth inferior to you, and no longer will we suffer it. Effacince is justice—it is equality!"

Prometheus glared as he contemplated the detestable effrontery of his fellow Gods: their foul jealousy, their evil intent, *but then*, their pitiable stance, their sorrowful state, their mournful envy, victims of jealousy and ugly ideas, he thought—*victims*.

"This…is a strange thing…you ask of me."

"We ask it not," snapped Zeushin, "It is *ordained*. It is law."

Shorter was the silence that followed. Fuller and louder was the voice of Prometheus.

"These are the musings of madness, the fruit of evil notions set amid the crowd and fanned until the culprit's desires are come to fulfillment. No—this thing I will not do!"

Growls rattled the earth and shook the foundations of the city. Quailing in horror, the councilors stared fixedly at Lord Prometheus, their fear building as a froth-plumed comber in anticipation of a rebellion they had not the power to stay.

"MY KING! MY KING! LORD PROMETHEUS! PLEASE! Please, let us not succumb to violence!" imploringly shouted Counselor Gorthang, as he rose from his seat and hurried across the rotunda's floor.

"Please, my Lord," pleaded Gorthang in a whisper, stepping nigh Prometheus. "We are but five hundred councilors and Zeushin. Should you choose to fight, many you will slay before the Royal Guard arrives, but please—hear me first, my Lord."

Scowling at Gorthang, Prometheus checked his escalating fury and grudgingly nodded. Thereupon, Gorthang—drawing a methodical breath—spoke rhetorically to the Royal Court.

"You are indeed *great*, Lord Prometheus, the most powerful of the Gods, but are you not also the most honorable?" asked Gorthang, a single brow arched as he cast a sideways glance at Prometheus. "Have you not spoken, even more eloquently than I, on the duty of obedience to the rule of law? Indeed, are you not the author of our laws?

"Are you not the most loyal, the most faithful to our kingdom? Yea, have you not rebuked lesser Gods for their lack of faithful ardor?"

Throwing his arms wide, Gorthang glibly asked the court, "Would he who condemns the thought of rebellion—rebel, himself?"

The anger quickening Prometheus's pulse now ebbed as Gorthang's questions touched principles Prometheus held dear. This, too—the mood in the rotunda was succumbing to Gorthang's oratory.

"Are you not the most peaceful, Lord Prometheus?" asked Gorthang, his head tilted toward his bemused audience, a smile on his face that thawed not the cold cunning of his eyes. "Have you not lectured your listeners on the virtues of civility?

"Is it not also true that the heart of Prometheus feels more acutely, more deeply, the suffering of others? Will he then withhold his mercy or revoke his grace when he is found to be the cause of suffering?"

Walking slowly across the rotunda, gathering his thoughts, checking with furtive glances the faces of his audience, measuring the effects of his guile, Gorthang smirked. "Are you not the most charitable? Indeed, if it were not for your charity, Prometheus, there would be no Vedyah."

Halting nigh Zeushin, Gorthang sweepingly turned toward Prometheus and sued, "We ask you to evince your duty to the rule of law, your loyalty to our kingdom, your desire for peace and civility, your sympathy for our suffering, and your charity for our needs.

"Lord Prometheus," he continued, now with the posture and tone of a suppliant, "your face yet shines with the light of creation, a glory and magnificence *we* can never know. Your friendship we desire, yes, your presence and your works we desire; but in your face, we see the undying memory of our inferiority. Will you not grant us reprieve from the misery you cause? Will you continue to make of us—victims?"

His eyes now soft, his countenance mournful, his spirit stricken with grief, Prometheus calmly looked into the councilors' faces.

"My heart aches for your anguish, the depth of which is only now revealing itself to me," said Prometheus. "I am, as Gorthang declared, a defender of my kingdom. I am a champion of its laws. I am an advocate of peace and the doing of charity brings me supreme joy, but I am most deeply concerned with the suffering of all creatures and the marring of this world. I have sought to succor the injured, subdue the misery of sorrow and repair the hurts that afflict us…. I cannot bear to know that *I* am the source of your pain…. I have no choice. I will grant you reprieve from the misery I inflict. I will don the shroud…Effacince."

A solemn applause, kindled by Gorthang, surfeited the rotunda, spilling its clamor into the streets: echoes of celebration, portents of tyranny. With a twisted grin, Gorthang declared that Prometheus's decision was most *wise*, exceedingly *moral*, and utterly *just*.

Gliding from their perches, the councilors swarmed round Prometheus, and watching from on high, Zeushin smiled fiercely as Prometheus gathered Effacince into his trembling hands.

Fingering the ugly material, the once proud visage that Prometheus had worn was become dim, a doleful resignation that crept through his every pore. Verily, as a dark cloud eclipses the Sun, so too did his surrender eclipse his majesty.

And thus—though none could recall the moment the mask covered his face—it was done. The inherent brilliance and power—that no army could conquer—yielded by its own volition to the serpent's bite of a secret foe, and the disfiguring guilt the venom engendered.

In the hands of those who hated him was now the power to destroy him: their promise of equity as a lie, his hope for fairness as the longing of a fool.

Nigh after the masking, the laws that Prometheus had written were turned against him, and a new narrative of the ages issued from the organs of governance, a narrative in which Prometheus was mantled with anonymity and crowned with infamy.

Never again was Prometheus celebrated, for to do so was to celebrate inequality. Never was he permitted to forget his guilt, to atone for his "wrongdoing," to recompense for his "offense," for to permit him to doff his guilt would undo the victory of envy, of those who clad their jealous deeds in righteousness, and called the act of bringing him low—equality.

4.3

Prometheus rarely ventured from his haunts after the masking; rarer yet did he attend the opulent celebrations in Natteley.

Where once he graced his onlookers with grandeur and power unrivaled in the cosmos, he walked now as one crippled by guilt and shame, faceless and broken. Yet friends he still had, for these had no part in the doings of the Royal Council.

Repudiating the edict of the black mask, even when these thoughts and acts were deemed repugnant by the authorities, they spoke ever in his defense. And though small were their numbers, counting some few hundreds of Gods, they refused to abandon him to the rancor of the masses.

At length, however, when slander was joined by vicious persecution, fear shut the mouths of many and stayed the deeds of most; for the cunning lies of Gorthang, so deeply poisonous, so infectious, had so stirred the kingdom to malice for the Faceless God that he who championed his cause was assailed by malice— implacable as the tides, unceasing as the seasons. Yet even against this storm, some there were who remained as faithful to the Lord as the Morning Star: island flames amid a sea of growing darkness.

Odious was their persecution, for history was rewritten. Though the Gods recalled truth, truth was forbidden, declared to be hurtful, a bane, a blight, an error, and those who spoke of it recast as unclean: alleged to be vile monsters because they knew neither compassion nor respect for the "victim"—vile monsters deserving neither compassion nor respect.

Many names were these Gods given. Traitors they were called, enemies too, conspirators and evil they were also said to be. Yet these were not the only names by which they would be known, for the distant future would know them as the Faithful, the Incorruptible, the Banner Bearers and many more names of splendor and renown.

As a reckoning upon a tireless steed, the Lord's champions would come to be shunned by the enemy as a portent of doom, feared as an avenging force, dreaded as a cleansing fire, for in truth they were the Valaroma—the Riders of Vengeance.

4.4

Nimble indeed was Gorthang's tongue, unctuous were his words and powerful were the spells he cast upon his hearers. Far better would deafness have been for those who harkened; for within his artifice, which he sowed ever and anon, was the promise of progress, of reward and liberality, of harmony and joy as each in his heart interrupted the vision.

Here lurked the potency of the spell; here was laced the creeping deception that empowered the entranced beyond his talents. And yet dearly bought was his boon, for he who harkened surrendered his will to the will of Gorthang, and though free he walked and choices he made as if free, indeed, he was—in truth—Gorthang's vassal. And with his gifts, and with his industry, he did Gorthang's bidding, blindly convinced that the bidding was his own.

By great effort and cunning, Gorthang concealed the influence he wielded over Crown and Council, convincing the masses that these were the sources of judgment and decision, preventing the masses from suspecting *him* as the secret master of their thoughts, the hidden dictator of their deeds.

Consumed by a lust for power, a lust for Zeushin's throne and an unquenchable desire to reign as master over a planet of thralls, Gorthang worked without tire, gilding the words with which he advanced his dark designs. For Lord Gorthang believed a delusion born in madness: that he alone was *chosen* for greatness, and that by treachery he would assume his rightful place—standing upon the backs of the *un-chosen*.

Many centuries passed before the fruits of Gorthang's cunning came afresh to the vine: gravid, ripe, and ready for harvest. So it was that yet again, Prometheus was summoned to appear before the Royal Council. There, in a scene reminiscent of the first, Prometheus was ordered to don a black cloak: decreed as justice, woven with hatred.

The cloak, Genosiliant, was fashioned to conceal the radiance of Prometheus's body, which remained a continual affront; for though his face had been purged in the name of equality, blotted from the pages of history for the solace of the inferior, his body served salient as a reminder of inequality, of his unmatched glory.

And the old arguments, so successful in shaming and guilting Lord Prometheus, were unearthed and resurrected: written now upon new banners, put into new songs, dressed in vogue fashions—and the stale made *fresh* with copious perfumes was carried into the battle of words and ideas.

Yet the attack went unchallenged, for Prometheus, bent and broken by shame and guilt, believing he deserved punishment, desiring to demonstrate remorse, yearning to atone for his *wrongdoing*, gratefully wrapped himself in the cloak.

Thus, as a hooded figure enveloped in the many folds of Genosiliant's sable cloth, scorned as one worthy of scorn, punished as one worthy of punishment, he withdrew from the Court Rotunda—consoled not but by the thought that his suffering was due and penance.

4.5

He was not honored. He was not thanked. In his name there was no celebration, no praise for making a *just* decision and no appreciation for donning the cloak. Rather than false gratitude, he was now vilely condemned as one who had unjustly lorded over others; indeed, many asked—in pompous tones—if they had gone not far enough.

It may be that even then the long memories of the Gods were succumbing to Gorthang's agenda, who, seeing history as a living refutation of his designs, redrew its vista, recast its players, rewrote its pages.

With calculated lies, the annals of history were revised to appeal to each God's self-image, self-worth, and self-pride: falsely magnifying his or her achievements while diminishing the debt each owed to Prometheus. Such lies desire to be believed and are oft blindly adopted as truth, even as they crawl on poorly cobbled limbs under truth's long and disproving shadow.

Whereas Prometheus had been well-nigh the source of all creation, faithful servant of the kingdom, most tender of all hearts, his role in history was now that of a beast, an exploiter, a scapegoat for the failings of the Gods. He was become Prometheus the Villain: said to have stolen the ideas of others, perverted their "mighty" works, sullied their "inner glory," corrupted the "truth" of their achievements, and usurped their "creations" to magnify his own.

His name, it was commanded by the Royal Council, was never again to be spoken in reverence—or even disinterest, for to do so was to incite evil's resurrection, a canker on history and a reminder of the past.

Here it can be said that much of the truth was inadvertently revealed, for the memory of the past—unencumbered by its new interpretation—evoked in the Gods the memory of the truth, the truth of *his* glory, *his* deeds, and of the supreme injustice of the actions taken against him.

It was thus only permissible to utter Prometheus's name in hatred and disgust: a metonym of evil, of exploitation, of oppression. No longer was it said that Prometheus accepted the mask and cloak of his own volition, but that the collective, for the good of the smallest and weakest, for the goals of equality and progress, had forced it upon him—the outlaw and outcast: cruel in heart, guilty from inception, richly deserving of punishment.

4.6

A great green wood he was known to haunt; yet, so rare were the sightings of the cloaked figure upon the limb of that enchanted place that he faded from memory as a character on a yellowing canvas.

Not unlike the opaline blur of a dragonfly's wings, centuries flitted by before Prometheus was again summoned from his dark abode. None of the councilors recognized the cloaked and masked figure that crossed the rotunda's floor. His gait was short and broken, his shoulders bent with defeat, his head hung low as one so drained of vitality, so averse to mastery, that in him the will to live spoke not with a young and vibrant voice, but with that of the senescent wrapped in stained sheets, melting inexorably into its deathbed.

There, in a scene reminiscent of the previous two, Prometheus was prostrate before the court, yet his reception was unlike to those earlier injustices. Whereas he was deftly guilted with cunning words and deceptive reasoning in days ancient and remote, he was now openly condemned as uniquely evil, an oppressor and exploiter.

An enemy of the collective, responsible for all of its misery and failings, he was ordered to divest himself of his birthright, to renounce his due, to cast off his powers and send them to the rim of Vedyah, there to reside beyond reach in the deeps of time.

"*You* have been above while *we* have been below," blustered Gorthang, his voice aflame with righteous indignation, the councilors and Zeushin feverishly nodding agreement.

Naming Prometheus's birthright and due *privileges,* Gorthang disparaged Prometheus, saying if it were not for his exploitative privileges, he would have accomplished nothing.

"It is now," Gorthang declared, "time for *you* to take your place beneath *us*!"

Gesturing submission, the hooded figure sent forth his powers, and as those powers yet sped from the confines of the world, the fullness of the cloak diminished so that it remained limply aloft, rippling listlessly atop tenuous currents.

Speaking with a voice as one who whispers by inhalation, he who had become wraith said but this to the assembly: "I am guilty."

4.7

In the ensuing centuries, hatred of Wraith-Prometheus was joined by the simmering fear that it would arise and avenge itself. Such was the fright that seized those responsible for the Wraith's punishment that *justifications* of the most fantastic imaginings were joined to the indictment. Many voices clamored for its imprisonment; among these, most ardent was Gorthang.

Yet, while most imbibed the Royal Council's edicts, drunkenly accepting the dubious narrative disseminated as historical and contemporary "fact," few there were who suffered not the weakness of mind that crippled the rest; for these few were beyond the deceptive reasoning, beyond the lies and half-truths, beyond the jealously that spurs the under in conspiracy to destroy the over.

Immune to the treachery of Crown and Council, they gathered themselves into numerous groups, some secret and some overt. Friends they had been of Prometheus, friends they were now of the Wraith, loyal to the Crown, but enemy of the faith. By their counsel, the Friends of the Wraith sought ever to change the minds of their fellows. Yet most heeded not their heretical wisdom, for the hearers were as cringing devotees of the ideas deemed *moral* by the Council.

In time, aversion grew hot for the Friends—for those unwilling to embrace the faith of the realm and its obligatory opinions. The Royal Council, fearing unrest among the masses, concerned they might heed the exhortation of the Friends, heed the unconvoluted telling of history—the undeceptive reasoning, devised punishments for those reluctant to submit to the new *truths*.

As conditions worsened, as the future dimmed, the Friends of the Wraith came secretly to its haunts and there passionately implored it to rebel, sharing that beyond the horizon the Royal Council purposed more punishment, and beyond that unhappiness lay the unspeakable. Yet the Wraith, having come to believe in its own guilt and innate evil, and unable to reconcile rebellion with obedience, civility, charity, and sympathy, believed that it deserved its punishment, and that redemption could only be found in suffering.

Withdrawing to the Lands of Fire and Ice as a craven, seeking—if it might—to postpone judgment, the Wraith sat in its hidden lair and waited for the inevitable. For, though it had removed itself, ensconced a little more remote than it had been before, it was, in truth, no more beyond the grasp of the Royal Council than when it fled.

Not long after the Friends admonished the Wraith to action, a legion of the Royal Guard approached the base of a restless volcano, its crown ruffed in cinders and framed by tenebrous clouds, its jaws violently lashing the earth with tongues of liquid flame.

Even without its powers, the Wraith struck such fear into the hearts of the Gods that their captain, Hathem, dared not ascend the mountain, but beckoned the Wraith from the comfort of the plain.

"Specter!" hoarsely cried Hathem, his voice disdainfully echoing. "Specter! On the order of King Zeushin and the Royal Council, you are ordered to surrender yourself to me!"

Wafting submissively from the darkness of its lair, the Wraith emerged, its cloak tattered and wayworn, a long, cold cry springing from the stones that it passed. Over the dull grey heights of the sheer walls the Wraith descended, dust swirling in its wake. When before the legion it drew, its appearance elicited revulsion and fear.

A hissing whisper, like that of a serpent, spoke to Hathem from the void of the hood, "What is the purposse of the summonss?"

"We are come to escort you to the Hon-Drowgleer...where you are to be imprisoned. That range will serve as your haunt, and death shall be your rod should you depart," said the captain icily.

Surrendering to its jailers, the Wraith was led to the Hon-Drowgleer, an extensive range of jagged peaks as of rows of teeth, and deep valleys as of hungry gullets. A place of wastes and hidden beauty, the Hon-Drowgleer would come by mortal man to be called Drowfear, and Teddelmarnahr, and Kawcus—and many other names in the distant ages that were yet to be.

The Lord's Revelation

5.1

And the work of the Friends was a work of love. And the work of the enemy was a work of malice. And the sacrifice of the Friends was a sacrifice of love. And the sacrifice of the enemy was a sacrifice of malice. Thus, the years grew and the years wilted, but few there were that passed ere the Friends began slipping past the sentry-laden girdle of the Hon-Drowgleer.

Over the wastes of those forlorn lands they scoured, searching the crumbling hills and broken peaks. At last, espying the Wraith from afar as a daemon enwrapped in the shredded rags of its wayworn cloak, they came to the dwelling of their ancient friend.

High atop the ashen wall of a bold precipice, the Wraith made its home in a cave, deep and dark as the moonless night. There, its friends would come and ever urge it to awaken from its torpor and apathy, to heed the true purpose and designs behind the oft fair-sounding edicts of the Royal Council, to rouse it to rebellion and freedom. But though the Wraith moved not to their impassioned pleas, seeds were yet planted in its thoughts. And it was for these tiny victories that those who later would come to be called Valaroma risked their fortunes, their freedoms, and their lives—for he who sows truth while darkness reigns, shall lack not a harvest when the Sun returns.

5.2

The stillness of the day lay upon them as they approached the yawning hole, cloud wisps mutely passing above and below.

"Prometheus!" shouted Halumae from the lip of the cave, his voice coarsely echoing into the cold, solid darkness. "Prometheus, it is I, Halumae, and with me, Orluna. May we enter?"

"Come…," breathed a voice as a hissing of writhing snakes.

Here let it be said that though the Wraith was friend, and though Halumae and Orluna, like many hundreds of Gods, had gone secretly thither time beyond count, the entering was like entering the cage of a restless animal, so that every step into the abyss was marked by mounting trepidation, every thought burdened with doubt.

Descending into the cave as a stone falling into the lost-memories of a well, the Gods probed the darkness with their thoughts, even as their hands groped the craggy walls. As they neared an elbow in the cavern, the faint orange glow of torchlight slithered from a hidden chamber and glinted on the stones, a flickering blaze that strove with the deep shadows in a haunting ballet.

There, the two Gods entered a small, unadorned hollow, torches sizzling upon the walls, cinders falling like shooting stars. In a corner that crawled with shadows, Wraith-Prometheus sat motionless upon the floor, the hood of its threadbare cloak hanging bent over its head.

"Lord, may we sit with you…awhile?" beseeched Halumae.

"Ssit," hissed the Wraith, unmoving yet unwillingly conveying the potential of sudden and deadly force.

Crouching, the two Gods rested in silence, studying the shadowy corner and the dark, dust-covered robes that stirred not to their presence.

"My Lord—it was there, rooted in that very spot I saw you last, more than three years ago. Has *nothing* changed?" said Orluna, her hope and her faith in the rising of Prometheus burdened to the point of breaking.

Unexpectedly however, the Wraith slowly lifted its heavy head, and from the folds of its garment slid dust like the sand of an hourglass, twinkling in the torchlight as it showered to the floor.

For the first time, the horror and weight of Effacince gripped Halumae and Orluna as they watched the mask devour the torches' glow, a plague of torment and misery filing the room so that a sickened twilight was all that remained.

"Much hass changed, for the day fast approachess upon which I will fulfill a purposse I have long concealed," sibilated the Wraith.

"What is it, Lord?" asked Orluna eagerly, noting something different, something expectant in the voice of Wraith-Prometheus. "We will aid you with strength and cunning."

"Long ago—a work I envisioned…the greatesst of all my creationsss—a thought as the rising of a thousand Sunss…even as I gave life to Vedyah. I have pondered it beyond the counting of time, planning itss every detail, carefully sselecting the moment in the deepss of time at which…to it—I shall give being…for I purposse to make it in my own image, and I have named it—Man. Thesse will be my children, and I their Father. Yea, even as we wane, they draw nigh."

"How, Lord? By what means can this be done?" said Orluna bewilderedly. "Beyond the portions confiscated by the Royal Council, only the unfriends, Masule and Sairren, were permitted to retain Cosmic Clay. And of the three Flames of Life yet unforged, they burn brightly upon Zeushin's golden crown."

"I have not the Flame, but the Clay I do have," susurrated the Wraith, and drawing its arm forward, unleashing more dustfalls from the folds of its cloak, an invisible hand cradled a portion of Cosmic Clay, which it placed on the floor before them.

"My Lord, how can this be…the counting and confiscation of the Clay—" said Orluna with a puzzled expression.

"Every home was searched," interrupted Halumae.

"Indeed, Halumae, every home wass searched—but the only prison wass overlooked," said the Wraith smoothly.

"But what of the Flames of Life, Lord? They are on Zeushin's brow and no power will move them," said Orluna sensibly, though secretly hoping Wraith-Prometheus would stir to rebellion, for rebellion alone offered the promise of mastery and life.

"It iss—my hope…Zeushin and the Council will hark to wisdom…that having heard of my…desire…to create things like ourselvess…things that we may teach, and guide, and love…their pity my plight will sstir…on me they will have mercy as mercy I would have on them…treating me fairly as fairly I would treat them…they will releasse me…permitting me to give *life* to Man so that we may come together in joy," responded the Wraith, doubting its words even as it blindly put hope in them.

Alas—as it has always been, so it shall always be. To the good and the fair and the gentle, the thoughts and deeds of the wicked are met with surprise, but only do the credulous and the craven, the simple-minded and the lazy suffer more than once, only these refuse to believe in an enemy whose presence warrants war, valor, and sacrifice.

"When has Zeushin or the Council harkened to wisdom? Never! Why do you continue to look to your enemies for approval and mercy, Lord? You will have none. You *must* see this by now," said Orluna sharply. "Their kingdom is not the kingdom to which *you* and *we* pledged our loyalty and lives.

"By Gorthang's chicanery, the council now reigns as tyrant—and Zeushin governs all according to ideas having not their origins in his own thoughts, but in Gorthang's rhetoric. Scores they have put to death for resisting their despotism. The laws…the laws *you* wrote are no longer obeyed by the Council; why then do you still obey them?"

"We will fight for you, Lord," said Halumae imploringly, his fist raised before his chest, "but you must fight with us—lest ours be a sacrifice for naught but glory."

Wraith-Prometheus lowered its head, and the light swelled, and the gloom receded as emptiness in a chalice is chased by cascading libation.

"These truths I musst ponder. You may come again," responded the Wraith ominously, and the fires upon the torches leapt into the air—and vanished.

5.3

Though Wraith-Prometheus was yet to begin its greatest work, it shared freely its vision of Man, unaware that treachery lurked behind the semblance of friendship. For, though most of the Friends were true of heart, some there were on unseen tethers, moored to fingers in distant lands.

Alas, long had Councilor Gorthang watched the Friends. Long had he known of their efforts to rouse the Wraith. And seeding their number with those secretly in his service, he observed their activities, influenced their agenda, sullied their reputations, and corrupted their works.

Tidings of Man, therefore, came by way of a traitor among the Friends, a lowly, nefarious God that reveled in the Council's despotism, for it was a tyranny that leveled all, making "equals" of the unequal, thralls of the thrallherds.

To Lord Gorthang the traitor flew, and receiving the news, Gorthang deemed the tidings good, for a wicked design took root in him, and it scrabbled with barbed fingers upon the walls of his mind until at last, reaching for the world, it unfurled the poisoned petals of a ghastly bloom.

Laughing, laughing as one stricken with madness, cackling as the deranged beholding the spider springing upon its helpless victim—so did Gorthang laugh a cold, piercing laughter. At once, on his order, the councilors were summed to the Royal Court.

There, he weaved a web of deceptive reasoning, saying he had received *unimpeachable* information, a revelation that the Wraith was planning *rebellion*. It had defied the Royal Council by retaining Cosmic Clay, and it was planning to build an army of servants, an army called Man—with which it purposed to assail and conquer the kingdom, crowning itself King of the Gods.

How the powerless Wraith would give life to these soldier-servants, Gorthang did not or would not say, though he gravely reminded the chamber of the power once wielded by the Wraith, saying that the *innately evil* cannot be trusted, even when the means to its power and designs cannot be discerned.

Drawing his hearers upon the strings of his guile, Gorthang, peerless in sophistry, master of thralls, incited his spellbound audience to swift action, to bring the Wraith—bound in chains—before the Royal Court, to answer for its many crimes, to force it to admit its guilt in the planning of insurrection.

Yet more he proposed, for Gorthang argued that they should compel the Wraith to instruct the council in the creation of these servants, so that they might make of them slave and soldier: vessels of carnal pleasure, enforcers of edict and decree, expendable lives in the service of the crown.

Though much he revealed, there some he concealed, for deep amid the black roots of his heart—the tangled webs—the burrows of his thought, he secretly purposed to use Man to abridge the kingdom's remaining laws and to silence all dissent. And further he devised, planning to use Man as an army of his own, to overthrow Zeushin and to crown himself—King of the Gods.

Yea, an allegation when it convicts his foe, an aspiration when it yields him the throne.

All roared assent, but alone Gorthang knew it for submission, for long had he prepared the ground to receive each of his calculated steps. Thus, more he could do amid the *urgency* of the hour, more he could urge upon the council. And he goaded them to kill the Wraith when at last it had revealed the building of Man—because, he grimly intoned, they should rid themselves of the Wraith and fear no more its rising, worry no more its recovery, dread no more its revenge.

Verily! at the moment Prometheus yielded to guilt and became scapegoat for the ills and shortcomings of the *Others*, this doom was cast.

And the councilors cried in a single voice: "Kill the Wraith!"

The Rebellion

6.1

Alone. Adrift in the stillness of the cave as a cloud tiptoeing on sleepy waters, the Wraith brooded in silence. Coiled in a nightmare of impenetrable darkness, nothing but its thoughts stirred to the fore-wind of an army of Gods as a gathering tempest: wrathful, their nerves set upon a saber's edge, the belly of the storm on rails of lightning. Though a guess upon their errand drew well-nigh the truth, the Wraith fled not their coming.

At length, the discordant sound of shod feet upon the craggy floor shattered the bitter silence.

"Wraith…! Exploiter…!" shouted a disjointed chorus of angry voices. "We've come for you! "Cave dweller…! Oppressor…! Vagabond…!"

Brave and bold, with insolence and disgust—the thick aroma of contempt astride the language of disregard—these were the sentiments of the Wraith's hunters.

No longer did they approach in fear, memories of its glory and power haunting their thoughts, for now they advanced upon the Wraith as one advancing upon vermin: viscerally hated—death deserving.

The light of their torches rounded the eaves of the hidden chamber as Hathem stepped into the hollow. Four Gods laden with heavy chains followed him, and beyond this vanguard the Wraith sensed, as a heaviness upon the air, a current of Gods in the thousands.

"Up with you," ordered Hathem. "The Royal Council has summoned you. I know not why your presence they desire, but if filth is their want, then filth they shall have—and this, too, I have been ordered to retrieve."

Bending, Hathem seized the Cosmic Clay.

"The counting and confiscation was for the general good. It seems...the exploiter remains unrepentant...and uncured," jeered Hathem.

Enmeshed in a heavy web of chains, the Wraith was violently dragged from its prison and driven like an animal—league upon league—to the gates of Natteley. There, the Wraith was paraded through the streets, its tormentors mercilessly striking it with barbed whips, the raucous crowd defiling its name.

Scattered among the heaving throng, moved many of the Friends, their faces grim, their voices silent—no aid could they render.

Through the grand and ornate doors of the Court Rotunda, over the pristine marble floors of the wide halls, and into the cavernous sanctum they dragged the Wraith as a beast so stricken with pain it lay in a swoon. Below and before the sumptuous and gilded throne reclined a long black table; there, Hathem deposited the Clay and proudly addressed Zeushin and the assembled councilors.

"As you have willed it, so has your will been done," he said, motioning to the Wraith on the floor. "I have brought forth the wretch, and its Clay I too have confiscated. Give me but a nod and I shall cleave its head from its body!"

"*THAT* glory belongs not to *you*, Hathem," came Gorthang's shrill voice as he scurried down the steps from his seat behind the throne.

"Unchain it now…and when finished—*you*, and the other guards—are *dismissed*."

Bowing, Hathem and his fellow guards did as bidden, and leaving, closed the gleaming doors behind them.

"Get up, exploiter," spat Gorthang icily. "Get up— usurper of others' creations—land-thief—smotherer of others' potentials…."

Straining, the Wraith compliantly swayed to its feet.

"By retaining Cosmic Clay, you have defied the will of the crown—and for that crime, heinous as it is, you are unquestionably guilty. Yet," continued Gorthang airily, "this is not the greatest of your crimes, is it—oppressor? For you purposed to use this Clay to build an army with which to overthrow the just and legitimate rule of this council. Is that not so? IS THAT NOT SO?" he shouted, his face flush and twisted with rage.

Compliant yet inscrutable was the Wraith, silent, a haunting image, a tattered cloak atop tepid currents.

"Can you not speak?" demanded Gorthang. "Look here, my fellow councilmen, this conspirator—plotter to stifle the glory of its betters…plotter to exalt itself with the works of its betters…schemer turned subversive…it has lost its power of speech," he crowed mockingly.

"Well, we who are enlightened and principled…we…we need not your admission, *wretch*. Know this, on this day you are found guilty of fomenting insurrection," thundered Gorthang, a sharp finger condemning the Wraith.

"Your punishment," Gorthang softened his voice, "your punishment *would* be death—but our hearts are without bound, our charity without limit—and even for oppressors…deserving of most grievous punishment…we are…so gracious…we are able to *forgive*."

On his face a twisted smile, and under his words a dripping oil, he went on, "We ask only this, Wraith: instruct us in the building of Man, and we, *we* who are tolerant and fair beyond measure, will permit *you* to live."

At that moment, the Wraith was sundered by inflicted guilt and its will to mastery, sundered by every principle it had known

58

and cherished, and the knowledge that now new was the context in which these were become bane. And rising at the last, the heat of courage to face the awful truth, the Wraith, peering from beneath the lip of its hood, saw the blade of a venomous dagger hanging under Gorthang's robes.

It was in that hour that a thing remarkable but imperceptible was come to pass, for there the first sparks of an unquenchable fire were kindled, and a new destiny written upon the stars.

"We are the defenders of the weak," Gorthang continued. "You have forced us to take ugly measures against you, Wraith. Come, let us put an end to these *misfortunes*…. Come now—will you not atone for your evil deeds? Will you give your solemn word that you will instruct us in the making of Man, and consecrate your oath before Zeushin Almighty?

"An oath, we know, you hold as an unbreakable sign of your honor…a determinant of the value of your character; will you make such an oath? Will you lead us now in the fashioning of this—*Man*?"

The Wraith nodded.

"I sswear a most solemn oath…to you and the king and the councilorss of this assembly…that I will instruct you in the building of Man. Mine, Lord Gorthang, iss an oath and a bond as good as those…with whom I make it," sibilated the Wraith from under his hood.

The oath made, Zeushin descended from his throne and approached the black table even as the Wraith, flanked by eager councilors, drew himself up across from the king. Bowing to Zeushin, the Wraith hissed as a serpent, "A flame from your crown, my king."

Zeushin removed his crown and plucked the brightest of the three Flames of Life from its brow.

"This—I give freely for the making of Man. Let the glory of my gift pass to the creation," gravely intoned Zeushin.

Taking the flame, Wraith-Prometheus placed it beside the Clay.

Behind him, Gorthang positioned himself to deliver the fatal blow when the fashioning of Man had been revealed.

"The hood—iss heavy," sibilated the Wraith, and reaching, slid the hood from his head, exposing Effacince, which devoured much of the light in the rotunda.

"What is the meaning of this?" snarled Gorthang.

"The cloak—iss a burden," continued the Wraith, loosing Genosiliant, which fell and clung limply to the floor.

"We gave you no pardon!" shouted Gorthang hysterically.

"The mask—iss a hindrance to my identity," hissed the Wraith, and pulling Effacince from his face, he held it aloft for all to see.

Standing naked in his thoughts, Wraith-Prometheus addressed the Royal Council. "See here the ssymbol of my surrender, and see now—*my rising!*"

Even as Gorthang withdrew his dagger to deliver the fatal blow—knowing he and the king and the council were betrayed, Prometheus swung Effacince as one swinging a hammer, and smashing it upon the edge of the table, spilled its darkness as a rushing vapor that engulfed the hive of councilors.

In an instant, Prometheus, the Cosmic Clay, and the Flame of Life—were gone.

"GUARDS!" rang out the alarm, "GUARDS! The exploiter has escaped!"

The rotunda detonated with bedlam. Beset with dismay, the councilors shouted and shoved as they fought to flee the court.

"Gorthang!" angrily roared Zeushin, the blackness of Effacince lifting as a dayfall's mist that lingered overlong and was smitten by the Sun. "Where is it?"

Stunned, Gorthang swiveled where he stood, his eyes scanning the wild confusion, his mind reaching out but there— thwarted by Prometheus.

"My king…I know not…," jabbered Gorthang, astounded and terrified.

Like turbulent streams vying one with the other, the councilors struggled to free themselves from the rotunda as the Royal Guard fought their way in.

"This—idea…was *yours*, Gorthang…and now the Wraith is gone…so too is its Clay…so too is *my* Flame!" bellowed Zeushin ferociously.

Gorthang fell to his knees, pawing at Zeushin's feet, "It…it is not my fault my king…," he tremblingly sputtered.

"I am a victim…Councilor Fador and Councilor Vrass…they were nigh the exploiter…they should have taken hold of it before it smashed Effacince…and it was Seraficc, my Lord…Seraficc who conjured this scheme…I swear…he is to blame, not I…shall I have him seized?"

"UP…Gorthang!" ordered Zeushin. "Find the Wraith. And when you do—kill it!"

"Of course…of course, my king," said Gorthang as he stood and bowed deeply, regaining his composure.

Turning on his heel, he snapped his fingers and three guards joined him as he, too, fled from the chamber.

Unbeknownst to all, the moment Effacince shattered, Prometheus put forth what little power he had retained and sank through the floor as one through water, Clay and Fire locked in his fists.

There, in a deserted basement he lay, setting forth his meager strength to frustrate the probing thoughts of the enemy. So great was the effort for the weakened Prometheus that he had not the strength to stand, but dragged himself along the floor to a remote corner, lest he be discovered in his refuge.

There he lay hidden for five days as the Royal Guard scoured the city.

On the sixth morning, having failed to discover Prometheus within the confines of Natteley, the Army of the Crown, led by General Theelien, departed in great force of number for the Black Forest and the Lands of Fire and Ice, believing that Prometheus, in his flight from "justice," would return to his haunts.

So weak was Prometheus that had he been discovered by even the least of the Gods, easily would he have been slain. But the genius of Prometheus, untrammeled by the bit and harness of guilt, reawakened to the vigor of mastery, now gave thought to peerless cunning, dissimulation, and deceit, realms of thought and action once mastered by Gorthang, bending now their knees to a new master.

From the deserted basement he fled as no more than a shadow of thought, slipping unnoticed along the sparsely crowded avenues of the city, passing over hill and dale, and finally, coming at length to his prison, the Hon-Drowgleer. There, he knew, they were unlikely to search.

6.2

To the gloom of his cave Prometheus did not return; rather, to a place he reared in the solitude of ancient wanderings he sped, a wayfarer as no more than a bird-shade that fleets across the earth. There, lost amid the innumerable wastes of the Hon-Drowgleer, he settled in a deep, fertile valley, a hidden island as it were—of bliss, hemmed by lands unyieldingly brutal and well-nigh pathless.

An enchanted river of the purest waters issued with spray and foam from under the mountain. Fed throughout the vale by sparkling tributaries and elegant falls, the graceful river nourished plant and beast even as it set upon the air a music of many waters. As a ring of battlements round the enigmatic vale, the peaks of the Hon-Drowgleer rose to dreadful heights; only the valley river, later to be named Cindillin—Spirit of the Stars in the Promethean tongue—carved a furtive and impassable route under the fortress walls.

Forests, splendid and thriving, gathered on either side of Cindillin, and many wide swards, green as glistening emeralds, swept along the banks of the river. Mirthful glades there hid amidst the trees, alive with bright and lovely birdsong. And grassy hills there were, sunlight dancing in the blades of their wind-kissed plumes. Many unseen places of wonder rollicked amidst the beauty of the vale, deep below its mountain sentinels, regal in their ashen robes and crowns of ice, haloed by the stars of heaven.

Standing in his naked thought near the Mouth of Cindillin, Prometheus beckoned his powers from the reaches of Vedyah. Then, utterly weakened from his secret flight, he laid himself down in the shade of the trees.

Shortsighted were those envious masses who would destroy him, for they believed his greatness lay beyond him, in the majesty of his environs, in the tools and knowledge with which he worked miracles, in the aura of splendor that seemed always to attend him, but these things were not the source of his greatness, rather they were the fruits of his greatness.

Verily, so long as Prometheus lived, he could not truly divest himself of his power and glory, for these things were spirit of his spirit, and their blazing resurrection needed naught but the spark of his will.

"Deception and cunning…I too can practice, Gorthang. I too…can master agendass concealed, and dissemble without peer. I too can bring death to my enemies—yea, more so than you."

And reclining on the soft grass, he slept.

The Making of Man

7.1

Heeding the approach of his powers, Prometheus rose from his slumber and drew himself down to the banks of the river. Being naked in his thoughts, he saw therein no reflection, yet therewith, in the mirrored skies below, there appeared a golden tendril as a great serpent, its gleaming body soaring beyond the limb of the firmament.

Light as the light of creation suffused the Lord, and as the long, gilded curls sank into its master, he was again become whole. There he towered, yet clothed in no more than his thoughts, a great and foreboding hill among the mountains.

Then it was that Prometheus assumed again the form he would later give Man. For days he reveled in the strength and vitality that to him returned, yet seeming now as unfamiliar things, strangers newly met and dearly received. But most poignant, *purpose* there was again in his heart, for if the body withers in the absence of nourishment, so much more the spirit withers in the absence of purpose.

At length, Prometheus turned his attention to the making of Man. As an author selecting his setting, or a painter his canvas, Prometheus chose a greensward for his milieu, wide and flat, hemmed by a sparsely wooded forest and a tame run of the river. Nigh upon that place there were shallow pools and brooks that wandered through undulant meadows, verdant and thriving. So too were there wildflowers in crimson, in violet and yellow, worn like mantles by hill and by dale.

Edible plants and game abounded amidst the meads and waters of that place. The leas were dappled by trees, and the trees towered as living islands, casting their boughs like open arms from their trunks. Beyond the nigh woodland and down the mountain's side, lucid rivulets cascaded as shimmering veils in numerous and splendid waterfalls, unfurling evanescent rainbows from measureless heights. Up the valley were natural gardens of thick verdure and vivid florets, blossoming trees and aromatic bushes, while below lay brindled plains and underwood, bounded by heavy wealds and sapphire lakes.

Prometheus sat himself down upon the fragrant grass, the Cosmic Clay and Flame of Life by his side, and there he began the building of Man. Carefully, he fashioned the Fathers of the Promethean Nation; nine there were, older than those he was yet to make. To these alone he would speak in the beginning.

When finished, he fashioned their raiment and clothed them therein. Gently—he placed them upon the grass, and there they lay as living things in the deeps of sleep ere life to them was given. Like unto these, thousands more he made, yet younger were

67

they: in the prime of their physical might. Small, like children's toys were the figures that lay scattered upon the grass, but this was not their fate, for, when finished, Prometheus set upon them a spell, and like unto seeds in the womb of the earth, they grew and flowered.

As day drew to dusk and the stars bloomed in the dark soil of the wheeling sky, Prometheus withdrew himself to the edge of the forest. There, he proudly beheld his children lying upon the greensward in their lifeless sleep. The night deepened. The waters raised their arias to a prancing breeze. The fires of heaven scintillated upon the cloudless vault, and Prometheus sent forth the Flame of Life—and his children awoke.

Yet not to the world did their minds first gaze, but to a dark slumber stirring with the wing strokes of a marvelous dream. For in the darkness fluttered a form like to a butterfly, and it had a light of its own, and its wing strokes were as a music that hailed from distant lands, a melody borne on a warm wind that thawed the frosts of doubt.

Though they were yet to take their first breath or to rise from the deeps of slumber, they lived a boundless enchantment, for Prometheus began a song as beautiful and as terrible as the world to which they would awaken: of good, of evil, of mastery, of defeat, of a struggle—and a fight, of a destiny—and a light. And though their ears understood the verses not, the lithe and magickal words formed pictures in their minds so that each, according to his or her talents, perceived the threats and promises beyond the darkness of the dream.

Neither before nor since has through the ether come a song of such surpassing beauty and dread, for Prometheus sang to his children with a love beyond the reaches of loving, a hope beyond the perils of hope. When its final note his song had reached, the sleeping Prometheans took their first breaths, and filling their lungs with the fresh scent of the many ambrosial plants that grew in the vale, they heeded first the music of the waters— whither, even to this day, they harken in memory of the ancient dream, a longing to which their hearts are ever turned.

Forsaking the raiment of his body, Prometheus returned to his naked thoughts, and there he watched as the dreamers awakened. Slowly, cautiously, as a field of white roses blooming to the silvery lights of midnight's vault, they woke to the world and the echoes of the dream in the world about them. To the memory of the dream all turned and therein found the rudiments of speech. And taking counsel, one with another, great profit was made, for by design each had perceived a part of the dream clearer than the others.

Lush grasses softened their naked footfalls as they surveyed the sward, and taking to small groups, friendships they formed: singing and laughing and dancing with bodies nimble and voices sweet—lilting in the cradle of their birth, a young Nation, a vibrant Nation, a People in the bosom of the Earth.

In time, all turned toward the living stars in deathless wonderment, for much was sung in the dream of their beauty and of some import, that alone or in the taking of counsel with others, they could not yet discern. It was then, with subtle whispers, that Prometheus lured the Nine to the shore of the river, and in visions he spoke to them. Many things did he share, so that their knowledge and wisdom grew beyond the visions of the dream. When finally to naught the images drew, the Nine sat long in council and deciphered the seeing.

Felicity and wonder twined in the Promethean heart as a quenchless bliss, and when night's joy seemed an endless romance, the darkness waned as the pale blue of morn advanced into the eastern sky. Toward the unexpected marvel the Prometheans turned, and watching with unspoiled eyes, they beheld what later they put to verse as the First Rising of the Sun.

Cool hues of green, and warm tones of violet rode upon the crest of the dawn. Gathering, they breathlessly beheld a thin halo of crimson tearing through the lofty ridge, setting fire to its deep clefts. As dazzling rubies, the fissures flared, jewels upon the diadem of the mountain.

From beyond the rocky face that lay deep in shadow, they beheld golden beams that leapt across the sky as the strings of a gilded harp, igniting the cloud-plumes of morning, their bellies as lakes of fire upon the heavens. All shielded their eyes against the growing light, for the piercingly yellow flame of the Sun crested the ridge, sending columns of limpid radiance into the valley, dancing in sparks atop the water's surface, calling forth the morning song of many birds.

So it was that the Prometheans, looking upon their first dawn, which cast its golden roads into the west, have ever turned their desires westward—even when necessity drove them elsewhere. Putting their backs to the might of the rising Sun, they beheld a marvel beyond telling, for mirrored in their eyes was the immeasurable beauty of Cindillin's Vale, and swelling in that reflection were tears of wonder and of joy.

7.2

Much was written about the beginning of days in the ancient text, *Illurillion: The Voice of the Fathers from the Fount of Creation*. Here, the Nine named the greensward upon which the Nation woke "Illumenyiar," which signified Cradle of Awakening in the Promethean tongue.

Written therein were the folktales of those who opened their eyes to the splendor of the stars and the radiance of the dawn. Its chief authors were the Nine, and yet many there were who lent their voices to its creation. Gathered there were stories that told of the passage of many seasons ere the residue of sleep was lifted, for the Prometheans lived as though wading through a pool of dreams, a fog of somnolence rising therefrom that yielded not but to the winds of hardship.

"Ethelleyah" the Nine named the Creator in that ancient text, and with that name they said of him that he was both the Voice and the Source, a tongue that spoke from both the flesh of their bodies and the spirit within. Moreover, the Nine wrote that the innumerable stars gleaming upon the borders of the world were the keepers of life, which ever they sow as a blessing in their service to the Maker.

Illurillion's pages began with the beginning of days, tales that spoke of a stardust as silvern mist that showered the Earth from the reaches of the firmament, and winged amid these glittering mists were said to be flames that upon reaching the Earth—begat the Promethean Nation.

Thus, in that sacred book, the Prometheans first named themselves "Kristelyn," which signified life that is lit by the light of many stars. And many more names did they give themselves— some fair and some daunting; for they also called themselves Children of the Dawn, Bringers of Light, and Beings of Light. And they called themselves Wardens of the White Fire in reverence of the stars upon which they first looked in wonderment, and Sentinels of Darkness they too called themselves, and the

"Oulvleer"—those who keep the silent path—and many and more were the names they chose.

And when son and daughter were born to mother and father, knowing these were of man and woman, whereas they were of the dream, they called themselves "Alaywinne"—dream wraiths beyond the borders of the dream.

But lost long ago were the corpora of the Promethean Nation to which *Illurillion* belonged. Though of those books and those early times before the first of the great upheavals, many tales survive, for they were kept and guarded by the people—meticulously inscribed in the lore of the Promethean Nation by the courageous and diligent work of the Lore Masters.

These early tales were preserved in later corpora of the Promethean Nation, collections that continue to grow, surviving unspoiled by the arts of the Lore Masters. To these collections is given the name "Dunvaigan," and upon the first page of the first book is inked this scripture:

"For the Elect are the Dunvaigan, and only before their eyes will the conjuration take its secret form. To all others it looms as a wraith, ever beyond their grasp, cryptic and inscrutable. For them, the animating spirit of the Promethean Nation and its titanic works are forever impenetrable and mystifying.

Those who are able to hear and obey the Voice shall walk an unbroken path to mastery. For you, whose spirit soars higher than the firmament and delves deeper than the abyss, for you these visions are incantation that awaken in you what has slumbered overlong. For you they are the divine nectar that waters the very roots of your soul, being to you as a dispeller of poisons and an igniter of fires.

Let these words set fire to the winter of your apathy, for it is the Voice who summons you.

> *From the darkness to the light,*
> *from the shadows and the fright,*
> *to your king, to your fate,*
> *to your glory and the fight!"*

7.3

In vain, the great armies of the kingdom scoured the world for Lord Prometheus, yet one there was who thought to seek him in his former prison. Wearing the shape of a great and ghastly bird, Gorthang soared amidst the clouds; and espying a fertile valley as a lily atop a sea of slag, trapped as it were amid the unhappy gloom of the Hon-Drowgleer, he cast his long gaze upon the banks of the river.

There he saw Prometheus at unawares, weak and alone in his thoughts. Hatred and jealously, as only Gorthang could allege on the part of his victims, suffused the great bird, so that he turned on Lord Prometheus, and in a steep dive purposed to impale him upon his mighty talons, to tear through the sinews of his thought with a mighty beak.

Oblivious though he was, Prometheus found death not under Gorthang's gleaming claws, for even as Gorthang sped down upon him, a golden rope thundered through the skies and struck Prometheus, and he grew well-nigh the height of the lesser mountains, scintillating in the full strength and power of his former glory.

Fear as of frigid waters fanned throughout Gorthang's shape, and washing over his hate, his courage faltered. His eyes dimmed and he tumbled through the air, yet fear it was that also woke him to his peril. Regaining his senses, he hastened for the cloudveil, back to the anonymity of the shadows.

Fraught with dismay, Gorthang sped for his life. It was a flight of terror, reckless and blind, yet his passions cooled and his cunning returned, for he discerned that if Prometheus lived, and if proud he lived, unburdened by the heavy chains of guilt, he would be formidable indeed.

Therefore, Gorthang conceived, he would need not only the strength of the Royal Guard and the Army of the Crown, but vast swarms of men to conquer and kill Prometheus. Moreover, he thought to himself, here was the chance to revisit his former intent: to destroy Prometheus, yea, but to use the might of the slave soldiers to usurp the throne.

On that flight he envisioned a new design, and overcome by mad elation, he sped in haste for the lands wherein dwelt Masule and Sairren. There, he spun a web of words, and being more cunning than they, his tongue defter, effortless was the task to enmesh them therein. As conspirators, the three drew together the threads of their separate parts, and made ready the ground for steps yet to come.

Therewith, the three assumed the forms of birds and furtively returned to the Hon-Drowgleer. On a ridge, lofty and obscure, they watched from afar as Prometheus sat upon the greensward, fashioning Man. When the long sight of the craven birds had served its purpose, they returned to the airs and their separate haunts. At once, Masule and Sairren began the copying of Man, each according to his memory of the making, each according to his talents and powers, each according to his tastes and proclivities.

Though Masule and Sairren feared Lord Gorthang, and though for the present they intended to obey his orders, they were loath to heed his most urgent demand: that the men of their making receive and give seed in fruitful coupling with the men of Prometheus's making. Here, the vile artifice of Lord Gorthang could be seen at work yet again, for if to naught his martial efforts came, the desecration of the Promethean Nation might yet deliver him to victory.

Grudgingly submitting, Masule and Sairren did as Gorthang demanded, and yet secretly both envisaged themselves as kings of their own Nations, captains of their own armies, authors of their own designs for world domination. Indeed, Gorthang furtively encouraged these thoughts, hoping to stir in them a fanaticism and malice that later he would channel, twisting and bending in the service of his own objectives.

Even as Masule and Sairren busily formed the men of their making, Gorthang convened secret sessions of the council wherein he corrupted the minds of many. Ensnaring them in his new designs, he convinced them that he and he alone, of his own genius, had formulated the making of Man; that for the good of the kingdom and the reign of Lord Zeushin, he had selflessly shared this knowledge with Masule and Sairren, and that these had already begun the formation of mighty armies of men, men to contend with those of Prometheus's making, men to assail Prometheus when finally his refuge is discovered.

In obedience to Gorthang's wishes, these councilors came forth in great number and sued for audience with King Zeushin. Unwilling to entertain more of Gorthang's designs, Zeushin paid heed to the councilors who claimed Gorthang's ideas as their own. Verily, so nimble was Gorthang's tongue that many had come to believe the designs were of their own making, and accordingly they intoned conceit when of them they professed.

When all was told, Zeushin was ashamed; for in the quiet of his thoughts he questioned Gorthang's loyalties, yet here there were many who spoke highly of his deeds, revealing that Gorthang endeavored with all his genius to preserve the kingdom and reign of King Zeushin.

In awe of Gorthang's benevolence, his brilliant formulation of Man, his charitable sharing for the good of the kingdom, and with great respect for his selfless loyalty to the crown, Zeushin requested of Gorthang that he appear before the Royal Court.

There, Zeushin the penitent abased himself, asking Gorthang to forgive his wrathful words, and beseeching him as though on bended knee, to take the final two Flames of Life from his crown—that Masule and Sairren might complete their work, that the safety of the kingdom be guaranteed, and the ruin of Prometheus assured.

Drunk with guilt and the shame of guilt as one who has further aggrieved a victim, and spurred by Gorthang's words, Zeushin took hold of the confiscated Clay—Clay set aside for projects in the interests of many Gods—and awarded it all to Masule and Sairren: that their armies might swarm like the waves of the sea—an irresistible tide of conquest.

7.4

Of the advisors and aids serving the Royal Councilors, some there were who put first their loyalty to Prometheus— second was their allegiance to the crown. These were among the

Friends of Prometheus, and few were the secrets that passed the nets of their making. Hence, tidings of Gorthang's endeavors came at length to their ears.

The Friends guessed rightly when they discerned that Gorthang had found Prometheus, and that by some means, crooked or otherwise, stole the knowledge of the making of Man. Desiring to aid Prometheus, but having no sign by which to plot their course, the Friends remained vigilant, purposing to fly to his aid when to them that course was clear.

The Promethean Paradise

8.1

Hundreds of years after the Awakening of the Promethean Nation, the children of the Alaywinne were focused and resolute: unyielding in their zeal for victory, undaunted by the burdens of defeat.

Under the gaze of ice-armored mountains that stood as aged sentinels, nigh the cover of wild forests that beckoned with alluring mysteries, and by the banks of Cindillin and her many tributaries that hymned as cradlesong in the springtime of their youth, the Prometheans hewed survival from the Earth.

Most heartily did they feast upon the fresh fruits and vegetables, herbs, seeds, and nuts brought forth in abundance in Cindillin's Vale, but also did they fish and hunt, felling wild beasts for food and other necessities, beasts both great in number and diverse in form, which the Prometheans slew, admired, and feared. From the Earth, the Prometheans asked no more than their need; for the Earth, they gave no less than their best: succoring its wounds, enhancing its beauty, celebrating its majesty.

Affinity for innovation lured the Prometheans to the pursuit of knowledge and the unlocking of secrets. Swift were they in learning—and faster still in the creation of those things that simplified life and served well the purpose of Mastery. Cunning were they of mind, courageous in spirit, great in strength, long in memory, and clean of thought. From their essence came a love of discipline, honor, and daring. These were a vigorous people, an ambitious people, hungry for wisdom and adventure. Their minds and bodies were seldom idle as ever they sought the heights in all that was fair and boded well.

They made speech in keeping with the chronicle of the Dream, giving names to all things, composing lays of surpassing loveliness, combining lyric with verse and meter to conjure enchantment: language as a wand for the summoning of beauty and the clarification of thought.

Tools they made for hunting and fishing, for the hewing of wood, the gathering of ore, the forging of metals and the sculpting of stone. Complex ornamentation of pottery, dress, and jewelry they also conceived. Numbers did they count, and music with instruments and their many voices did they make—yea, in abounding beauty.

The songs and laughter in the Promethean paradise rang about the boughs of the ancient trees, singing in response with the wind in their leaves, echoing long as an ancient rill, beyond the quiet, beyond the hill, and amid the rush, and amid the still, the wheeling cycles of shimmering Moon, near but far, above the tune, and above the sky the piercing eye, its fires wide both near and far, the song it hails, the Morning Star.

Heedless, they sang as they were a thing unparalleled in the history of the world—undaunted by the shadow of adversity, inexorable in their drive for Mastery. Theirs was the bliss of the sunrise, when—awash in the dew of dawn—the forest and dale come to life in reverent song: to the cords of the Sun's mingled beams, and the honeyed flowing of its golden dreams—resplendence upon the Earth.

In the shadows of the austere mountains and over the variegated plains, the Promethean Nation endured and mastered the caprice of the climate. Fell and raw could this primordial world be, as injury and death stalked the living in many forms, yet none so grievous nor so many as to indelibly mar the triumph of the living.

In all ways were the Prometheans like to their Maker, and in no way was the mark of their Father more evident than in their drive for Mastery and the building of marvelous works. So it was that the Prometheans, yet whimsical of heart though focused of mind, built the roots of their kingdom near the Mouth of Cindillin.

Humble was its beginnings; for it was a village of chiseled stone and carven wood, modest but proud structures along the banks of Cindillin. Roads of polished stone ambled from the village to gardens lush and farms bountiful. Here, there were fields watered by streams that found their strength in the river, and in the rains, and in the waters that draped the mountains in the pale blue of shimmering curtains, showers as of liquid gems.

Discovery drove their curiosity as the precipice drives the cataract. The maintenance and restoration of health, the channeling of waters and the working of stone, the reading of stars and the working of metal, these and many other endeavors abounded and were nourished by the Promethean Spirit, which never bridled the hunger for knowledge, but ever refreshed, renewed, examined, and reexamined all things for the answers to their riddles.

Above all, the Prometheans prized the power and feats of the mind, and most heartily did they honor those who here excelled. But also they honored the bodying forth of beauty: paintings and sculpture, music, poetry, and prose climbed as flowering vines, sublime testaments to their Father.

Here, let it be told that the Promethean Nation looked to the Silver Ring for guidance and wisdom—a circle of nine, formed by the Alaywinne Nine, and passed on ere their deaths: to carry on their tradition and role, to harken to the Source when with subtle Voice it spoke. Round the Silver Ring was formed the White Council: a body as it were, of leaders of the Promethean Nation, formed by the Nine nigh the Awakening. Here also was started the tradition of the Lore Masters, for the Alaywinne Nine were the first to assume that honored role.

Now it came to pass that into their lands came various and wonderful creatures with hidden promise, whose coming was foretold. Long, over the wide plains did the Prometheans journey, searching for the beasts of alliance prophesied by the Silver Ring. And in the finding, made allies of them; and in the allegiance, *made* them. Steeds, companions, and more the Prometheans saw in them, and took to the labor of cultivation with all the joy of their father. The mightier, they increased to titans of awesome strength; the swifter, they honed like to the living wind. All made beautiful and proud, so were born the first Promethean beasts. Over them the Prometheans watched; by them they toiled; and with them prospered. On their backs they journeyed far and fast from the walls of their homes, mapping the unmapped, unveiling the veiled.

It was during these years, it is said, while quarrying the stone used in their structures, that they discovered vast seams of gems. Thereafter, tools they crafted for the shaping of gems, and polishing them to a scintillating fire, sowed them into their courtyards and squares—a foreshadowing of the glory of the kingdom to come.

8.2

Like the pages of a book that fan under thumb, so too did the years of bliss fan in the wake of the Awakening. Over a vast and dreamlike city well-nigh complete, the Prometheans reigned as lords and masters. As jewel upon the crown of that glittering city, there climbed the coruscating ramparts and shimmering turrets of a stainless palace; white were its walls and blue-grey its many roofs.

Against the snow-plumed mountains, scores of its ornamental towers soared. Like a white forest, the elegant pinnacles rose above ornate gables, sailed above ribbed vaults, and flew above wide balconies: towers upholding majesty, spires adorned with statues that ambled among the clouds.

Fair and lovely had the Prometheans become, but also hard and valiant in their city beneath the Sun. "Qwindellin" they named their palace, and "Sentilleena" the city far below. Enriched were the places within that city, so that burbling brooks took their course through its sacred spaces, so that trees rose and flowers bloomed, so that bridges arched over azure waters, so that all things fair and beautiful dwelt.

Grand pavilions, palatial avenues, and pinnacles stretching aloft, webbed and dotted the vast spaces like the branches and bloom-stalks of so many flowers. A golden light spilled from the sky's cerulean dome: obeisance of the Sun, a laying of aureate hands on magnificent structures, regal homes, and gardens meticulously wrought.

Within the palace, its wide halls, herculean arcs, and luxuriant atriums, there unburdened beauty abounded.

Embroidered hangings and painted scenes of Promethean achievements adorned the walls and high ceilings, and lain therein were Promethean histories: their triumphs, their hurts, their discoveries and creations, and the works of their greatest artists and thinkers.

Marmoreal paths networked the city, crawling beneath curved entrances and over grassy folds. Sculptures and fountains of precious marbles dappled the courtyards and gathering places, the euphony of their crystalline waters raised in hymns of enchantment.

If loveliness were to give itself a voice, or beauty a face; if genius were to don a form—or courage, or grace—the Prometheans they would choose; for on the paths that ran like lace, and from the windows and from the gates, and the towers standing tall, and the spaces big and small, their laughter came as music, their smiles as moonrise, their mirth like the buds of spring, the light of heaven in their eyes.

A breeze, pirouetting upon the yellow grasses that rippled like golden seas nigh the city, gathered perfumed petals from flowering trees and carried them throughout Sentilleena. Pink were their skins, edged in violet and white, and they capered upon rooftops and danced by open windows, whence came the ambrosial savor of succulent foods, a symphony of redolence upon the air.

Just beyond the borders of Sentilleena, whither cobblestone roads led, merry rills and deep forests abutted the foundations of the mountains. Copious and luxuriant pools, dotting the fair country, yielded seascapes from well-nigh every home—lucid waters glittering like gems: aquamarine in their shallows, sapphire in their depths.

8.3

Eight and thirty and one hundred years before the Coming of the Source, a vision on satin wings descended on the Nine whilst they slept. Cradled in the Lord's power, they dreamt of a fair streamlet and shallow pool beyond the margin of Sentilleena. Therein grew water lilies: some of pink petals rimmed in yellow, some of lavender with shafts of white, and their palette was as a music of color, sublimely foretelling of prophecy to come.

On the appointed dayfall, ere the rising of the Sun, the Silver Ring and the White Council gathered round the streamlet and pool to which the Silver Ring had been summoned, the Nine taking positions on either bank—even as they had seen themselves in the dream.

The White Council, several hundreds in number, took positions on the hills and among the trees, there to watch the Nine commune with the Lord. Eager yet anxious, they awaited their God. And by this fashion came suddenly Prometheus, for a bouquet like the fragrance on the fore of the storm swept over the milieu, and the councilors shuddered.

Thereupon, the Lord spoke from the shallows, transfixing the councilors, setting upon them bewildered joy and astonishment; for he foretold of his coming, to walk among his children as Father, to reign as king and protector, to love, guide, and teach, to be among them—as one of them.

Then he called upon his children to put forth their peerless powers of imagination, industry, and genius, to build an opulent chamber and throne within the bosom of Qwindellin—a tribute to their high Lord Ethelleyah—and more, a testament to the grandeur of the Promethean Nation.

8.4

At the last, amidst the vast halls and titanic chambers of the palace, amidst the bounteous meadows, forests, and lakes of Cindillin's Vale, there came that hour when was complete the habitation of the Promethean Nation—and the mansion of Lord Ethelleyah.

In accord with the will of the Lord, a chamber of radiant beauty was built within the bosom of the palace. Four prodigious corridors led thence, and they were lit by seething flames that leapt from lanterns of an antique gold. Here, burnished statues of Promethean heroes mingled with marbled colonnades, marching along walls of glittering stone. Silver fountains dotted the halls in twain, singing with the lovely medley of their waters, scintillating beneath the lanterns' coltish fires.

Beyond the great halls nested the Royal Chamber: a colossal space roofed by an immaculate dome, a canopy as a reflection on the nighttime sky, stars aflame and twinkling in their heavenly abodes. Up and away from the dais grew a coliseum of eminence and grandeur, and set in walls resplendently embellished were great windows of stained glass and tracery, infinite in their beauty.

Heavy columns girdled the chamber as the ribs of a great beast, and there, in the heart of the beast, the heart of the Promethean Nation, upon the stage of the arena arose the glittering throne as a tongue of fire. A mighty cathedra wrought of canary diamond, it balanced atop a perfect sphere that swelled more than thirty feet in height.

Midnight black was the obsidian sphere, and upon its glossy surface was there inlaid, in silver and gold, a map of the Earth, so that the sphere itself was a mirror of the world, as the image of its wide lands and measureless seas came in visions to its builders. Round the girth of the great sphere, as if lit by a living fire, glistened the lithe script of the Promethean tongue. And there, upon a pedestal of diamond, in the polestar of the chamber before the throne of Ethelleyah, the White Council placed the divine opus—*Illurillion*.

8.5

In the same wood where Prometheus sang to the Alaywinne, the gilded leaves of the woodland's canopy sailed atop shadowy seas—shade currents stroked by the wind's breath, probed by vines of amber light. Thus inhaled and exhaled the long years until, at length, the Coming of the Source drew nigh.

By divine vision were the Nine and the White Council instructed to gather and set themselves upon the greensward, Illumenyiar. Though the edict went no further, none were deterred. Indeed, all of the Promethean Nation assembled near the sward—there to witness the coming of the Lord.

Late was the hour. Black was the firmament. Lustrous were the stars as on the night of Awakening. None approached the limb of the forest wherein Prometheus had sung to his sleeping children, for they felt a power issuing from the night shadows therein, a power that lit fear and trepidation in measures no less than joy and anticipation.

They stood in silence amidst the silence of the night, their numbers covering the tors and the gullies and the groves nigh the sward. And edging the crystalline pools and fringing the quiet river, their bodies were adorned in their finest raiment and jewelry, their faces beautiful and stern, many trembling, some with tears in their eyes.

Most brought gifts of flowers and works of the hand, and others carried torches that glowed through the darkness, bathing themselves and the waters in light. A quiescence had come upon the world for which there was no rival; for there stirred naught but the cool of the night adrift on a breeze, wind wisps running their fingers through Promethean hair, mingling with the torch fires in *pas de deux*.

Thunder! quivered the earth beneath their feet, and thence bellowed the rumble of a terrible wrath.

Sunder! fissures on the slopes, and the distant sound of cascading rocks came falling to their ears.

Breath seized in their chests as they reached into the night with eager eyes, contending with the shadows even as the last airborne stone tumbled to silence.

Distant—came a resonant voice in song, clear and rich and infused with power, a haunting tune filling the void as wine the golden goblet, a night-clad melody that took wing and soared amidst the clouds, summoning memories deeper than thought.

Suddenly—a presence amidst the trees, a knowing that no sign betrays, and then an unlight as of a deep purple or darkness made visible, nigh imperceptible, buried in the depths of the wood like a shadow amongst the shadows.

The host gasped, for this beacon was no phantom of a waking dream, but a thing as themselves, visible and living. And they watched as the unlight grew, rising as a black Sun upon dark waters, a bead in the depths, leaping and swaying, rendering itself with the power of a great storm advancing upon howling winds.

Columns of unlight threw themselves between the trunks of the trees, night shadows as long stalks that swayed upon the grass. From the darkness of the wood there came the shimmer of mail, the gleam upon a breastplate, a rippling cape and an onyx flame caged in an iron torch, a human form nigh tall as the trees, eyes luminous, and sharpened by ancient betrayal.

There, mounted on the brow of the form, were glistening spires of silver, ornately hewn and infused with a cryptic magick, casting beyond the pinnacles of the many spires the silvery fires of the midnight sky. A crown it was, without peer, for there blazed with the scintillation of a thousand diamonds lit by the fires of a thousand Suns—the Crown of Stars. And striding forth upon the greensward before his beloved children—Prometheus Ethelleyah, High Lord and Maker of the Promethean Nation.

The Coming of the Gods

9.1

Assuming the natural breadth and height of a man, Prometheus mounted his coruscating throne, and there he sat astride the world, a God-King of ineffable splendor and magnificence.

Like four redoubtable statues arrayed round the border of the world, white as the foam that flies from the prow, glinting as the spray when awash in the noontide Sun, there peacocks impassively stood, regally adorned in snowy feathers, their great fans unfurled and majestic.

Wrapped in silence around their God, rapt by his every utterance, so were the esteemed members of the Silver Ring and White Council. To their ears came his voice like an enchanted music, falling like spring showers into lovely pools.

As Father, he spoke of his undying love for his children, his pride for their many victories, his sadness for their pain, his joy for their happiness, and his hope for their future.

As king, he lauded the peace and tranquility of the realm, the harmonious ordering of all things, the progress and refinement, and he set decrees he had sent not in waking dreams.

As Creator, he spoke much concerning things in the deeps of time and of distances unfathomed, revealing the histories of the cosmos in spells that unfolded in visions too copious to convey with words.

Thus, the Prometheans came to know much of what was, what is, and what yet may be. But all his words were not lithe, nor so quick to set sail on the currents of sunshine that rained through the windows.

"Darkening my joy is the loom of a heavy shadow," said Prometheus gravely to the assembled.

"For though I extend my will that we may here remain hidden, confounding those who probe the world with the tendrils of their thought, I have long endured an unquiet—a fear that others there were who harbored our secret. Why these few reined their tongues…I knew not. But in time and by stealth I peered through the brambles of their thoughts—and therein found black obsession.

"There are three who keep the secret of our kingdom, but friends they are not. They are Gorthang, Masule, and Sairren. Long…in error…I dismissed the pleading counsel and warnings of other Gods: seers, prophets, observers, witnesses of the enemy's designs…. For theirs were ugly accounts, burdensome accounts as in the hearing the body was obliged to action…. Thus—the truth, I did not desire.

"Long I refused to believe and act upon *even* what I felt in my *own* heart to be true—that Lord Gorthang, cringing devil and puller of strings, desired above all things and prized above all life, to be ruler of the world—a cupidity and a claim of rightful inheritance based in wicked delusions. Ever did he conceal his lust with gilded words and fair motives, seeking with guile and treachery to undo, to alienate, to murder *whosoever* barred his path or made difficult his long road.

"Loyal, indeed, were Masule and Sairren to Gorthang, for profit they made in his service, profit beyond their grasp without his support, yet the season of their allegiance has changed, for each now conceals secret thoughts of his own—within burns the desire to rule the world as lord and master. And with strength *newfound*, they purpose to scatter the cinders of their designs—even do they plot to surmount Zeushin. Such are the musings of the wicked.

"The source of their new strength is in men. But they are unlike to you, my children, for, though similar are their forms, contrary is their spirit. They are not a creation made in love; they are a creation made in your despite, a creation made in mockery and hatred of the Promethean Nation, a hatred that was essence of their making—and of which they were born.

"I have seen these—*men*, and I have touched their hearts, their minds. Just as you are *my* reflection, these men are the reflections of their creators, reflecting their talents for mimicry, their capacity to contrive where memory has failed them, but also their tastes, their lusts, their proclivities, their characters—their thoughts.

"Both Masule and Sairren purpose to marshal their men, gathering them into great armies. And once amassed, they shall loose them upon you as an angry river—to destroy you, to *unmake* you…. And if by force of violence you cannot be unmade, they have devised *other* means…. For they have so fashioned their hordes that life may be had by a union of their children and mine, and thereby your unmaking achieved, for I have made you as ethereal beings in my own image, white petals upon a supple flame that once drowned in the mire cannot be reclaimed. Tarnish the flame and it may rise again and again, but plunge it into darkness, and no spark can rekindle its fires.

"To endure, you must master yourselves, and that journey begins by looking within. Know that *you* are the reflection and that you cannot understand yourself without understanding *me*…to look within, you must look out from the mirror, my sons and daughters—and into the face of your Maker.

"There is no escaping this truth, for the creator is in his creation: a blessing—and a curse. The spark of your intelligence shines as the white-hot birth of a star, a light that yields to nothing. Your creativity is as the azure skies, boundless and eternal. Your imagination—from which your creativity chiefly flows—can scarcely be contained within the borders of your mind. Your compassion is as wide and deep as are the seas, yet sooner will the waves be silenced than your compassion diminished.

"From that compassion arises a selflessness that gladly calls upon you to forfeit your life that you may save another, and therefrom also springs a charity that sings in the giving and knows no season that would silence that music.

"You are a courageous people, a folk of valiants. Hot within your breast burns a fire that stands ready to fight for honor and Nation. Many enemies will come to know and dread the bite of your vengeance.

"Your minds are powerful beyond compare—your thoughts given wing to soar above the flesh of the body and the dust of the earth, and there to seek objective truth among the heavens. And more, for you are an innocent Nation, trusting and peaceful—a glorious civilization can neither spring nor last in the want of such traits.

"You are many things, my children, more than I have spoken—and yet none more so than this, for you are masters of destiny. Insatiable is your desire to master the unknown, to master sickness, to master ignorance, to master the turmoils of the seasons and the limits of the flesh, yea! to master all things—and this I say unto you, let there be no pall or shadow that stunts that hunger, for it was *I* who made Vedyah, and *I* am its Lord, a gatekeeper I have placed upon its workings, a gatekeeper that yields *to naught*—save Mastery.

"But heed this above all else—heed *this* or decay: for all your strengths can be turned against you; all that might carry you to the stars can be made to bind you.

"This you must guard against with all vigor and sleepless diligence: for your innocence and trust could fall prey to forked tongues—your intelligence and creativity become engines of interests other than your own—your compassion, selflessness, and charity, a means to your waning and the waxing of others—your imagination, a tool by which your life conforms to false and harmful beliefs—your lofty thoughts that seek objective truths become bound to notions that make a sacrifice of the *spirit* on the altar of an *idea*.

"These are warnings that know not a winter, for they are evergreen—*ever* must they be reckoned!"

A disquiet settled upon the chamber as the grave warnings gathered in the hearts of the hearers, and then, with a pace quickened by need, Prometheus continued, "More urgent are matters concerning Masule, for he has already broken with the others, though they know not of his treason.

"So great are his failings: his miscount of his prowess, his hunger for violence, his heedless indulgence of cruel whims, his incessant self-celebration—he has become as one divorced from reason, devising in his madness to march upon you in great force of number, for he has spawned and bred his horde like maggots, so that he may count *one thousand* of his children for every *one* of mine.

"Not yet are they afoot, but I forebode they shall cross the wilderness and draw round our country before fifty years is come. Prepare, then—for war. An army you shall raise and I will aid you: infantry and cavalry, brandishing the weapons and clad in the armor I inspired in vision, and for which you saw no purpose beyond beauty—though now grim, that purpose is clear.

"This first I shall do: while you are yet busy with your works, I shall delve caverns as the webs of a great spider beneath the mountains. These darkling roads shall serve us in war—and perhaps…escape. Go *now*, my children; our time is short."

As Prometheus spoke his final word, a whisper filled the Royal Chamber, and his form became as a thousand butterflies. Black were their wings, hemmed in yellow flame, and their flight was as a bustling of leaves lashed by the wind, shifting and climbing, a sinuous shape of fire and shadow, fading as toward the heights they soared, cinders on heated winds that suddenly—were gone.

9.2

Ere autumn of the hundredth year following the escape of Lord Prometheus, Zeushin halted the pursuit. Believing that

99

Prometheus had fled the confines of the world for starless voids innumerable and uncertain, he again turned in tyranny upon his kingdom.

Hundreds of years of disquiet followed the end of the hunt, but Gorthang cared not, for he perceived that his treasonous designs were advancing according to his lusts. He longed for the day when he would come before Zeushin's court and there announce, with unctuous pageantry, that mere days earlier—alone and with terrifying peril to his life—he had discovered the *Promethean pit* amid the forlorn rubble of the Hon-Drowgleer.

A day it was for which he had to wait, surmising and counting at the inception of his design a span of time anchored by his coming revelation, a span of years for Masule's and Sairren's hordes to swarm like grains of sand upon the desert—two armies of men and the Army of the Crown: a host, he surmised, that would devour Prometheus and his *wretched* Prometheans.

Nonetheless, Gorthang yet needed to convince Zeushin to refrain from personally joining the battle—lest his plans come to naught, for he needed the Gods loyal to Zeushin to be swept like shriveled leaves before the scalding wind of Promethean wrath; thus, vulnerable and heedless, they would fall as prey to his plan of ambush.

Masule and Sairren, Gorthang did not expect to survive the war, for he perceived they would fight alongside their hordes and thus come to their doom. Therefore, Gorthang smiled in his thought; for their deaths would give him—and the Gods secretly in his service—mastery over a vast and sprawling tempest, armies of men seething with rage over the deaths of their Fathers.

And lo, they would search for answers, hunting with clenched teeth, open to the suggestion that Zeushin was to blame, that had he but entered the fray, rather than refusing to sully his hands, their Fathers would yet live.

"If apace my design continues," Gorthang mused, "we shall ambush Zeushin and his weakened forces as they recover in the city—and I shall take the crown for myself."

But no sooner had Gorthang outlined the final details of his designs to those in league with his purpose, counting little more than twenty years before the next phase of his plan, than Masule—speaking as a wan fog atop Natteley—triumphantly, flamboyantly, arrogantly announced to the kingdom that *he* had unearthed Prometheus, and that he and his "omnipotent" army—"...strength unrivaled in Vedyah; mightier than a union of Prometheus and Zeushin"—would soon march to vanquish "the thief and oppressor."

So enamored and deluded were many of the Gods with Masule's boastful claims and vainglorious self-celebration, and so filled with hatred were they for the "exploiter," Prometheus, that a third of Zeushin's kingdom departed the city forthwith, purposing to join Masule in his desert redoubt, to march with him and his army against the Prometheans.

The news of Masule's treason filled Gorthang with quenchless hate, yet as his wrath subsided, a new plan he devised to attain his purpose, and coming at once to Lord Zeushin, he found him livid with horror and rage.

"The exploiter's burrow is mere leagues from the city, and he went unnoticed! A third of my kingdom has abandoned their king!" cried Zeushin in a frothing rage. "I shall marshal the Army of the Crown, and we shall pursue the thankless traitors…blood for treason! And then we shall turn to Prometheus."

"*No,* my king—they will destroy themselves," protested Gorthang pleadingly.

"Masule is an insolent cur, and those who have joined him we may count as no loss. Let him march against Prometheus. If he should prevail, we shall slay the survivors with ease—and take his men for ourselves. But I think it more likely he and his rebels will fail—a weakened Prometheus they will leave behind: no match for the Army of the Crown and the men of Sairren. With one stroke, we can destroy the traitors and have our revenge on Prometheus."

Zeushin's face—volcanic with rage, his brow tight and furrowed—softened in the wake of Gorthang's words. A smile twitched at the corners of his lips, and then a wide-mouthed laughter grew therefrom, a haughty laughter that sent its echoes about the chamber like the cackle of crows, for it was come of a blindness and power that contracts with evil and is lost therein.

"*This*...is a stroke of genius, Gorthang," said Zeushin. "We shall watch from afar as the winds of Masule's army crash upon Promethean mountains—then, we shall make our move. But idle I shall not sit—members of the Royal Guard I shall dispatch, nighthawks to survey Sairren's deeds. Should he, too, contemplate treason...they will slit his throat."

"A most wise decision—my king," said Gorthang, bowing as one who ingratiates himself to mask his control.

9.3

To the distant south of the Hon-Drowgleer lay the far-reaching sands of a vast desert; "Chargaroth" it was called by the Gods, "Mumndeeb" by Masule's revolting spawn. Here, Masule and his horde made their kingdom.

The forlorn estate was hemmed by a swift and turbulent river that stretched beyond the horizon, the beaches of which were bordered by swathes of wild though habitable lands, soil rich and fecund. Too numerous to count were squalid dwellings along the banks of the river—primitive huts made of sticks and skins, reeds and mud—these were the dens of the Masulian host, the Masule-azai.

Amidst the windswept dunes, rolling as the swells of tawny seas, scowled a garish citadel made of sand, a palace of ugly ostentation, hewn and mortared by naught but Masule's will. Round that citadel and astride the end of a long road turned an undying storm, roaring as a maniacal beast, a cyclone of sand, the summit of which reached for the firmament, the walls of which no glance could penetrate, no flesh could endure, for the speed of the airborne grains, hissing as they whirled through the air like the cries of the damned, cleaved skin from the meat and meat from the bone.

Yielding only to Masule and his appointed servants, the winds and the sands they carried leap over the road. An arch there would form—a long, dark and howling tunnel. High and wide that tunnel gapped for the arrival of the perfidious Gods, come to pledge themselves to Masule and his kingdom.

Macabre was the month-long celebration that followed. In honor of these "most honorable" Gods, demented festivities were made, for the rape, the murder, and the consumption of man-flesh brought wicked joy to Masule and his iniquitous children. Hotbeds of inhuman torture became the huts of the Masule-azai, women enmeshed in rallies of rape, the gagging screams of each beneath the sweat-soaked, writhing backs of many. The weak were mirthfully slain, the dead dismembered and devoured.

Demonic their faces, the Masule-azai, large their teeth bespattered with gore—gleeful as they ate, gleeful as they raped.

9.4

Valindeal, a member of the Nine and the royal commander of the Razorum, the Promethean army, lay asleep by his wife in their darkened bedchamber. In a dream, he trod over golden sands, watching birds that blithely tossed about on a fragrant breeze. Upon his face rained the warmth of the noontide Sun, and from the shade a cool bed of grass beckoned him.

A river drifted under his gaze, sparkling as though liquid diamonds swam through its waters. Birdsong played against the whimsical tangle of branch and bloom beyond the river, a fountain of music plumed by effervescent notes. Curiously heavy, Valindeal thought to himself, seemed the weight of their many voices….

"…Are they prepared…."

"…The enemy…make haste…."

"…What of the archers…."

"…He is waking him now…."

"Sir…Sir, the watch reported new stars in the night's sky— and they are afoot," gruffly whispered a soldier, his lantern's warm glow captured like sparks in his blue eyes.

Valindeal rose to a seated position amid the weight of anxious voices spilling into the room from the hall.

"What of the scouts beyond the vale?" asked Valindeal, squinting against the lantern's light.

"Nothing…they're dead…or the enemy isn't on the road."

105

Starting shirtless from his bed, his body lean and sculpted, Valindeal ordered, "Sound the alarm—wake the Silver Ring—and send for Moorlin."

The soldier rushed from the room as Valindeal went to the window and drew back the shutters. Amid the night sky, he descried the luminous bane, cadaverous flames that quavered as the candle's light against the draft.

"They have caught us at unawares," he thought angrily to himself.

"What do you see?" came the honeyed voice of Valindeal's wife, Elaylinne; she had raised herself onto her elbow, her lustrous, long hair and fair skin silvered by moon- and starlight.

"The enemy is come," replied Valindeal, his eyes fixed on the falling stars as his mind raced. "To the other room and get dressed—you and the children must leave for the palace at once."

The Razorum was yet to rally, but the Rizoria Rangers were afield and in position to ambush the descending lights. Though he saw them not, Valindeal knew they would be ready to strike.

Reaching forward with his right arm, he called for Prometheus with his mind's voice—but he heard and felt nothing in response. Thrice he beckoned the Lord in vain, and though bewildered, he made ready for battle.

As Valindeal dressed in the night's pallid hue, there came a knock at the door; Moorlin, his adjutant, entered the room, a swinging lantern in one hand and the pommel of his sheathed sword in the other.

"What devilry is this, my commander?" asked Moorlin breathlessly, an angry tone of apprehension in his voice. "Are we to fight the Gods, or are the Masule-azai winged like bats and aflame like cinders?"

"Gods or men, winged or no, here they will find naught but death," replied Valindeal.

At that moment, the long, dour note of a horn hastened over the kingdom, the vibrations of the blast rendering themselves to the flesh as much as the hearing.

Swiftly, what few lights burned across the city went dark, and in the distance, many new lights blinked amongst the ramose trees of a creeping forest—a decoy city to bewilder an attacker.

"What of Lord Ethelleyah?" asked Moorlin as the horn faded.

"I know not," replied Valindeal, lacing his boots.

"But we will need him."

"And he will come," said Valindeal confidently, rising from his seat. "Go to the White Council and the Silver Ring in the Royal Chamber…tell them what we know—and to prepare for war."

"What do we know?" shot Moorlin.

"By dawn—fire will fall by the sword, or Sentilleena will burn."

Slipping past Moorlin, Valindeal entered the hall at a trot, two soldiers at his bedchamber door departing with him.

The bare streets were become as lunar-shined arteries aflow with Prometheans—some speeding to safety, others to danger. Soldiers assumed posts across the ramparts and in Qwindellin's many windows, even as women, children, and the elderly hastened for the palace and the refuge of its thick walls.

The mingled sounds of officers bellowing orders, the clamor of weapons and the grunts of beasts pushed to their limits splintered the stillness of the night. Men on horseback galloped through the darkened streets, carrying messages and speeding to positions. Regiments of soldiers hastened as windswept lace amid the night shade, winding toward the wide plains, the luster of their arms as the sheen of starlight upon the foam of an angry sea.

Followed by his personal guard, attendant captains and messengers, Valindeal raced toward the plain as a grey ghost atop a silvern steed, the beast's white hair aloft and gleaming in the moonlight, its muscles churning as furious cords beneath taut skin, its hooves gouging the dark earth and hurling it skyward, eager as its master for glory.

"Commander!" shouted Remlokk, a Ranger captain with a short red beard and long red hair, an old tangled scar across his ever-young face.

Valindeal espied Remlokk in a thicket of trees paralleling the plain, and there he joined him. With Remlokk were several messengers and soldiers. Their helms and armor, which normally blazed, were cloaked in dun raiment. Shadowed were their faces under the flaring cheeks and proud nasals of their helms; their eye-slits were as haunted chasms, expressionless and grim.

"We're in position. As soon as they alight, we'll pin 'em with a volley…maybe two…then we'll charge…hew 'em where they stand," said Remlokk hoarsely, the fierce determination in his voice spreading its doughty fire to his eyes.

"What is their count?" asked Valindeal, his personal guard pulling round the group, their horses snorting, muscles quivering, hides wet with sweat.

"Five hundred—maybe more," dismissively replied Remlokk, pulling his helmet down over his face.

Valindeal followed Remlokk's gaze toward the vault and the shooting stars.

"What creatures are these that attack from the heavens?" asked Valindeal.

"I know not. No more can be seen with the spyglass," grumbled Remlokk, shaking his head.

"They will land before the Razorum is in position," observed Valindeal, drawing the cold steel of his sword from its sheath, a shrill cry leaping from the blade as the point slipped into view. "We are few, but we are great—our sacrifice for the immortality and glory of our Nation."

Valindeal's guard drew their steeds around him, and they made ready to charge into battle.

Extending his arm, Valindeal called for Prometheus once more, but there, silence he did not find, for a fog of voices filled his thoughts, a confusion he could not disembroil.

"What is it?" shot Remlokk, noticing Valindeal's puzzled expression.

"Something muddies the waters. There are many voices…I think…or a single voice that comes through endless echoes."

Remlokk gave a sharp nod, and through gritted teeth, he ordered his men to prepare to fire.

A note from a small horn went up and was joined by others as the descending lights took hue and shape, though still some distance beyond the pinnacles of the tallest trees.

Even as the night waters buoyed the stars of heaven, serenading their sojourn with the music of tiny ripples, the soldiers girded themselves for war: the slow, quiet slide of the arrow's shaft, the crepitating of sinew and wood under tension, the silent menace of the sword's edge, thirsty for blood. To this, men added the choppy breath of dread and mingled mirages, of the laughter and smiles of those whom they love woven with visions of struggle, of the clash of arms, of screams, of gore.

"I see them," eagerly reported one of Remlokk's aids, studying the descending lights with a spyglass. "Gods...I believe...of varying scope...the less glorious are borne by the greater...not injured, but carried."

Remlokk raised a spyglass and examined the enemy. Then he lowered it as though it were a burden, lowered it as one resigned to fate. Muscles flexing in his jaw, Remlokk raised his arm and growled, "On my order."

"Wait!" cried Valindeal. "Our Lord speaks."

"Join me, Valindeal—here, before the fires in the sky."

Scouring the darkness, Valindeal marked Prometheus in the effulgence of the falling stars.

"Stand fast, Remlokk." ordered Valindeal. "Our Lord meets the invader alone and without fear. Look there—he is upon the field."

As a horn signaled the order to stand down, Valindeal coaxed his steed into a trot across the plain.

Springing from his saddle, he joined Prometheus before the invading swarm.

"My Lord...the shooting stars...," said Valindeal confusedly, motioning to the hundreds of shimmering Gods alighting upon the earth.

"I sensed the cries of the Nine, and yet my thoughts were consumed by the divine heralds, ancient powers whose voices could not be quelled. I came at once from my labyrinthine labors in the grottos and chambers beneath the mountains.

"I felt my children gathering for war—and their great leader, Valindeal of the Nine and Royal Commander, speeding with all haste to the contest—to the sacrifice of his life in the service of our Nation.

"I am proud to call the Prometheans my children, my heirs, yet not this night will you lay down your lives or wet your swords with blood—for these are the Valaroma, the Riders of Vengeance, allies of the Kristelyn, enemy of the horde, friends who have come in our darkest hour."

By the wise it has long been held
that the joy of this fateful night
that the bravery and the fright
that the moment of the sight
has thus sown by some means unknown
Promethean affinity for the falling star
for by light of shooting star came salvation from afar
and some yet hold among the wise
mirrored in the tears of suffering eyes
there again will fall the shooting star
a gleaming omen of salvation
and its healing light upon an ancient scar

will join the ties of a wayward Nation.

9.5

Little here is told of the fellowship and merriment that flourished between Promethean and Valaroma, yet let it be said that much rejoicing festooned Cindillin's Vale for a time all too brief before the coming of war—and the war's aftermath: the fragmenting of the Promethean Nation, named—even in those days—"the Sahnderring."

Felicity and profit were had by both men and Gods, for both marveled at the other, seeking eagerly to learn with as much vigor as each sought to teach, cherishing the days in the cheerless knowledge that their like would neither share another sunset nor celebrate another dawn.

Transfixed were the Prometheans by the sudden spectacle of the Valaroma, for though none drew nigh the power and glory of Lord Prometheus, they were nonetheless more powerful than themselves, and yet like to themselves—unequal in their talents and abilities. This, then, was the basis for the many classifications that men gave to the Gods, classifications that persist in myriad terms and fluid definitions.

To the weakest of the Gods they gave names like unto warlock and witch, and mage and magess. These were divine men and women, scarcely more powerful than the Prometheans. Stronger and quicker were they—and keener their senses. Small objects they could move if they wished with naught but their will, and flowers they could coax into bloom in the palms of their hands. They could sense the Clay in all things, as one who peers through a heavy fog and descries shapes therein, so that at times they seemed to speak with animals or to commune with the elements of the Earth.

With great effort, the mage and magess could take to the airs as if upon wings, though the skies were not their domain and their time aloft was brief. Storms they could summon and dispel—though they could not control them. Fires they could throw, and the thoughts of those whose wills were weaker than their own they could plumb.

Beyond these were given names like unto enchanter and enchantress, wizard and wizardess. In their formless thoughts, all Gods could walk, forgoing the raiment of their bodies, yet none weaker than these could clothe themselves in different shapes, assuming forms like unto creatures widely known or shapes of their own designs. These could rise as hills among men, swells upon storm-lashed seas, white-crested and tall, dark and terrible to behold.

Though diminished, weaker and with less endurance, the wizard and wizardess, and those greater than themselves, wielded in all ways the magicks of the greater Gods.

Beyond these were given names like unto sorcerer and sorceress, demigod and demigoddess, and beyond these retained the titles of God and Goddess. But even of these, none were like to the power and splendor of Prometheus: for he wielded the powers and subtleties of all others in excess, and yet he evinced magicks far greater, the limits of which he alone could fathom.

Joyous and yet sad were those days, for none who lived could fail to heed the coming of darkness, yet their memory is not lost, for remembered in song, in story, and lay, are the tales of halcyon times, and none more blissful nor so mournful than the brotherhood of Gods and men—in the fair city of white Sentilleena under the reign of Prometheus Ethelleyah.

The Battle of Arn-gelwain

10.1

Dranggist, a potent sorcerer wearing the likeness of a great ebon eagle, descended through azure skies toward white Sentilleena, his brindled feathers rustling against the warm air, his ash-blond talons outstretched for the paving stones of a bright lane—the eagle's cry, piercing and shrill.

Alighting upon the earth, and again in the shape of a man as though stepping from reverie, his long blond hair fell silkily upon princely robes, his deep green eyes glinting in the sunlight. Taking the glance of none, he hastened toward Qwindellin's gates.

Within the palace, a gallery echoed with the thrum of gravity and grace. Touched by the craft of the artisan, svelte candelabra grew there like stalk and stem of flower and vine, and maps there were, beautifully embellished, exceedingly detailed, some arrayed upon the walls and others unfurled upon desks.

Prometheus, Valindeal, captains of the Razorum and Rizoria, and Gods and Goddesses examined the maps in meticulous study. Of interest was Arn-gelwain, a region that lay upon the marches of the Hon-Drowgleer. There, prostrate lay an unremarkable lowland bordered by a horseshoe plateau and the tributary gorges that twined the heights.

Though safer paths there were through the wastes of the Hon-Drowgleer, it was here the Masule-azai would likely pass, for no paths other were as straight or as accommodating to their stunted foresight. And though Masule, their maker and leader, reckoned himself a great thinker, he had never displayed profound thoughts of his own; thus, the most obvious route would spring to him as genius—and to his mind no other would come.

This, the Prometheans believed, would be the March of Masule, and with this fact they were well pleased. For of the countless burrows Prometheus had delved under the Hon-Drowgleer, not few wound their way to the gorges of Arn-gelwain. There, the many gorges bordering the plain invited ambush upon the luckless or witless who trod its naked paths.

At length, Dranggist entered the gallery, and all drew breath as he swept into view. Saluting Prometheus, he spoke gravely to the purpose of his errand.

"My Lord, the Masule-azai are upon the road; they are not more than ten days' march from Arn-gelwain, and thither their path leads. Yet—more grievous is the March of Masule than conceived, for a third of the divine marches with them."

The gravity of the advancing threat struck deep roots into the pall of silence. Impassive were the Gods' faces, yet those of the Prometheans hardened with courage—and darkened with certitude.

"Against us there is kindled a great fire of hatred, of guile and ferocity, of conquest and cunning," began Prometheus. "Extremes that must be fought by extremes. With greater venom and more wrath, with deeper guile and hotter ferocity, with less mercy and crueler cunning—we will meet the invader.

"Upon the plain of Arn-gelwain—there we shall carry the banner of our Nation against the foe. None shall withstand our coming, and none shall pass our leaguer. Yea, as parched hills are blackened by the feral flame, may we desolate the Masulian horde!" thus spoke Prometheus the Lord.

Raucous was the cheering in that hour, for the battle cry had been raised as a sorcerous intonation upon the airs, and by it the courage of both men and Gods were driven as if by divine bellows, a white-hot flame—ravenous and insatiable.

Turning to the Rizoria Ranger and Razorum captains, Prometheus ordered: "Fly with all haste through the darkling caverns; fly, and come not forth until I deem the hour ripe."

Ere the horizon climbed over the Sun, the Rangers entered the shadowy tunnels on horseback, laden with supplies and smoke-roiling torches. And the following morn, hauling loaded wains with creaking wheels of iron and wood, the Razorum began their long march through the belly of the mountains.

Seven days' journey it was from the Vale of Cindillin to Arn-gelwain. Two or three days would they have—no more—to rest and prepare before the coming of the horde.

10.2

Even as the long columns of the Razorum slinked like burnished snakes into the caverns under Qwindellin, the Gods were not idle, for they had convened a momentous gathering in the Royal Chamber. And so it was that upon the eve of war, Prometheus Ethelleyah sat upon his coruscating throne in the center of the lofty coliseum, white peacocks of elegance and bewitching ocelli standing as enchanted guards before the limb of the world, encircled by an army of Gods and a marshaling for war.

Therewith, Prometheus spoke much about the coming of war and the duties of the Gods, addressing his legions, saying, "If you have pledged your loyalty to me, then let also that loyalty pass to my children. If you have linked your fates to mine, then let also your fates be linked to those of my children, for war is come upon us, and we must fight even as I have trained my children to fight— as a single Nation—a single mind—a single heart."

As one conducting music, Prometheus held forth a discourse ranging far and wide, yet he spoke not alone, for he was interrupted by Odindayne, a God of great prowess. Tall and fierce, he had championed Prometheus's cause when fear had sewn shut the mouths of others. Silver was his hair, crimson was his mantle, and withering was his glance.

"My Lord, we have done much to rouse you from torpor, from groveling deference and willful ignorance, from participation in your own oppression—we wish it not that you would come forth to battle, risking all we have so long endeavored to preserve.

"In our youth, I was as far from attributing evil intent to the self-styled *exploited* as they were from intending good. I denounced the prospect of their conspiracy against us with as much vigor as they conspired against us. Yet I could not and would not deny facts when to me the truth was revealed by others.

"Forgive righteous indignation when its shield is wrath— and justice when its sword is reckoning. My will is strong, Lord. My hatred for the enemy—small though it was, now blazes within me. Does the seed once planted and carefully tended break not the soil? How much more does the passion of retribution strike deep roots when planted in the debilitating soil of guilt, and tended diligently by the self-proclaimed *victim*?

"If oil lights the lantern and yet threatens the abode, has guilt not lighted the enemy's path and yet threatened to consume him in flame?

"Well, Lord, I am the flame burst free of the lantern's cage; I am the fire that shall devour the enemy. He who is persecuted in the name of equality by revenge, and has thus become vengeful, shall brook neither persecution nor set limit on vengeance.

"Trial has tested me. Sacrifice has proved me. If the Lord permit it, let proof of my sacrifice be tested in trial once again. Let me lead the attack against Masule and his profane horde. *Pity*, I will show not the enemy."

"Nay, Odindayne," objected Prometheus, motioning to his throne and the world beneath him. "For what cause would I assume these royalties if I were but a craven? Wherefore would the Crown of Stars rest upon my brow if I refused as great a share of danger as esteem? No. To him with the greatest reward must go the greatest hazard. Prometheus Ethelleyah will go to war, and you will be by his side. Together, dear friend, *pity* we will show not the enemy."

Saluting the Lord as one whose honor is met by honor, Odindayne returned to his seat, harkening with great interest and vengeful delight to the address that Prometheus then made to the weakest of Gods.

"Many are bound by strengths little more than those wielded by my children, yet this need not be so. For those who wish to be more and greater and yet endure a changeless sacrifice, I offer this: come forward and I shall put upon you the form of your choosing—and more, for I shall invest in you more power and glory than was your fate.

"The form you cannot change, for I will not further diminish my strength by amending my work, and you will have not the power to reverse the making. But hear me; some must take a shape of *my* choosing, for I purpose to raise an army beyond terror—quenchless in its wrath."

10.3

On the morn of battle, white Sentilleena blushed with the rose of dawn as silver trumpets greeted the rising Sun. Bright were the many banners that billowed from the stainless turrets of Qwindellin, and glimmering were the rainbows that played upon the white fume of the many falls at her back.

So it was that even as the Sun rose on the blanched fields of Arn-gelwain, thick with the advancing swarm of Masule-azai, a music of trumpets and a beauty was put upon the airs as a garland and blessing upon the valiant defenders—silently waiting in ambush.

10.4

The wide plain of Arn-gelwain lay submerged beneath the thronging Masule-azai, and yet more there were—far more—for the great bulk of their force lay throttled in the gulches and ravines to the south of the plain, and still more in the wild, uncharted, and nameless lands beyond.

In the van of that profane host, cocooned in a bronze fog and trailed by his cortege, marched Masule; gaudily adorned was his battle helm and raiment of war, a boastful and grotesque spectacle. Towering twenty feet over the Masule-azai, Masule was followed and flanked by many Gods, most of whom had drawn themselves to similar height. But more Gods there were in the midst of the Masule-azai: some as men of normal height, some as men striding amid swine, and some in the shapes of birds that flung great winged shadows over the writhing horde.

Only the Masule-azai elite, marching in the vanguard behind their Lord, could be said to resemble an army, for their raiment and weapons had been fashioned by the Gods. The remainder of their host, though strong-limbed and bestial-tempered, came to war wearing naught but grasses and skins, wielding little more than sharpened sticks and reed baskets brimming with stones.

Great landships laden with supplies were driven by Masule-azai, helmsmen that hoarsely shouted and fiercely swung barbed whips, thick and angry coils, thongs covered in blood and flesh. Savagely they lashed their luckless countrymen, who, bound by their necks, heaved upon ropes anchored to the looming prows.

The thrum of the masses under the scorching Sun was as a sonorous din: the in- and exhalation of countless lungs filling the air with a putrid breath; the churning of the landships' great wheels upon the hard, desiccated turf; the shuffling of innumerable feet as a grievous portent to the city of Sentilleena. This evil, and yet more, gathered as the strident chords of a demonic hymn, rising from the plain as a thick and listless bedlam, choked by the churned earth that lay as a death shroud upon the swarm.

Flecked by frayed nerves and hostile tempers—screams and angry howls of fratricide—the Masule-azai plodded mindlessly toward the promise of rapine, of sexual feasting upon Promethean women and children, of beautiful homes in which to squat and fine adornment to don in garish excess, of succulent foods to swill and of glittering riches to wreath vacuous lives.

As the van of the Masule-azai drew in upon the northern rim of the wide plain, the host abruptly halted as though it were a prey herd alarmed by the sight or scent of a predator, for at that moment, a presence blocking the path came as an icy wind to their hearts, a deathless foreboding of ruin and pain.

With divine eyes, Masule gazed northward and yet saw nothing—his will checked. Yet, from the air as though stepping through a fog, there strode a large and menacing warhorse: black was its coat, black as the abyss before the coming of light, crimson were its eyes as though pierced by darts and swirling with blood— haunted was its saddle.

Though unblinking, none spoke as the warhorse drew near: high was its doom, a vision of horror that crawled like worms through flesh, and with each stride it grew until it soared over Masule as a horse over men. When at length, the beast drew within a bow's range, a rider, as if gathered on the breeze, took shape upon its back.

The Masule-azai were dismayed, and some in the van turned from the march; with their weapons they cut through their brethren, fear driving them through many wounds until breath escaped through many holes. But if these were smitten with horror, the Masulian Gods were no less disheartened, for they guessed rightly his name who upon that dreadful beast sat, and all but Masule deemed true the change that had come to the Black Rider's heart.

Together, Rider and horse were as a nightmare, the likes of which the world had never known, for the Black Rider wore a hooded cloak of fire and smoke, tongues of ruby flame leaping amid coils of raven fume, hands of jointed steel gripping leathern reins.

Nigh the beast and its rider, the stones and dust of the earth smoldered beneath the withering blaze, and above, a halo of swimming heat soared atop invisible vapor: a horror that probed the weaknesses of onlookers as with needles of ice, and slipping through raiment pierced the flesh.

*Clop…clop…clop…*went the hoofbeats of the warhorse as it drew in upon the host—*clop…clop…clop…*went the sound of doom under a cloak of fire.

When death it seemed would swallow them all, the warhorse halted, growling, its blood-filled eyes streaming, and probing. The cloak's fires hissed and the smoke writhed upon the whisper of a breeze, and Masule recalled the courage that had failed him. With great effort to restore his flagging spirit, he forced himself to laugh haughtily, and then he spoke to the rider in hostile derision.

"Now I see clearly…foolhardy malcontent…outcast," said Masule hubristically, a mocking chuckle punctuating his words.

"It is the exploiter himself…an agent of insurrection…a hater and an inciter of hatred…the thief…the oppressor."

Cavalierly turning his back on the Black Rider, arms flung open in a gesture of arrogant disbelief, Masule put a spell upon his voice so all could discern his contemptuous words.

"Look now, my children…see here the hater…the thief and oppressor has come. HA! To parlay…perhaps? To beg for mercy and forgiveness for his exploitation of others—I should think! HA! A captain with no army. Outcast! Thankless is he. Impudent! Not upon a steed, but come he should on bended knees—begging for my mercy and forgiveness."

Turning to the Black Rider, emboldened by his silence and inaction, emboldened by the Masule-azai's screams and rumbles of cacophonous laughter, Masule arrogantly continued.

"I see you have fashioned a new cloak…. I like it not, but do conceal your guilt and shame…exploiter. If it were not for *my* genius and labors—"

"From you, Masule, naught of value has ever come," issued the minatory voice of the Rider from under the hood.

Deep as the grinding crusts of the Earth, powerful as the collision of worlds upon the moment of impact, so too was the voice of the Black Rider—a power that shook the hills and drew crying winds about his foe.

Fear flashed in spasms across Masule's face, a shadow of doubt growing heavily upon him as he quailed before the Rider's power.

"What did you say?" he shouted, hastily stirring his rage, dismayed by the Rider's indifference to his words, expecting the Rider to submit, submit as he had in the past, submit as he had to words and to words alone.

"Get down, oppressor! Get down and crawl on your knees. Beg me for forgiveness! Outcast…outcas—"

At that moment, the Black Rider took hold of naught, which was become a stainless white staff as a pillar of marble, crowned with a great vermilion stone. Masule fell silent, and he

127

gazed at the staff in horror; but with pretentious rage, he suffocated his growing fears.

"Get down on your knees. Persecutor! Exploiter! Get down!"

In the midst of the shouting, the Black Rider leveled his staff: a sourceless shadow leapt from the crowning stone, and it struck Masule as with the force of a great hammer. The sky roared, the earth heaved under foot, and Masule catapulted backward, sliding, scattering rocks, gouging the ground, tumbling through rank upon rank of the Masule-azai, crushing them with the weight of his body.

The staff then twined about the Rider's arm, limber as silken thread, taking to itself the form of a great white serpent, hissing like volcanic fissures, scales like virgin snow. Lissomely it coiled about its master and steed, its scarlet tongue flicking the air, fangs dripping amber venom, vermilion eyes gleaming and murderous.

Rising, dirt and gore falling from his back, Masule leered at the Black Rider, and yanking his sword from its scabbard, marched fiercely across the shattered earth.

"You…insolent…thief! Get in your place."

Saying naught, the Rider threw back his hood, and there, in his undiminished glory, was the face of Prometheus Ethelleyah: a stern countenance, a wrathful countenance, and a dreadful helm upon his head. For there, perched atop the helm, gleaming in the sunlight as an adamant fire upon liquid silver, a likeness of a fell beast unknown to the world: jaws gaping, wings outstretched, a monster beyond terror—a *dragon*.

"Words will not avail you," said Prometheus with a dark and mirthless laughter. "Dull has the edge of those weapons become—for *guilt* haunts me no more.

"Your path is well-worn, but here lies the end of your road, for I come bearing the helm of war, the Dragon Crown, and upon its crest rears the sign of your doom. Go back to your depravity and send word to your allies that *I* am Prometheus Ethelleyah, father of the Promethean Nation. Kindle our wrath—and you kindle your pyre."

"Proud words for an exploiter," answered Masule, a tremor in his voice betraying his fear. "A ruler…of hatred…father of cravens more like it—where are your children now? Their leader comes to war while they cower. HA! I think today…my children and I…and the Gods of my kingdom will slay the mighty— *oppressor.*"

"You have chosen death," said Prometheus coldly, his eyes seething with rage.

At that moment, as though all Vedyah gathered to heed, the hills and gorges of that wide region came alive with the baying of the Promethean horns of war, bewitching the enemy with terror, enkindling their imaginations with visions of indomitable men, unflagging warriors who slay with grim purpose and laugh in the midst of combat. So dreadful was the wailing of those horns that not few of the Masule-azai became crazed, scrambling like the rodent that flees the long sight and sharp bite of the merciless hawk.

At the baying of the horns, the Promethean host leapt forth from the gorges and hills in sudden onslaught, curling like a toppling wave racing for the shore, the light of their arms as a fire upon glittering spires of ice. From east and west the Promethean banners assailed the enemy so as to take the Masule-azai as between hammer and anvil. So swift, so fell was the onset that through the horde they hewed with hindrance little more than grain resists the reaper.

Unchecked by the will of Prometheus, Masule sensed the presences of the Promethean Nation; and in his heart, he counted their number even as the clash of arms rang stridently about the plain.

"Your children...they are too few, Prometheus...not a whisper against the roar I have assembled. Even if each of yours slays hundreds of mine, yours will yet be overwhelmed...far beyond the passes to the south stretches the train of my brood...and to this counting I have added not the measure of Masulian Gods."

"I too have brought friends," said Prometheus, dropping the veil of his power behind which the Valaroma had lain hidden. With great ferocity, they came forth upon the enemy, and despite their inferior number, the Masulian Gods quailed before them.

Most were in their natural forms as of men and women donning the implements of war, yet others there were who came forth as great and fearsome beasts. From the blind of ambush, some fell upon the enemy in shapes alike to wolves and warhorses, others as serpents and hounds, and still others upon the airs as eagles and bats.

Then it was that Prometheus loosed his final strength upon the foe, for a great, dark cloud appeared upon the limb of the pale vault, and it moved against the wind as it descended in haste. Down swirled the mountainous thunderhead, snarling, roaring, cleaved with lightning that became as glistening talons and serrated teeth, a legion of dragons winging over the plain, hurling jets of liquid fire.

The choking screams and desperate cries of men washed over the pitted fields of Arn-gelwain: throats pierced by spears, veins severed, geysers of black froth, lungs filling with blood round the tusks of jagged darts, flesh melting under the dragons' inferno, fighters fighting, fighters killed. And the ground streamed blood.

Hard was the charge of Prometheus, and leaping forth from his galloping steed, leaving the warhorse and serpent behind, collided with Masule with such force that a tremor ran through the world. Dragging his stunned prey toward the heavens, he was followed by half the Masulian Gods, seeking, if they might, to aid Masule in his mortal contest. But aid the Valaroma lent not to Prometheus, for they knew his children needed protection from the Masulian Gods who remained—a number, though halved, that yet was greater than the Valaroma.

Like Arn-gelwain, the heavens were become a field of combat, cast into a rolling madness of vivid colors and deafening explosions, hammering the earth with thunderous shockwaves, hurling men and Gods from their feet in the midst of combat. Thrice at the outset, Masule fled the contest, and resting upon the peak of a mountain, nursed his wounds and watched in horror as Masulian Gods fell lifeless from the firmament—their mangled corpses crashing upon and near the earthbound combatants.

Under the vault's glowing tumult, the mail-clad Prometheans shone like rivers of steel. Wielding gallant swords and long spears that bristled like a forest capped by shining petals, they smashed into the thick-skinned Masule-azai, leaving blood and gore in their wake.

Shrill were the cries of the Masule-azai as Promethean heroes cleaved through their ranks, piercing them with lethal darts, caving their thick skulls, and hewing their legs from under them. Yet, as evenfall approached, the tide of war turned against the exhausted Prometheans; for their muscles burned, and their arms no longer had strength to wield their shattered weapons.

Ever did fresh Masule-azai pour from the ravines to the south, slowly pushing the Prometheans toward the gorges whence they came. In their retreat, they no longer trod over earth, for strewn under foot writhed a mire of the slain and dying. Here, atop two, three, and four bodies deep, no footing could be found, forcing the Prometheans to fall back toward the darkling caverns, which increasingly beckoned as the hope of escape.

In that desperate hour, the Wilding Kingdom went to war; for their maker and Lord, Prometheus, summoned them to the aid of his children.

From the pits of the earth sprang venomous creatures that punctured with lethal thorns the naked legs of the enemy. Birds there were that vexed the attackers, or as raptors fell upon their faces and dug their eyes from their heads. Great cats, wolf packs, and bears emerged from their caves, and they slew the Masule-azai with red claw and razor fang. And herds of rams thundered down slopes, smiting the enemy and shattering their bones: fragments tearing through flesh, marrow swirling in the dust.

And more there were—animals of every description assailed the enemy, fighting and dying even as men fought and died. But not only in Arn-gelwain did the Wilding Kingdom go to war, for wherever Masule-azai drew breath, fell beasts and the small but many legged monsters assailed them.

There, to the south of Arn-gelwain, the Masule-azai reinforcements were waylaid by the onslaught of the Wilding Kingdom, and away in Chargaroth—armies of ants and hooked fanged spiders bit with venom and stinger. And monsters of aforetime drew themselves up from the rivers; with snapping jaws they took the Masule-azai at unawares, wreaking much havoc before a defense could be made.

With the confusion wrought by the onset of the beasts, the Prometheans cleaved their way back to the mouths of the gorges and there formed defensive positions: impenetrable walls of barbed spears upon which the Masule-azai foundered in grisly eddies of death.

Ere dusk, Masule, the last of the Gods to strive with Prometheus beyond the heavens, fell therefrom, and crashing upon the jagged shoulder of a mountain—lay dead, vanquished by Prometheus Ethelleyah.

Turning his attention to the south before joining the Valaroma as they strove with the remaining Masulian Gods, Prometheus discerned that the battle went ill for the Wilding Kingdom, for there they were unaided, fighting alone against the Masule-azai.

Beckoning them to hasten for cover, Prometheus raised his thoughts to the ether: stygian clouds there formed over the nameless and forlorn lands, gaseous mountains plumed with roiling black crowns, their feet upon the ceiling of the sky and their heads bowed by the reaches of the vault. Winds churned therein, roaring and swirling and reaching toward the earth with sinuous fingers, whereupon they became as grey pillars of madness, gorging themselves upon the enemy.

Then it was that Prometheus alighted beside Masule's lifeless body, and drawing himself up to the height of a towering and monstrous hill, he held aloft the corpse in his hand, causing a surcease in the battle as every warrior studied the grim spectacle.

Bellowing so that none failed to heed his words, the voice of Prometheus rained as thunderbolts upon the field of combat.

"Here is your God; and I, Prometheus Ethelleyah, have slain him. Your king is dead!"

And with these words, he threw the disfigured corpse to the plain below; heavy, it fell amidst the Masule-azai.

He then loosed the dreadful cloak which yet hung about his neck. As the raven-coiled flames fell to the earth, he stepped forth in power and majesty: armor clad and coruscating as a silvern sunrise, eclipsing and joining the power of the setting Sun, bathing the earth in mingled beams of silver and gold.

Descending the mountain in fury, Prometheus tore the earth asunder so that fissures opened across the plain: great and angry mouths, effluvia-breathed, thrust molten tongues from hungry gullets, lapping Masule-azai as they fled.

With the aid of their Lord, the Valaroma slew the remaining Masulian Gods, but pyrrhic was their victory, for more than two hundred Valaroma and thousands of Prometheans had succumbed to the dreamless sleep, lying dead about the field like flowers freshly cut from their roots.

Soon after, night flung her dark cape as she wrapped cool arms round the weary combatants, and though silencing not the cries of the maimed and dying, nor subduing the perfume of death, she brought reprieve from the Battle of Arn-gelwain—of which all is now told.

10.5

All the dead were mourned, but of Valaroma, some there were dearer to the Prometheans than others—and their passing more grievous. Among these was Sauouel—the "healer" he was called, for his joy was in the mending and curing of Promethean pains. So too perished, Kaluva, Morren, Es-tay, and Illeera, pedagogues of unequaled patience and perseverance.

And fell also the "gardener," so named for his love of all things that lived with root and leaf: his true name was Arnum, and

136

he drew his last breath in the form of a red dragon—yellow eyed. So ended his coequal, Fingonne, for he also was a keeper of plants and trees, and like Arnum, in the form of a dragon amid the heaviest fighting, he was slain: charcoal were his scales and black were his wings.

Perhaps second only to Prometheus, most beloved was Airehdelle, for like a mother she sang with an enchanted voice to the children of her adoption, the Prometheans whom she dearly loved. In joy, the Prometheans called to Airehdelle—gladness in hymns of beauty. In reverence, they spoke of the Lady Airehdelle—a vision of bewitching elegance. In longing, they cried to Airehdelle-Alass—their solace and sacred mother.

A Goddess of great prowess, she was a figure of momentous glory, for aloft in her eyes burned the triumphant flame of creation, paralyzing with wonderment those who looked upon her splendor. Oft she was seen with Prometheus, and for a time all too brief, the Kristelyn viewed the pair as father and mother of their Nation. Much gladness, it is held, was kindled in Promethean hearts when toward one another they turned with subtle smiles and lingering stares. And what joy more when rumor found them hand in hand to have walked the many gardens of Cindillin's Vale.

Supple was her skin, long was her hair, yet changeful were the silken strands, for at times they glimmered as though bodying forth the Sun, shone with the silver of the Moon, flared with the ruby's eye of the flame, enchanted with the rich pallet of the earth, seduced with the darkness of the night.

Hers was the loveliness in the stars' frost upon the twilight before dawn, and her coming brought forth the flowers into bloom. With a clarion voice as pure as the firmament and as enigmatic as the music of creation, she sang and it seemed that round her voice welled the sounds of many fair and lovely instruments.

In Sentilleena's enrapturing places, its many ambrosial gardens, its moonlit fountains quicksilvered by the night, and beyond—by the limpid pools in the vale, and upon the cool turf nigh the verdant hills, Airehdelle, mother of the Promethean Nation, poured forth her music, filling her children with wonder and delight, enchanting them with a mystifying and radiant magick.

Her mellifluous voice oft spoke as a whisper unlooked for, a euphony and redolence that lured suppliants along whimsical paths and through hidden forests. Thus, like a specter she moved through their lives, a song from afar that soothed the ailed and incited the strong.

So it was that she brought a new beauty to Cindillin's Vale, and in the measure of that beauty naught can compare. Yet many ages would pass before Promethean eyes would look again upon the mother of their Nation; for she was wounded to the death, and would have died indeed had it been not for Prometheus, who, having found her on the fields of Arn-gelwain in the waning moments of life, cradling her in his arms, brought her back from the limb of death with the tears that rained from his eyes.

So grievous her wounds and so long the span for their mending that Prometheus hid her in the deepest hollows below the mountains. And though her clarion voice and luminous beauty were long remembered and preserved in song and tale, she was seen never again until The Odyssey of the King.

In the Hymn of Arn-gelwain, it is sung that the battle ended when the first stars of dusk lit slate the night clouds that feathered the sky; soon after, the Promethean wounded and dead were gathered and taken homeward upon numerous biers, rimmed by torches and adorned with wildflowers. In many songs and lays now long forgotten, it was recalled that though joyous was their victory, bitter was the taste, for many valiant warriors had fallen to the foe.

Upon the fields of Arn-gelwain there fell the mighty Raddigan beneath the slain bodies of fifty Masule-azai. And there fell Dwarin of the noble house of Callunsey. There also perished Halrod, Graw, and Marmakk, valiant captains of the Razorum. And slain too was Galmunde Ümber-mane, and Loyalad, whose eyes gleamed green like emeralds in shallow waters, his heart pierced by a Masulian sword. And by his side was found his brother, Winnom, his eyes lain open, brown as richly polished wood, still moist with tears—his body he used as a shield to thwart the defilement of his slain brother. And in Eredain's lap died his eldest son, Felori, a man of three and twenty years, though ever his father's baby boy.

And many more Prometheans there fell, as valiant and as fair as the world has ever known. It is said that amidst the celebration of victory when finally home the heroes returned, long there echoed an endless dirge of changing melodies, a lamentation lit by many lamps—for the dead, and for the living.

Of the Masule-azai, there is little more to tell, for few survived that had gone to war, though these in their flight went not far from the field of combat. Returning when once the Prometheans were gone, they took that dreadful country for their home: and with the carrion beasts, and with the writhing maggots, feasted long upon their fallen brothers.

Ere Masule took his final breath, the storm that churned round his redoubt fell as it were a long curtain from a lofty rod. Thence, it was looted and occupied by the most savage Masule-azai. As a Nation, the Masule-azai splintered into countless packs, each tyrannized by the most robust and bloodthirsty male: a hideous and bestial blight upon the lands in which they dwelt.

The Battle of Fallowsgate

11.1

Sairren sat himself down and made his dark kingdom in a land lying many leagues to the north and east of Cindillin's Vale; named "Oradüme" by the Gods, by many names did Sairren's children, the Sarraneem, call their country: "Shie-kawa" and "Yawahns," "Clangshee" and many others.

In that distant place, the Sarraneem, as numerous as had been the Masule-azai ere the Battle of Arn-gelwain, built countless stone dwellings: diminutive and grotty, thatched, bleak and squalid. Theirs was a land of steppes and heaving verdure that embraced the seeping Fens of Hhóm, a country that stood on the marches of a vast everglade, sweeping from south to north along the eastern borders of the land. Here was an outland of jungled bogs and mires that served as the haunts of biting and stinging insects—countless in their swarms.

Central and westward, the murky swamps released the turf as it climbed ever higher into the plains, giving way to grasslands that were thickly veined, wrinkled and furrowed with nameless rivers that branched like foaming lightning toward somber lakes. Upon the steppes of that land, Sairren built Mongzching, the Sarraneem's capital city. Nigh that city's center, his garish palace sprawled behind leering ramparts, stone walls queerly embellished, portalled and barricaded with the snarling teeth of wrought iron gates, behind which another wall and another gate rose from the earth in numbers uncounted.

Like to a shelled beast in form and countenance, the serrated palace clung heavily to the earth. It too resembled the roofless walls that ringed its courtyards, for within mounted wall upon wall behind which, in its innermost chamber, squatted a gruesome disharmony of hide and bone, organ, fang, and claw: a throne he called it, and from that seat Sairren governed his Nation.

Beyond the palace and its many ramparts lay the mean homes of the Sarraneem, maundering from knoll to lowland and down to swales and back to hillock. These were a people more intelligent than the Masule-azai; though like their father, their prowess lay in learning rather than creation.

Much like the Masule-azai, the Sarraneem were inglorious and in arrant discord with the harmony of the world. Oft were they disquieted by strange thoughts that huddled like carrion crows round formless shapes, and from these issued grisly notions that rendered gruesome acts, for the Sarraneem prized the devouring of uncommon beasts, coveting most highly those parts rejected by the predator: the stomach, the intestines, the reproductive, and the waste. These, they lied, brought them magickal powers of agelessness, health, and sexual prowess.

Had this been the depth of their depravity, wicked they would rightly be called—yet deeper they delved into madness, for the flesh of the Sarraneem unborn was prized above all others. Rumors and tales of fanciful boon passed from village to village. And the rending of the soft meat, and the ache of swollen bellies haunted the lands, staining them with horror.

But the murder of the pregnant and unborn was not wholly embraced, for many who would refuse not such tender morsels were yet dismayed, and thus laws they passed to restrain their hungers, and order was put to their lives that stood above the Masule-azai in as much as it fell below the Prometheans.

But more than their own lusts haunted the Sarraneem, for great fire-breathing worms stalked their lands ere their departure for war: some with legs strong but short, and others legless, traversing the earth like great lumbering snakes. These were fearsome monsters with snapping jaws and brightly colored scales, spirits of malice that rejoiced in hunting Sarraneem.

From dark lairs they crawled on their bellies, yet from these dungeons they were not come. For these were the beasts that Sairren called dragons, creations of his will but not of his conception; rather, they were a likeness of what he beheld when at the Battle of Arn-gelwain he watched from afar, studying with apprehension the Promethean dragons.

Then it was that Sairren hastened to Natteley, and there induced nigh two hundred Gods to change their forms, promising powers and glory beyond their due. As were the men of his making, Sairren's imitations were a mockery of Prometheus's work, for his dragons were flightless and weak flamed, great hideous worms that tormented the weak.

Though from Zeushin's kingdom these dragons were drawn, and though Sairren they named their captain and Oradüme their home, Zeushin was untroubled by their going. For their allegiance to his kingdom they did not renounce. Moreover, Gorthang had seeded their number with spies and assassins, Gods who would murder their captain at the behest of their masters.

Perched atop his morbid throne, his knees nigh his ears and his arms 'tween his legs, Sairren took counsel with none but himself. There, he formulated scheme upon scheme to topple Zeushin and Gorthang, plans so cumbrous and slow to ripen that they were reliant on a changeless world—and thus utterly feckless.

But though he plotted to crown himself as king, Sairren hid his intent under a mask of content, and following Gorthang's orders, marshaled his army not more than one year after Masule's defeat. For the Sarraneem had a great trek, and Gorthang desired not that Prometheus would find strength and vigor in peace; thus, as an army of terror, the Sarraneem set forth in double haste, purposing, if they might, to come upon the Prometheans at unawares and while yet their spirits were shaken.

11.2

Even as blood runnels yet slithered and sank as crimson webs and wine-red pools into the parched folds of Arn-gelwain, even as crying death throes hung funereally about writhen echoes over the horseshoe plateau, Gorthang madly sought to dissuade Zeushin from his war decree, for Zeushin had ordained that the Army of the Crown and the Royal Guard would go not alone to battle. Rather, they would serve as the impenetrable flanks of a great army that would leave not one of his subjects behind.

The decree stunned Gorthang, and thwarted his designs. For it was the headstones of the Army of the Crown and the Royal Guard that would pave his mutiny. Thus dwindled, Gorthang and his supporters, bolstered by the leaderless Sarraneem, could strike the kingdom and deliver its deathblow.

It was now likely, Gorthang surmised, that many of his supporters would fall in battle, that the Army of the Crown and the Royal Guard could return unscathed, and that Sairren could survive, forestalling his desire to take lordship of the Sarraneem. But not even lies mingled with truth, not even the great dexterity of Gorthang's tongue, could sway Zeushin's decision.

It may be, perhaps, that Zeushin looked with keener eyes than Gorthang upon the power and strength of Lord Prometheus, and therein saw that victory obliged the full might of his kingdom; or perhaps he guessed that treachery was afoot and that a uniform weakening of his host would guarantee his dominion. Nevertheless, the forces that would change the world were set in motion, and neither man nor God could arrest their momentum.

11.3

Craggy and riven were the mountain passes to the east and north of Cindillin's Vale. Here, hundreds of ravines mutilated the earth, gouging the lands like the claw scars of a colossal beast. In fitful bursts, the monstrous rents gave way to deep valleys, but to pinched canyons and shadowy walls they always returned.

A mighty chorus of furious rivers roared upon the land's southern border, and below the throb of their song a silence clung to the wastes, disturbed not but by the hiss of the wind stripping the stones. This inhospitable land, the Prometheans named "Fallowsgate," for here they would clash with the enemy.

Peace was again lain upon the altar of war. Armies raced toward the clash of arms as the landslide that consumes and destroys, hastening with mounting speed, striking the earth with rolling fists, venom, and thunder. And thus the wayworn Sarraneem drew nigh on Fallowsgate, and so too the war-weary Prometheans.

Death was come again ere memory could dull the pain of death, for even as the Prometheans gallantly drew themselves up for battle, the defiant challenge of their silver trumpets singing toward the rising Sun and swarming Sarraneem, Zeushin and his kingdom sped to war upon winds of malice.

11.4

As the Prometheans trod the cavernous tunnels to the sanguinary fields of Arn-gelwain, so too did they pass to the wastes of Fallowsgate. Six days they had to establish their defenses in the numerous ravines through which the enemy would funnel, a foe crawling and boiling over the earth as hungry broods of black-fanged spiders.

When once their fortifications were complete, the beleaguered Prometheans awaited the army of the Sarraneem, an army surging like hastening waters toward living dams, Promethean bastions that bristled like fields of polished reeds, spear points ablaze like whetted tongues of fire.

Thick and sluggish was the air amidst the channels, resisting the draw of the breath as though it were a burden, starving the Sarraneem as they marched. Nevertheless, as the seventh Sun struggled beyond the dark limb of the world, the gasping Sarraneem were sighted by the watch wardens.

Unlike to the Masule-azai, the whole of the Sarraneem were clad in the tackle of war, though of an ignoble and stunted mastery: wicker helms and shields braced by animal hide and bone; swords, spears, and darts of inferior metals and poor quality.

Lecherous were the Sarraneem for the riches of the Promethean mind and the beauty of Promethean flesh, but frightened were they when they beheld the watch wardens on horseback; for never had they witnessed men such as these, tall and broad and fierce—and never beasts such as these, gallant and noble and suffering the Prometheans to sit upon their backs. Verily, many perceived rider and steed as one, and with a gnawing sense of foreboding, fear wriggled like cold worms in their bellies.

Upon hearing the riders' bugles crying a strident warning to the Promethean host, the Sarraneem let fly a volley of arrows. But too swift were the watch wardens, for they vanished behind the many bends of the coiling defiles.

Daunted, but whipped into covetous fury by the words of their God, the Sarraneem drove on through the hard, indifferent shadows, the sharp stones biting their heels, the lofty walls leaning over them, the crump of their march and the clatter of their arms as ghostly omens.

But to their ears came rushing the keen music of silver trumpets, clean and bright as the notes of heaven: the Promethean challenge of war. The hearts of the Sarraneem stuttered and quailed in their chests, for never had they harked to a challenge so pure and powerful, so mystical and triumphant.

A deep silence followed the Promethean challenge, but ere long a rumble, as of thunder gathering in distant realms, sped toward the invader, and rounding the bends like a racing torrent, it flew against them as a great energy upon the airs. *DOOM-doom…DOOM-doom…DOOM-doom* hammered the Promethean war drums like the heartbeat of a great beast, voracious and on the hunt—*DOOM-doom…DOOM-doom…DOOM-doom…*

The Sarraneem's resolve grew cold in that fearful hour, for the thunder of the great drums crawled through their bodies, and the rocks groaned under their feet. Then, in the midst of the drumming, there came to their ears the horror of ghastly horns, wailing like the piercing cries of daemons.

The Sarraneem wavered, as rank upon rank in the many vans refused to press on, crippled with terror, unwilling to turn the final corners and there to find the beast that put its madness upon the air.

*DOOM-doom…DOOM-doom…DOOM-doom…*and the scream of the daemon shattered the thunder.

The knees of the Sarraneem buckled beneath them, some fainting, others digging in their heels, fecklessly resisting the momentum of thousands.

By after knowledge, the wise held that here the invasion teetered on the brink of dissolution, for the Sarraneem were become possessed of a fear that made numb and heavy their limbs, crippling their minds. But again, their God enflamed their lechery and greed with visions of Promethean riches and beauty, stirring the lusts and courage of many. Thus, there was laid a carpet of flesh of those whose hearts misgave them, smitten with fear and sprawling on their faces.

DOOM-doom...DOOM-doom...DOOM-doom...and the daemon's voice cried.

At length, the Sarraneem turned the final corners and there looked heavily upon the death that awaited them. Many now stained themselves with urine. Many convulsed and vomited as they swayed over legs that pawed for the earth. Others fell and were devoured as it were by spinning gears, trapped between the rock of the earth and the weight of the march, for before the advancing Sarraneem rose an army, blazing eerily in the shadows, their faces hidden beneath the shade of their regal helms, their eyes haunted and forbidding.

Then it was, from behind the Promethean lines there came the music of many bows, and a great fog that climbed toward the heavens, and therefrom somber clouds bared glittering teeth, raining in great sheets upon the Sarraneem as the storm driven by the gale. Hundreds wailed in agony as the whistling arrows plunged thickly into flesh, and clutching wildly at the shafts that jutted from throats, shoulders, and chests, the Sarraneem thrashed the ground in death pangs, the darkness tightening its noose around them.

Answering, the Sarraneem loosed volleys of their own, sending arrows skyward upon high arcs, yet most reached not the

Prometheans, and those with flights both long and true clattered broken-tipped upon Promethean armor.

Again and again, the Promethean bows sang, felling the enemy in swollen heaps: hideous, crawling, screaming mounds over which the Sarraneem lurched like the dead yet living, the defenders between them and the prize of their lusts. Bereft of their senses as one driven mad by the jagged screams and echoing visions of dying men, climbing and descending hillocks of stinking flesh laid open under the cleaving velocity of sharpened darts, there issued from their parched throats a scream of madness as over the shrinking gaps they charged.

From the direful collision there came a sickening crunch of wicker against metal, and the snapping of Sarraneem bones like dried twigs popping underfoot. When once their momentum was checked, there issued Promethean spear thrusts, perfect in their unison and symmetry, cleaving wicker and sinking through tissue as glowing steel through virgin snow.

Driven mad by lust for Promethean women and riches, the Sarraneem hurled themselves upon Promethean meat hooks, and there lay dying at their feet, loosing their bowels, their lives speeding from eyes gone cold. Repeatedly, the Promethean lines redeployed as the dead and dying rose as gruesome platforms from which the Sarraneem assailed the defenders. And thus waxed the Battle of Fallowsgate in the deep wedges of the many defiles.

As the struggle raged in the fissures below, Prometheus strove with Sairren in the heavens, for Sairren had come to war with his brood, forsaking Zeushin's summons—though the penalty was death. And yet death he found—swiftly—at the hands of Prometheus, who, having slain his foe, cast his corpse from the cerulean vault. Without witness, it crashed upon the turf above the ravines, broken and disfigured.

Turning to the aid of his children, and sensing that Zeushin would come not to war until the following morn, Prometheus descended in wrath upon the midpoint of the enemy, and there waded as a mountain with its roots in the depths of the sea and its zenith amid the heights of the stars. Then it was that he spilled lands and cast flaming bolts upon the foe, careful though he was to spare his power, for he knew he would need his strength with the coming of the morrow.

11.5

Here it must be told that even as Prometheus brought death and ruin to the Sarraneem, there began that battle which was remembered long in song and tale; for upon a wide plain before the eastern threshold of Fallowsgate, a field was fought: "Sythzehar" it was called in later days—Battle of the Dragons.

It was upon that land that Sairren's great worms contemptuously craned their bulbous heads, and there espied Prometheus's dragons descending in wrath, their great fingered wings reaching for the horizon. As jets of liquid flame sped from the dragons, answering columns rose from the worms below. So terrible was the inferno where those currents vied that it seemed a winged spirit of the Earth had arisen in fire.

With the surcease of that volley, the great worms lashed the sky with flaming whips, and they filled the heavens with darts of fire, downing many dragons that took many hits. As these crashed to the earth, the worms fell upon them in great force of number. There, the fighting was most fierce, for like snarling dogs they writhed through the dust with snapping maws, each dragon contending with many great worms.

But the airborne dragons circled back and picked off their prey, snatching them from the earth, and others hurling ropes and balls of fire, and still others landing, pinning the worms beneath their feet, opening their bellies with mighty jaws. Thus, the sky and the field were become a confusion of battle, rife with dragons and blaze.

Lord Faiden, captain of the dragons, wheeled low over the great worms, drenching them in his black fires. Kindled darts he dodged and he took—but he stayed aloft, and eyeing Grong, the worm master, he seized him and took him up, piercing his armored hide so that blood surged red over keen white talons.

For a few strokes of his great wings, the earth fell away, and he gathered speed as Grong tore at his grip. Therewith, Faiden released him, tossing him back to the earth like the hawk the gangly serpent. As Grong fell, Faiden rolled and banked and passing nigh the worm captain smote him with a searing fire.

Tumbling and gnashing his teeth in fury, Grong howled in a fell voice, his flaming hide billowing with the roar of a banner lashed by the wind. In vain, he whirled in search of Faiden as the fires consuming him burnt out, and he streaked through the sky as a ribbon of smoke before smashing upon the ground—a shattered heap and waves of dirt ringing the impact.

Landing heavily before him, the earth quivering with the noise of torn soil and shattered rocks, Faiden reared and unfurled his colossal wings. Gold gleaming, dazzling in the morning's light, he rose before Grong as a terrible reckoning.

Naught but Prometheus was said by the wise to be as beautiful and menacing as Faiden in that fateful hour, for his outstretched wings caught the Sun like shimmering sails, his gaping maw ringed with teeth as of ivory and ice—a furnace therein alive with writhen flame, and all nigh him bespeckled with golden stars in the shapes of his scales.

Drawing a seething breath, Faiden unleashed a withering fire that roared as the breaking of waves and hissed as of water leaping to steam. But well met was the captain's fire by Grong, for he had unleashed a torrent of his own, yet the wingless dragon was soon overmastered. As the flames engulfed the worm, he writhed upon the earth in limitless rage, his lambent, multihued scales charred to the black. In a bed of broken glass, the terrible worm shuddered: agony from the blaze and anger from the agony.

Folding his wings and falling back to all fours as he regained his breath, Faiden passed aslant to Grong. But even in the midst of anguish, Grong was overcome with such terrible hatred that he drew himself up and hurled his mangled body at the golden dragon. His forefeet clutched round Faiden's throat, and the points of his talons pierced the armature, spouting blood and tissue that rose as geysers and coursed as streams.

Their jaws clashed with the ring of sabers, teeth upon teeth, fang upon fang as the captains fought for mastery, each raking the other, each vying with his monstrous jaws for the neck of the other, and falling like two great pillars, they crashed with murderous cunning amid the pluming dust of the earth.

There, tangled in wreckage and flailing madness, Faiden found Grong's belly, and yanking, ripped him open, spilling his glistening bowels: worms of the great worm uncoiling upon the ground.

As Grong roared with wild agony, Faiden seized him by his throat, and he shook him lifeless as a wolf its prey. So ended the worm master on the stoop of Fallowsgate.

Yet Faiden found no reprieve in victory, for Arreth and Azane, two great worms, ravingly vaulted themselves onto his back. But ere they could do him grave injury, Limbalin, a white-silver dragon with pearlescent wings, tore them from his captain and flung them to the rocks.

Madly wheeling, Limbalin loosed an annihilating flame: white was its issuance, but blue it kindled in all that it smote. High was the fire that leapt from the coiling worms, and ghastly was the image on Limbalin's breast; for his relucent scales were the like of white mirrors, and amid their gleam echoed the field's turmoil in ghostly hues: gaping maws hurling ropes of flame, teeth tearing through hides, corpses charred and lifeless—reflections that to him returned for the remainder of his life, for, unbidden and unlooked for, the images of that day would awake from slumber as though, seething, the battle yet raged.

Thus stormed Sythzehar until not one of Sairren's great worms dragged its belly upon the field. Therewith, the Promethean dragons turned upon the bloodthirsty Sarraneem, assailing the fore of their army's final third: smiting them with infernos that withered them to cyclones of ash, smashing their ranks with tails like the trunks of great trees, and hewing them to shreds with blades springing from their feet and sprouting from their jaws.

11.6

Elsewhere along the enemy's march, the Wilding Kingdom went again to war, for they fell upon the enemy at unawares, assailing the rear third of their army. The sudden onset threw the

Sarraneem into chaos, for they cried in their madness that possessed were the beasts by nature's spirit, and now, for their wanton defilement of animal dead, for their insolence toward the Earth, a sacrifice of their lives was due.

And lo, as Chargaroth had bled, so too was Oradüme assailed. For in those lands, mighty herds of beasts, crowned with great antlers, destructively swept throughout the country, impaling and trampling the enemy, gathering Sarraneem like dangling trophies amid their many-fingered horns.

Cats there were, well-nigh the size of steeds; through doors they crept as through leaf-litter they stalked, and amid the screaming darkness of the forlorn huts they raked the enemy's flesh to sodden braids. And along the coasts, and even deep into the firths where sustenance jumped from the waters, fishermen were taken by monsters that threw themselves upon the beaches, catching the Sarraneem in mighty jaws and barbed arms, dragging them screaming and pawing into the red wash of the tide.

So grievous was the assault of the Wilding Kingdom upon the rear third of the Sarraneem, and so terrible were the losses toward the fore of that third, where dragons wrought death and destruction, that the scattering remnants forsook the battle and fled northward as a starless night fell heavily upon them. But night brought them no respite, for the monsters of the night assailed them from turf and sky, crippling and killing many with dreadful wounds.

In the deep wedges of the many defiles, darkness gifted reprieve to the weary combatants, and skyward, Prometheus ordered the dragons to join him upon the broken spine of a mountain; there, the majority of Valaroma were unspent and preserved hale for the battle to come.

11.7

With the ominous creeping of a pale dawn, the riotous assaults on the Promethean lines were renewed. Weakened Protheans fought valiantly; continually supplied with new weapons, they deftly slew Sarraneem as quickly as replacements filled their ghostly voids. But for all their matchless valor, it was but a few hours before the Razorum began to falter under the weight of the enemy.

Before the lines could be sundered and its valiant warriors beaten into the dust, a wail of horns echoed from deep behind Promethean lines—a signal, for the linemen forsook the defense and fled to the valley walls as the Ranger cavalry charged the Sarraneem. Thunderous were their hoofs in the thousands as they beat the earth in quickening wrath, noble Promethean banners whipping in the wind of their speed, gleaming knights like the specters of the slain come again to wet their weapons in the blood of the enemy.

Quicker than the rush of thought, the Rangers descended on the Sarraneem, sweeping their heads from their shoulders, puncturing their chests with deadly spears, riding them down and breaking their bodies under the galloping legs of their mighty steeds.

Deep into the ranks of the enemy was the charge of the Rizoria Rangers, and thus followed in its wake, the battle become mêlée, for the Promethean captains loosed their final reserves upon the dismayed Sarraneem: man against man and bawls of agony, swords crashing upon shields and bodies thudding to the earth, and the singing of Promethean arrows as they again began whining and whistling across the field of combat—pinpointed messengers of death come to the aid of Promethean warriors.

11.8

Beyond the ravines of Fallowsgate, the Sarraneem northwarders arrested their reckless flight of the previous day, reassembling on a wide plain nigh the march of a dark forest.

As russet and auburn leaves eddied on a chill wind under a cloud cover that clung to the treetops, the Sarraneem captains erupted into heated debate: some urging they resume their war against the Prometheans, yet others there were, though their numbers were fewer, who argued against the war—homeward their hearts were turned.

Some, and Captain Weenchen chief among them, held forth that if only they renounced their war against the works of Prometheus, they would return unmolested to their homes. But the decision was given not to these, for louder and more numerous were the voices of those who cried in rapine and lechery. Thus, there was a splintering of their force, for a fifth of their number rebelled, decamping with Weenchen and other captains of like mind.

Those who remained, and Captain Zouween prominent among them, foolishly hardened their hearts, turning their feet westward to the carnage and devastation of war. But never would they come to the ringing clash of swords at Fallowsgate, nor would they ever lie in their beds or look upon Oradüme again, for from the east came hastening their doom as an early winter that wraps the world in ice, binding it under the chilling winds of a merciless embrace. This, long recalled by the Prometheans in canticles of similar name, was the Last March of the Wilding Kingdom.

It came to pass, as the Sarraneem prepared to march westward, that a soldier from the rearguard of their column cried in horror; for, beyond the wide sweep of a deep champaign, great beasts stood in a manner not wholly unlike a military formation, as proud and regal as any mustering of men the world has ever beheld. Theirs was the banner of Prometheus and the Earth, an alliance with the Promethean Nation, a mortal struggle against those who would mar the works of their Lord.

Under the hurrying cloud wrack of the low-hung sky, the Sarraneem captains wheeled their army as the trumpets of the Wilding Kingdom sounded, their lines leaping forward, hastening to war. Down they spilled, down over the rim of the distant hill, the agile pulling away from the herd, crossing the void at unthinkable speeds. Up there came, up from behind the hill there bloomed great black clouds with outstretched wings—a fierce music of roar, hiss, and scream.

Shuddering, the Sarraneem captains ordered their fear-stricken men into battle. And with a torturous resolve, they witlessly leapt from their position—down into the sloping plain, swords drawn, shields held high, crying with fell voices.

If the ocean had gone to war with the sea, no greater and more fierce would their clash have been than that of the Wilding Kingdom and the Sarraneem; for men wildly hewed at the naked hides of the beasts, but the fury of the beasts was quenchless, and though mortally wounded, they slew men with skill and rapidity beyond reckoning: jaws snapping bones and rending meat, claws that tore through clothing and opened flesh.

Then it was that the dark clouds, resounding with the beat of countless wings and the shrill cries of lofty predators, hungrily descended upon the Sarraneem rear with honed beak and sharpened talon. That fresh Sarraneem could not be brought to bear, and that their wounded could not be pulled to safety, was owed to the mayhem inflicted by the aerial onslaught.

For a single hour the battle raged—no more—yet the Sarraneem defeat was foredoomed.

From a promontory nigh the conflict, Captain Weenchen reproachfully watched the bloodshed. Withdrawing his sword, he cast it disavowingly to the ground, and renouncing his war against the Promethean Nation, the Earth and its beasts, he besought Prometheus for forgiveness.

In peace and safety, Weenchen and his men passed from the field—and here too, they pass from this tale.

11.9

At length, as the Sun burned like a cold pearl behind the morning mists, Zeushin and his kingdom, astride an angry current beyond the grasp of the firmament, drew nigh the region of Fallowsgate.

It was then that Prometheus Ethelleyah rose to the challenge as a great golden bird wreathed in flame. Behind him, he bore aloft upon a train of his thought those of the Valaroma who were earthbound, and behind these followed the remainder of the Faithful, like hundreds of rising stars from the spine of the mountain, blue-white in their ascension, with long tails that lingered, reaching like great luminous shafts for the heavens.

Beyond the somber canopy, Prometheus raised his wings and intoned a hymn upon the winds, and the winds took up the melody and the whole of the region vibrated with its cadence and majesty. It was thus held in Promethean lore that in that hour Accalobain-Iedolin, War of the Heavens, was begun.

But not by sign or roar of violence was the battle opened, nor could the waxing or waning of conflict be seen or heard, for throughout the morning the Gods strove with their wills alone, a struggle for the positions from which to wage war, rather than war itself. Yet the signs and roar of battle would come, for ere the day's noontide, the sky ran red as the spilling of blood, and naught remained as it was before the horror that followed.

Sickly was the last flickering of the Sun behind the bloodstained curtain of the sky, and long the Earth would wait to bask again in the warmth and favor of its radiance.

Ere the horizon eclipsed the light of day, the crimson canopy boiled as though it were become a poisonous brew: volatile, popping and hissing with explosive madness, thunderous detonations galloping across the heavens that painfully drummed and numbed the hearing, rupturing rock and fragmenting the earth.

Promethean, Sarraneem, Masulian, even the faces of the beasts turned upward in horror as clouds unrivaled took monstrous shapes, speeding across the foaming skies, plunging below the mountains' peaks, towering as if from the Moon poured the swirling vapors, tenebrous as though flowing from the gloom before light.

Black and roiling was become the firmament under the fists of living nightmares: scarlet flames licked from the vault like columns of fire under an undulant canopy, and bolts of red and sallow webbed and bombarded the lands with relentless fury.

Amid frenzied neighing and desperate shouting, the Prometheans struggled with their fear-stricken horse teams. Riders were thrown from saddles as vivid limbs leapt from shattered rocks, piercing the firmament with bloodstained shafts that lit with horror the glowering darkness, casting the Earth into unholy twilights.

As the last of the northward Sarraneem fell to the Wilding Kingdom, their countrymen in the many ravines of Fallowsgate fought on for the reward of their lusts—though their end was also near. Their captains faltering in the face of a rout, their men bedraggled, wavering and nigh steerless, had taken to flight so as to regroup and resume the attack.

But there would be no reformation of their flagging throngs, for magnificent were the glorious Prometheans that pursued the enemy, and cutting them down as the woodman the luckless sapling, left not one to witness the coming horror of the Longest Night.

By after knowledge, it was revealed that the surviving Sarraneem in Oradüme turned their gaze in dread upon the unnatural skies, and they took it for a sign that their Lord had been slain. Fearing that the beasts would again take up the banners of war, they fled into the wilderness, heedless and without bearing. Like ash on a stiff wind before a withering flame, the Sarraneem were scattered, taking with them little more than the memories of the monsters that haunted them.

As a Nation, they spread themselves in numerous villages throughout and beyond the borders of Oradüme, most taking readily to a life of squatting indifference, submerged in strange and ghoulish fantasies, meekly enduring the callous tyranny of hermetic chieftains.

11.10

The Prometheans fled for the darkling caverns as the land groaned under the war beyond the firmament. Though dreadfully wounded and fatigued, their thoughts were given to the fate of their fair Sentilleena, for in the skies they saw death devouring the world.

Days they traveled in all haste beneath the lofty mountains, explosions, earthquakes, and the din of wreckage reaching them in the deeps of the earth, driving them as one in sight of pleasure and pursued by pain, for they yearned to see the faces of their families: loved ones hunkering in fear under the firestorm in the heavens.

When from the dark passages the gallant warriors emerged, frayed and overtired from the battle and the homeward flight, they were startled by the throng of Prometheans miserably crowded into the palace, and the leering spectacle of supplies piled like hillocks near the mouths of the caverns. Further were they dismayed when they learned that Prometheus had sent a terse message to the Nine: *Make ready for flight.*

"The war goes ill!" many in the crowd wailed in desperation, wiping tears from their eyes and consoling their frightened children.

"All is lost!" cried others, sickened with grief and worry as they peered through Qwindellin's windows upon the end of days.

"Let us join the battle!" bellowed the valiants, their weathered hands fingering sword hilts, eager to aid the Lord, but knowing not how.

Many voices were raised in lamentation, so that a confused chorus of sorrow and panic resounded within the halls, plunging deep into Qwindellin's bowels, echoing up its tall towers, pinnacles once glorious and lovely, now mantled and stained by ringlets of smoke.

Much of the Promethean Nation huddled in the chambers and corridors of the palace, the remainder finding cover as nearly they could to Qwindellin's battlements, for gossamer flames had been cast from the heavens, killing hundreds in the fires that raged, kindling Cindillin's Vale with amber flame—hot as the poker that glows in the coals.

Braids of smoke rose from the fires as though ebon fingers tended the blaze. Torrential rains flayed the earth with the snap of whips and the clamor of thongs—loosing mudslides and swelling Cindillin, drowning much of what was not alight.

From the many windows of the palace, the Prometheans beheld a world in the grip of torment: soot-laden winds roaring over lands, uplifting trees and hurling them as seeds, the Earth wailing, its flesh crawling, heaving skyward and then falling.

No count was there made of the dying days in the maw of Accalobain-Iedolin, or it may be that their number has long been lost, yet it is told that at length Prometheus sent message to the Nine, urging them to gather in the grand courtyard and gardens abaft the palace. There, three of the wisest, noblest, and hardiest houses of the Promethean Nation—Aemriel, Wenya, and Adamanta—willingly took refuge under the elements, spiting the weather's wrath and the blazing darts of the enemy.

No sooner had the Nine assembled by the charred ruins of the courtyard's colossal fountain than Prometheus, and the surviving Valaroma—few more than three score—alighted upon the field. Prometheus they could not see, for he had not the strength to manifest a body. So great was his effort to restrain the enemy, that his children and Valaroma might flee through the caverns to safety, that naught but his diminished words marked his presence.

"Make haste for the tunnels," spoke Prometheus's disembodied voice. "Divide yourselves into many hosts and follow separate roads. The tunnels, the Valaroma will also tread, but with you they will go not, nor will they go together, for their lives depend on solitude and the hiding of their thoughts from the enemy.

"This doom I lay upon you, my children: the survival and mastery of the Promethean Nation is now yours alone, for the Gods live not forever—but in you is the potential of eternity. Preserve and ennoble yourselves and you shall rebuild what here has been lost, but forsake your making and naught but the hollow semblance of this glory shall you ever achieve; yea, less still…should you drown in dissolution.

"I alone shall contend with the enemy…. I will come for you if I am able…. No more can I say…. Go now—while you still can…."

Save for Valindeal, who remained with his house in the courtyard, the remainder of the Nine hurried back into Qwindellin and hastily began the evacuation. Yet even as the Valaroma fled for tunnel mouths in the hills nigh the palace, the three Promethean houses refused to depart, saying: "Lord…alone—we shall not leave you. We who are Promethean owe everything to

168

you, our Father. Yea, the father may urge his son to flight in the face of danger, yet the son is guiltless in refusing to abandon his father in the hour of his gravest peril. Send us not away; send us not to the haunting imaginings of our Father ringed by ruthless enemies; if you must fight, then we too will fight…and if victory be yours, then with you we will share in that victory…but if death be yours—then, even in this, we will share in that destiny."

Though they saw him not, they perceived that toward them he turned, and that pride lit his eyes even as sorrow darkened his words.

"No less haunted are those who depart…as those who remain behind…. Some who enter the dark roads will come never forth, and those who do may wish they too had perished rather than endure the persecution of the enemy and the devastation of the world, yet I would that my children survive…even if I succumb…."

He paused, and they sensed that he winced from pain.

"It is…for you, my children…that I willed Vedyah into being, for you were in my thoughts—even in the beginning…."

His voice abruptly fell as one who stays the onset of tears, or silenced by a dawning comprehension of sorrow beyond reckoning—of its breadth and depth, of the cruel murder of innocence and bliss, of the bitter onset of hardship and misery for those he loved above all his works.

"So—it has come to this," said Prometheus with renewed vigor and determination, as if he had again grown tall and glorious. "As I go to my final battle, I am comforted by the Promethean Nation—no greater sacrifice could a child make for his father. If in me there are yet miracles—you shall not perish this day!"

At that moment Prometheus vanished, in truth, from their presence, and reappearing, he perched himself in Qwindellin's tallest tower, taking the bodily form to which he was accustomed—though grievously haggard and injured it now appeared.

Having no longer the strength to restrain the enemy, he gravely awaited the coming of their wrath. There, he wearily stood beneath a large windowless arch, sadly beholding Cindillin's Vale: its green floor, once laced by the sparkling threads of its waters, now engorged with blackest horror.

Reaching forth with his thoughts, he touched the thoughts of his children, and terror he felt therein, confusion and sadness greater than the babe who has wandered far into danger, and there to find himself alone, no mother or father to answer his cries or catch his tears, no arms to take him up.

And like to the anxious parents of the child lost in a sea of dangers, crippled by sickening visions of their love become prey, fearful tears rose in Prometheus's eyes, glistening misery that wet his cheeks in worry unrivaled. Never have tears been loosed in greater sadness, nor shall any know sorrow as deep as Prometheus that terrible day. For no more would he hold his children's hands, or light their eyes with gifts of happiness, or take them lovingly to his chest.

His gaze upturning, he was recalled from woe by the invader descending as points of flame upon the sky, and hardening his heart, Prometheus summoned his final strength. Against the enemy speeding into the vale, he raised his arm, and grim was he become, grim as only he who stands before the summation of days—and yet boldly treads the gauntlet of its fires.

A sourceless scream there then arose in deafening ferocity, a horror that felled many of the invaders with the violence of its voice. A toppling wave of winds then gathered, and storming against the foe, briefly checked their gain with the sharpness of its fury. Stones climbed upon his slackening will, and flew like bludgeoning and piercing darts, afflicting the attackers so that many fell lifeless from the heights, and were thus borne away like autumn's leaves upon the back of the gale.

Against the last strength of the Lord, the battered enemy— the crazed enemy—wildly advanced through the lashing torrent. Their progress he marked, and he ripped the ground asunder, and mighty Cindillin fell away as a dream replaced by thunder. And from the void the heart of the Earth came forth in volcanic madness: lighting many like the tinder—brightly to flame and swiftly to ashes.

Ever potent waxed the storm, ever more the enemy fell, but onward—still onward they drove. The Girdle of Cindillin he caused to rupture—the mountains he hurled, but while many saw in those acts their end, onward, still onward, they drove. A skyward rent he opened that caused to cease those near its horror—their bodies, their essence, to dust, to naught. But onward—ever onward—they drove.

The roar of the light and the light of his fury went forth from the world in power unrivaled—a voice and a terror yet living, though its fires and furnace have long gone cold. Bright in his head burned crimson his eyes—naught but those coals glared out from the storm. Still onward, ever onward—they drove.

And yet, serenity swept through the madness, for a great flock of swans sped northward—beyond the death, beyond the carnage. And their sudden onset, and their regal beauty was as the final note in an enchanting music that had come to its dreadful end, and with it the fall of Prometheus Ethelleyah, High Lord of Vedyah, and Father of the Promethean Nation.

The Flight of the Prometheans

12.1

Labyrinthine threaded the darkling roads below the broken peaks and frowning valleys of the Hon-Drowgleer. Bewildering in the complexity of their ranging networks, these were comfortless grottos that rose and fell and wound their way through the earth like the empty roots of a colossal tree: hard, joyless, and confusing.

Whereas undulant were their walls and roofs as though placid swells rolled through frozen seas, smooth were their floors, so that foot, paw, hoof, and wheel passed untroubled through the darkness. In their beginnings, these were the pathways by which Prometheus had purposed to provide his children with passage beyond Cindillin's Vale. Every road was so hewn that it joined or was itself a route that discreetly surfaced beyond the Vale: some emerging a few miles beyond the mountainous girdle, others slinking for hundreds before crawling toward the light.

But awry had gone the purpose of many: their courses broken, blocked, or impossibly frustrated, for so disastrous were the effects of Accalobain-Iedolin that some were crushed under the weight of fallen roofs. And others had drowned below frenzied waters, gushing white-fisted from breaches in the rock. And still others were so fractured and fragmented that they appeared no longer the work of Lord Prometheus, but were like unto natural caves in their dangers and cumbrous passage.

Yet more treacherous were some roads become, for some there were that now led to underground seas, cold and shoreless in their eerie darkness, brooding with enigma and malice. Many waters had cheerless faces turned toward shallow ceilings, while others gazed like the dead upon measureless vaults. Bright and searing were the vast lakes of fire by contrast, for some roads opened to blazing chasms, living hells with leaping fires, twisting flames billowing in heated gales. Here, the high roofs were aglow and barred by rocking shadows, pillared with crumbling shafts that climbed like otherworldly trees, lambent in the flickering light; their floors were of liquid fire, seething, bubbling, and churning as though these were the bellies of stone giants.

Some roads there were that broke in upon natural caves, pathless in their sinuate wanderings, wet with streamlets and virulent pools, forested by icicles of stone and spires of rock. Homes they were to the blind, the creeping and the wriggling monsters of the dark: long-fingered or haired, or else on leathern wing and shrill of voice.

Few roads there remained unbroken, but even these were not untroubled, for furtive waters crept through fissures and tumbled like wayward rills: unpotable poisons seeking audience with distant pools. And oft heavy and hard was the air, for nigh all the secret vents, so carefully wrought by Prometheus in happier days, had been broken or lost their way among the shifting tides of the land.

It was into this nightmarish underworld that the Prometheans heedlessly threw themselves, escaping the devastation of their fair country. Little foresight could there be in the confusion and urgency of that hopeless hour, even less did they consider the glowering peril that awaited them in the dark, inscrutable caverns.

Of the long passage of those desperate wanderings—the deaths, the births, the gallant acts of courage and self-sacrifice, the tears and the wailing and the personal surrender, and finally the triumph and the coming forth to the devastation of the world— much was told in the lays Izad and Üntamieren, of which naught but distant and lonely fragments are all that remain.

12.2

Beyond the many mouths and the black, crumbling teeth of the darkling roads lay a world of ruin and woe. Unrecognizable was the Earth in shape and hue, for vapors of fire and ash yet rode upon icy winds, baring naught but a pale, cold Sun.

Though the full might of the cataclysm begat by the war had relinquished the world from its terror, the great storms of hails and fires yet sped from the vault. Winds there also howled across the lands, carrying airborne soot as formless specters, poisonous and menacing. Lightning tore aside the darkness, thunder cracked its angry whips at those who cowered beneath its wrath, and rains flung their dirty waters as black tears upon the living. Heavy was the shroud of death that yet clung to the world—yea! with both hands.

Broken and rent was the world so that naught remained as it was intended: oceans were delved while others were drained, mountains were raised while others were toppled, rivers were carved while others were dammed, and lands were cast while others were drowned. Mottled with the putrid corpses of the dead and dying, glowered the ruined fields and forests of the world; and fetid pools of baneful waters beckoned the thirsty with kisses of death.

Great coiling reeks sprang from fissures in the earth, and the ground yet shook with tremors of agony. Sea monsters and fish lay dead and rotting on lands far from the sea, for the oceans had assailed the earth with faceless warriors: mountains of water that reached for the heavens, helmed and shod with foam, clad in blues and the deepest of greens.

This was the nightmare to which the Promethean companies emerged, a world smoldering in its ruin and smothered in darkness. Weeks they huddled by the mouths of the caves, fearful of the uncharted and hostile wilderness, yet hunger and thirst gnawed at their fears, threatening to drive them suddenly forth—heedless into the miseries of the world. Only then, famished, parched, and fraught with trepidation, did they depart. And so it was with a lessened host that the Promethean companies set foot upon a new world—and a new world order.

So arduous were the cavernous roads, that each company believed that they were likely the only survivors. For this reason, each took to itself a leader who had served as captain or councilor—and some of these would become the remote sires of the great kings and kingdoms that would spread themselves throughout the lands: a chronicle of the faithful, replete with triumph and grandeur, and a history of traitors—of blackest deeds, of evil and infamy.

Beholding the peril and desolation of the world, Promethean hearts yearned to flee for haven, or landmark, or some token of the past to which they could turn in desperation. Yet no landmark was found, no token remained from the past—there was no haven in which to repose.

Against the torrid winds, their eyes stung and their skin was scorched; and filling their lungs with wisps of noxious fumes that burned with every breath, they set out upon pathless roads in search of new lands.

Some companies there were that hopelessly endeavored to retrace their steps, to find the lands of their birth and there rebuild what had been destroyed, but never again did any of these look upon the white shimmering walls or the proud tall towers of Qwindellin, for it and Sentilleena and all therein—were lost forever, leveled by the war, razed to dust by the conquering foe.

Not even the Vale or the Girdle of Cindillin remained as a memorial of their past: too near was it to the contest, too much was it an emblem of Prometheus's prowess, too swift was its undoing to leave more than ghostly echoes of enchanting music, voices oft dismissed as fancy by lonely Promethean travelers—but music indeed, entombed in the winds and waters by the ancient power and majesty of its source.

12.3

Unable to find semblance of aught they recalled, and broken by sickness, hunger, and misery, the Promethean companies put their backs to the lands of their birth, journeying farther and farther afield, for the tumult of the world was greatest nigh the ruins of Cindillin's Vale. Beyond its borders, the wreckage of the world grew less complete.

Terrible was the passage and countless were the lives lost in the mounting years, yet at the last, the tattered remnants of the Promethean companies came to new lands, habitable, though perilous and forlorn, for the world was yet ill, brimming with dangers and offering little by way to survive. Moreover, from the squalid lands through which they trudged, a new enemy had come upon a mounting wave of decay, an enemy as merciless as illusive: silent hunters, consuming plagues.

Under this enfeebling spell and disorienting horror, each company strove to rebuild the order in which they or their parents were born, to resurrect the Promethean Nation as wrought by their forefathers in days now dim and distant. But hardship consumed them; hunger and thirst consumed them, and even when these were quelled for a time, the swift passing of hard lives thrust them back to the precipice of death.

From the majesty of their noontide, great had been their fall; for this illustrious people now scavenged for meals, clad in threadbare rags that had once been the regal ornaments of an august Nation, bequeathed from parents to children as tokens of yore. Yet even these reminders of ancient glory withered with the passage of time, so that naught remained but broken tales and shards of memory—an oral tradition, fading and fragmenting.

Songs of lamentation they made in their wanderings, for in the cruel adversity of their pitiless world, the Prometheans unlearned their high wisdom and culture, and they forgot the many devices that civilized and simplified the needs of the living.

Rather, they turned their peerless minds on the needs of the present, becoming masters of the hunt and shrewd in the knowing of all edible and medicinal plants. And the finding of water and the ways of the land they did also learn so that they were become expert and matchless.

Much they left behind in the dusky past, much was burned to ash or crumbled to dust, yet with them they brought that which matters most, that which brought being to all that was lost, that which would give being to it all anew; with them they bore what He had made, the fount of who and what they are and all that they bring forth, for within them—shaped by the hands of Lord Prometheus—was the spirit of the Promethean Nation.

So it was that the radiant Protheans were become a shadow folk, fierce and yet wary of the world; for the passage of uncounted years in the wild had turned them into a fell people, hardened by the struggle to survive, and yet fair did they remain— hints of their majesty alight in the swift, sharp glance of their eyes, the cunning of their minds, the might of their fists, the soft of their touch, and the melody of their voices. Young was the fire that burned in their hearts, and it harkened still to the echoes of glories lost—and visions of glories yet to be.

In years untold, their oral history ebbed into a rich folklore, and this into a fertile soil from which the stalks of many myths leapt up the spring rains of winter's fall. These were legends born of half-truths, tales that ennobled by recalling the past.

In the long wheeling of its endless cycles, the turmoil of the Earth abated, its lands becoming again like unto fair gardens for the beasts of the world and the three Nations of man. Swiftly, the distant descendants of the Promethean companies began again their march to mastery. New and many were the tongues with which they spoke, for long were they sundered from the past they no longer recalled. Promethean clans they were become, and many and diverse were the names by which they were known.

The seasons marched and the tides ebbed and flowed, and the Sun arched high upon the vault, and the Moon ferried waywardly across the sea of the stars, and the Promethean clans rose toward the heights of majesty. Bright was the spark of Promethean genius that grappled once again with culture, wisdom, and the manifold devices of civilization.

Numerous were the religions that sprang from the myths of the past, and many were the gods to which they turned in hope and dread, yet most were no more than phantoms of the mind. Though it is held by some, and indeed it may be, that the gods of their imaginings were shaped by the ancient stories of those who walked the Earth in eons dark and long forgotten.

Over the span of many ages, Promethean kingdoms flowered like white blooms across a sea of green; of these, one is most renowned, for it retained the tattered memories from the ancient past: here was preserved the authority and tradition of the Lore Masters, here was kept the memory of Prometheus Ethelleyah, Cindillin, Sentilleena, Qwindellin, and—the *war*.

But even in this illustrious house, the house of Ettahkarina, the fragmented memories were oft believed to be fantasies of desperate peoples, stories that comforted those who huddled round the fire's edge, globed in light that held at bay the screaming darkness—and the glinting eyes of nightmares.

12.4

As the Prometheans were become a divided people, here must be observed the fruits of those reunions that shaped, for good and ill, the Promethean Nation. For it came to pass that the Promethean clans grew hale, and in their newfound strength wandered ever further afield in search of lands more bountiful than those from which they trod.

During the age of these wide wanderings, as is told in the ancient texts, the long sundered people of the Promethean Nation were come upon one another in wonder and amazement, for it was as though the mythical tales were come alive, the characters therein stepping forth into the world of the living. These were fanciful stories that told of others like themselves, yet tales of demon men and monsters and gods there also were, so it was that the seeing of men was a fate accounted no less miraculous than the seeing of gods.

Glad were the bulk of these meetings, and great profit was had by the clans that met in friendship, reawakening ancient bonds below the surface of petty differences. Many clans there were that wed under the guiding brilliance of Promethean captains, yet there were other meetings that were unglad; for some clans, plagued by the lordship of wicked rulers, sought to increase their power by dominating the weaker and fleeing from the stronger: their poisoned tongues enlarging contrast and fomenting grievance.

And so it came to pass that one of the Vielem, the execrable crimes, held second only to Rofaynem by the Lore Masters, was inflicted by these wicked misleaders on their fellow Prometheans; for they drew crude weapons, one upon the other, and there committed Gorheerim, that is—folk slay: the killing of Promethean by Promethean when for the Nation's health the act does not serve.

But war in that time was fought not only between the children of Prometheus, for the children of Masule and Sairren, ever in the service of the purpose in their making, sought to murder Promethean men and rape unto death Promethean women and children. Thus it was that the Masule-azai and Sarraneem, like unto the Prometheans in that they too were dispersed into many tribes, brought war, death and ruin upon the Prometheans wherever their paths were mingled.

It was during this age that the Odiun, the unmeant, came forth, for many were the Promethean women and children abducted by the Masule-azai and Sarraneem. There, the first of their kind, the Promethean bed slaves, gave sons and daughters to brutal masters. These children were Masule-azai and Sarraneem indeed, yet diluted, ennobled by the Promethean Spirit and in all manner of Promethean measure, superior to their fathers, though inferior to their mothers.

Yet, in time, the tables of conquest would turn, for no longer did the Promethean clans travel heedlessly and trustingly, as is the inclination of their spirit; for they sought to waylay the designs of the Masule-azai and Sarraneem. And coming against them with cunning and in full might of arms wherever they dwelt, conquered and slew them to the last.

So terrible and fearsome were the Promethean clans become that many Masule-azai and Sarraneem cringed before them, owning them as unconquerable gods descended from the heavens, promising service and worship if only they might be spared, if only they might profit from the gifts of the Promethean Spirit.

Amunakkie and Anuaum, and many more such names they called their Promethean gods, and the Prometheans encouraged their crude imaginings with tales of homes nigh distant stars, and flights through the blue of heaven—captured in the eyes of many: a formula of force and fancy that served well such Prometheans, yet in the fullness of time delivered them to oblivion.

Grievous was, and is, and always will be the decision to take such peoples as subjects, for the error reaches out across time in dissolution, desolation, and ruin for the Promethean Nation. Yet too near were they to these decisions to see their outcomes, too blind were they become to the warnings of Lord Prometheus so long ago, too great was the profit and boon of many servants, for the ideas of Promethean minds were become empowered by many hands and many strong backs—so that kingdoms and temples and works of wonder arose under their guidance. Language, mathematics, arts and culture, things of the gods to the minds of the Masule-azai and Sarraneem were spread throughout these realms: the fastest-growing kingdoms in the world. For there were no limits to Promethean genius and no want for subjects to do its bidding.

Yet these great kingdoms were accursed from their beginnings, and their downfall as sure as the setting of the Sun. For though the Prometheans who governed these realms preserved themselves incorrupt for many generations, in time they took mates from their subjects and thereby encompassed their own ruination. In the wheeling of years, it came to pass that even the crowns of these realms yielded to the most loathsome of the Vielem, for they too became Rofayn, committing Rofaynem—spirit-stain, essence-profane.

With the sullying of the source, there is the perishing of the source, and so was lost forever the fount from which issued the learning, the might, the glory and high culture. So it was, as it shall always be, that these great kingdoms, even in their primes, waned as the aged, fraught with disease.

When at the last the source had been submerged, these civilizations returned to darkness, and forgetting nigh all they had been taught, to the wild whence they came, the Odiun, Masule-azai, and Sarraneem returned.

By the wise, it is held that from these unions sprang the mixed peoples of man, which are indeed the offspring of the three Nations of man. Deeds and time conspired to level the peoples and Nations of the world; for even as the latecomers reached the heights of their potentials, the three Nations, reckless in the preservation of the potential sown into each by their makers, became shadows of their making.

Unlearned were the lessons of the Aydemenocs, the great kingdoms built by the Promethean Spirit on the brutish toil of others; for the Prometheans and those rich in their spirit looked again and again to the labor of others to realize their matchless genius, only to find, without exception, that they were consumed by their own designs—and in truth! repeatedly delivered to oblivion.

12.5

Elsewhere, while Prometheans struggled to survive amidst the turmoils of the world, one fewer than all the Gods of Zeushin's kingdom lay crippled in Natteley. Few more than one thousand survived the war, and none escaped unscathed, for all were grievously maimed and lacked now the will to govern the world to their liking, lacked now the desire to sate their lusts on those weaker than themselves.

Victorious they were in battle, yet broken were their spirits, enduring in spite of their dispassion, waiting for what they knew not and caring little for the days to come. Natteley lay in ruins, its wide streets and gilded towers, its burnished temples and fountains proud broken and crumbling. Naught there was that gleamed in sympathy with Sun, star, or Moon, for too near was the city to the tumults of war to escape the upheaval.

Often, Zeushin would drag his mangled body to a forlorn terrace, and peering eastward, he wondered long what had become of Gorthang since the close of the war and his abandonment of the city. Though other Gods there were who fled also the city in the march of years, taking up secret abodes around the world, it was his memory of Gorthang that most troubled him. Of himself, he asked if all the ruin and sadness, if all the misery and now all the regret had not been, at its uttermost source, the doings of this silver-tongued demon: as hungry for dominance as he was skilled at cloaking his desire in the sanctimonious robes of obligation to the "victim."

But Gorthang looked not over his shoulder, nor did he look to the Gods who remained for his domination of the world. For in them he saw decay and death, whereas in the Nations of man and the peoples who followed, he saw the summation of his desire to rule the world and reign as king.

Eastward and northward he traveled, agonizingly limping on a gnarled stump under which his foot no longer hung, and coming to his hidden redoubt in the bank of an ill-favored hill, Gorthang rested and pondered long how he might gather the reins of power—and from that seat conquer the world.

The Vyresh

13.1

Wrapped in his black thoughts as the bat its leathern wings, the demon long sat upon his throne brooding crooked thoughts of malice. In time, as the roving spider stalks and leaps suddenly upon its prey, plunging hooked spears deep into its flesh, Gorthang alighted upon an idea blacker than any he had yet conceived. And rising, he burst from his infernal lair, setting out upon the world as a dark, effluvial fog—a reaper gathering the ingredients with which to brew his poison.

Now there came an evening when his errand was complete, and returning to the gloom of his lair, he began the brewing of his pestilential venom. Bent as if over a cauldron, the juices therein thick as mucus and boiling with fury, Gorthang—in the course of long years—formed and reared his poison in the likeness of its creator.

In his madness, he had abducted hundreds of Prometheans, Masule-azai, and Sarraneem. By cruel and demonic arts in the wretched and misery-haunted grots of his bleak redoubt, he wickedly fused his captives, making of them a new people, fashioning them in his own image, infusing them with his cunning malice and gilded treachery. Rearing them on offal and ordure, he fostered in them a mania he turned to his own devices, a mania that persists in their seed—even to this day.

Dank were the burrows under the hills: a people's womb wet with mud, crawling with pale, hungry worms, webbed by throttling roots that fell from the heights, and dark as the night that has known neither star nor Moon. Yet light there was, for Gorthang moved among the corkscrewing tunnels as a pillar of fire—a terror and a boon to his scions of evil.

When finally the toxin had reached the peak of its potency, he spoke to his chimerical brood, telling them of the world, and how *he*—in the goodness of his heart—had fashioned it and all therein as a garden for their pleasures: to shape or to spoil, to mold to their liking.

Of the Gods, Gorthang said little, declaring them inferior and that blackest envy had driven them in war against him. A battle it was for the kingdom of the Earth, Gorthang avowed, yet victory was his in the end. Well-nigh all the rebels were slain, and the remainder he cast from the kingdom's walls, imprisoning these in a dungeon—deepest and most perilous.

Of the universe and all therein he lied thrice: saying he was before all else, that he had fashioned the cosmos, and that his labors were naught but a matter of days. Of the beasts of the world he spoke strange riddles, for he told his children that many he made and diverse were their forms, but some he made in forms like to their own.

These, he said, were thus wrought that his children might have servants and play-things. These he called not by the names given them by their makers, nor by the names of their taking, but rather he named them "Ganyah"—beasts of the field with the forms and tongues of men.

Then it was that he named his brood after his most secret thought, calling them "Vyresh," though that name they no longer bear, nor many others they have donned and doffed to escape the infamy of their deeds. But though their names are manifold, and though a name, like raiment, may be changed, a people it makes not—for neither name nor raiment nor glad hand nor vow nor aught that might veil the fount of a people, alters, ennobles, or un-muddies the source of that spring, for the fount remains unchanged. In time, the deeds and desires that grow therefrom bleed through even the thickest of veils—a lustrous light of splendor, or a hard light of malice.

Further and more Gorthang ordained, declaring that all above and below the earth belongs to the Vyresh, saying that a Ganyah may possess nothing, for in the possessing he has proven himself a thief and may justly be deprived of his thief hoard. Only by leave of the Vyresh, intoned Gorthang, may Ganyah hold and use what rightfully belongs to the Vyresh.

Years Gorthang spent in the darkness with his mud-splattered brood, instilling in them the vast and subtle arts of seizing power in Ganyah kingdoms: that Ganyah labor may furnish the Vyresh with sustenance, enrichment, and pleasures of the flesh—and further, of the turning of that supplanted authority and the directing of that stolen force against those who have shown themselves stubborn and proud: beasts unwilling to be broken, unwilling to don the bridle and pull the plow.

Books of secret conquest he scrawled and gifted the Vyresh, calling the oeuvre "Megeela." "When in you superior force is held and the hour is come," ordered Gorthang, "whether by your arms or by Ganyah you control, come in all force against those who yield not to your lordship, promising amity, but brooking not peace nor plea for mercy, killing all—yea, even uprooting the trees of the earth."

At the last, Gorthang broke the seal to his hidden lair, and therein splashed the light of the dazzling Sun. Standing before his brood, he spoke, saying unto them, "Though it was I who made all, from the greatest even unto the least, it is you whom I have chosen to be—my *specials*."

Even as Promethean kingdoms bloomed like wildflowers across the lands, a mission Gorthang gave to his brood, a vision of world conquest. A satisfying of the cravings of the flesh beyond reckoning in them he immutably instilled. And sending them forth as pilgrims upon the world, they came indeed as contagions to the kingdoms of the world: harbingers of a decay they named virtue, would-be masters, secret slavers, tricksters come feigning as the tricked, victimizers come feigning as the victims.

13.2

In six hosts, the Vyresh set forth to subjugate the world. United was their beginning, but within each there quickly dissension arose; for those instincts so carefully crafted to foster a ravenous desire to live upon the backs of others, to reign as lords over squalid servants, to erode the unity, identity, and pride of the Ganyah tribes, served also to consume the Vyresh from within, to drive them one against the other—yea, to eat their own heads off.

Six there were, yet ere long they were become seventy-four, and twice more they trebled their number before coming to the world of the Ganyah. These were a merciless, conniving people, for they had no honor and were become incapable of truth, save only in matters when truth availed them. They made not good neighbors, for the Vyresh were driven by an infernal light to feign friendship while working to undermine, weaken, and conquer.

As cowards, they conceived no shame—not even in the basest ignominy; for they fled in all haste from the aroused ire of tribes stronger than their own, bitterly complaining, naming themselves blameless victims, saying naught of their guilt in stirring the wrath of their neighbors. But by scheme and sabotage they worked not all their efforts; for in those days, this self-proclaimed *long-suffering* people fell at unawares upon those weaker than themselves, raping and pillaging their victims, slaying all—even uprooting the trees of the earth.

Over the course of long years, it came to pass that the Vyreshian tribes had exhausted themselves in rancor—veiled and unveiled. So it was the Vyresh were dispersed as weed seeds upon the airs, infecting the beds of many gardens, strangling the roots therein, stealing the light of the Sun.

Thus, they were become guests of other tribes, and there reborn in them, by the scarcity of their number, was the fervent allegiance to the mission that surged through their veins, an allegiance that appeared to the benighted as benign, as not more than folkish loyalty to Vyreshian traditions and lore. By their efforts, they remained a people apart, and thereby—at the last—assumed the role that Gorthang had long prepared for them.

In the semblance they wore, no ill could be seen, and with arguments cunning they opened all doors. Envy and hatred filled their hearts when for the limpid riches and fair women of their hosts they lusted, but they hid their thoughts and dissembled their desires.

The Prometheans and those rich in their spirit they hated most, for their prowess and beauty galled the unlovely Vyresh, and so all the more did they humble themselves. All the more did they offer their services. All the more did they feign friendship.

Profit the Ganyah had from their counsel, and thus they harkened to ideas they ought never to have heard, for visions the Vyresh conjured in their minds, lusts and envy they kindled, and claims of injustice they spread with cunning unrivaled. Their addled victims were led to believe Vyreshian ideas were their own, and thus ever the Vyresh found fools to enlarge their lies and spread their poisons. *Problems* in these kingdoms the Vyresh counted, and to these *problems*, many solutions they offered that in their veneer appeared just and noble, but—in truth—unfailingly served Vyreshian interests.

Thus, into the Ganyah kingdoms the Vyresh were come; in they came with poisoned tongues, flattery sweet as honey dripping from their lips—self-abasing, ingratiating—preaching at first a doctrine of tolerance, yet in the coming to power an intolerance they preached for all who troubled the summation of their desires.

They were sowers of disunion and discontent, stirrers of treason and the fear of treason, supplanters of the healthy with the unhealthy, of the normal with the abnormal. Masters were they become of dissimulation: experts of speechcraft, adroit practitioners of the wire and lever, skillful in the art of shadow mastery.

As victims, they loudly and brashly heralded themselves, for in the civilized country the victim wields the glittering scepter: all must do obeisance to him, all must esteem deference for him, rendering aid in his need, deferring to his views, forgiving his insults, yielding to his will, abetting his boon. No transgression by the aggrieved is too grievous, nay! for as long he carries the banner of the victim, he cannot be begrudged, for even to question his banner is to magnify his claim.

In the land of the aggrieved—the most aggrieved is the king of kings, so it was that the Vyresh wove fanciful tales of their persecution, tales of woe so prodigious and grisly, of injury so monstrous and undeserved, of afflictions so numerous and enduring as to eclipse all others. Yet the Vyresh knew well the cult of the victim endures not when civility is abandoned, or when patience has been tried to its breaking, and so in it they trusted not their domination, but sought ever deeper and more complex the ways by which they might control the Ganyah.

In this, they sought to break the traditions and loyalties the Ganyah fostered for the principles and gods they held in reverence: declaring to the Ganyah that there was *one true God*, that he was the God of hordes, and that they—the Vyresh—were his *specials*. "Draug"—that is, unclean, vulgar, and wicked—they called those who worshiped the *false gods*, and Draug they called those who harkened to the accumulated discernment of their elders and leaders.

Vying with many subtle arguments, the Vyresh gainsaid all wisdom, setting the Ganyah on paths of ruin. Treacherous were these roads, for their purpose was treachery; of these, not the least perilous was the doctrine concerning the coming of man, for here the Vyresh declared that all are the children of Gorthang, and that in their beginnings all men were of like spirit. Fathomless ages and leagues of separation, they said, caused in them the changes in their spirits, which are a grief to the Lord.

And more they hinted, though guile stayed their tongues— guile urging that the idea be permitted to take root in their victims, growing nonetheless in the train of its secret keeper, coming to the only conclusion whither the path could lead: that if sundering is a grief to God, then reunion and the mingling of spirits is a blessing to God—an act that brings joy to the Lord and grace to the graceless.

But though the Vyresh called upon the Ganyah to abandon their false gods, to wantonly mingle their spirits and to own Gorthang as their Lord, they admitted them not to the people of the Vyresh, nor to the station of the *specials*, for the Vyresh said their station was a burden—an example of self-sacrifice to the world was their purpose.

But let it here be told that not all were deceived by their gilded tongues, for some rulers there were and some peoples there were who heard the Vyresh, but heeded them not. Loath were they to abandon the traditions and ancient wisdom of their peoples. For these, the Vyresh elders raised their voices in prayer to Lord Gorthang, beseeching him to do with miracles where words had failed.

And so it was that Gorthang heard their prayers: at times appearing to the hidebound as a stern face amidst the clouds, or as a polished serpent that spoke with the tongues of men, or as an unconsuming flame that tarried in the courts of the kings.

And by other miracles Gorthang sought to persuade the disbelievers, but in this, as with his moments of wrath, his will was not free—neither to do as great nor as much as he wished, for he desired not to rouse the curiosity of the Gods ere he was become king of men and master of the world, for then, he surmised— power he would wield insurmountable.

At the sight of these miracles, most of the Ganyah were moved to reverence for the Vyresh, yet some there were who hardened their hearts, repudiating both the miracles and the doctrines of the Vyresh, seeing—at the last—through their devious designs and the summation of their wicked purpose.

Then it was that these peoples expelled the Vyresh and drove them forth as a mighty tempest at their backs; for so are the ways of the world: that when the spell of treachery is broken, when the guile of the wicked is lain bare, a quenchless wrath is unleashed in those deceived, a righteous blaze ignited by the naked flame of the conspirators.

But the Vyresh suffered these peoples not, fleeing from their just anger, and calling upon Gorthang in prayer, they besought him to bring ruin to all those who dared to yield not to their mastery, to show no mercy to the Ganyah.

And so it was that Gorthang came forth from his dark lair, bringing death and destruction upon these kingdoms. Pestilence he unleashed so that masses were felled by invisible hands. Waters he swelled so that floods swallowed hearth and country. Storms of thunder and bolts he gathered that smote the rooftops and ignited the cities. Plagues of biting insects he conjured, and horrors many and more Gorthang summoned from the ether, smiting those who in their pride rejected the Vyresh.

By these and other evil devices, the world was bent on a path of subjugation; in time, the greater part of the Ganyah were entangled in the tendrils of Vyreshian ivy, the black ropes snaring their ankles and wrists, inching around shoulders, crawling over mouths, encircling throats: a creeping cocoon indeed—a feast for hungry roots.

13.3

In the reeling of long years, the Vyresh were come to hold positions of power within the kingdoms of the Ganyah, to sit behind the thrones of well-nigh all kings; and from those hidden seats they urged the Ganyah into doctrines, vices, and wars that served well the interests of the Vyresh, but worked terrible evils upon the minds, identities, and freedoms of the Ganyah.

From seats of power and prestige—seen and unseen—the Vyresh spread many doctrines. Some among the Ganyah, farseeing and subtle of mind, resisted these burgeoning movements, seeing clearly the budding of dangers in their deceptive tenets, the jagged barbs that lay in wait behind the sweet smell and fair semblance of the florid screeds. Yet these heroes were largely unable to thwart the infernal doctrines, for the Vyresh wielded the authority and might of the crowns, brooking not opposition nor even opinion at variance.

Though the Vyreshian screeds were many, and manifold were their themes, similar were their methods and goals: to corrode until breaking by endlessly condemning the bolsters of Ganyah identity and wellbeing, to mingle the spirits of the Ganyah so that from the unmaking of the disparate peoples and the melding of their cultures would spring a faceless horde—a servant host. And more, for the doctrines goaded their zealots with deceptive tenets that worked to fuse all kingdoms under a servile banner—a banner crowned by the tyranny of Vyreshian domination.

Of the universal screeds, the most pestilential was the doctrine of Saipist: She was a hideous Vyresh with a mind more cunningly evil and deformed than the body within which it was trapped. Saipist, however, wielded not the lordship of that doctrine for long, for her kinsfolk, jealous of her power, slew her and her children in secret, blaming the gruesome slaughter on Ganyah dissenters.

With these murders, the Vyresh made a martyr of a monster, magnified the potency of a doctrine, and at the behest of a horrified public that cried for *justice*, imprisoned dissenters and murdered their leaders. In defeat and fear of the grisly murders, those who yet secretly opposed the *Saipists*—as they were then become known—retreated to the shadows and there laid down their banners, cravenly surrendering their duty and struggle.

Like a contagion upon the airs, the Saipist doctrine spread from kingdom to kingdom, brought in upon the traffic of the wandering Vyresh. Great evil did it work upon the Promethean Nation, for in all things it named the Promethean *villain*—*victim* it named all others.

Too weak were the kings and lords become to resist the Vyresh and their insidious doctrines; for the communal and thatched might of the Vyresh had grown so prodigious that nimbly they toppled disobedient rulers, bringing them low by numberless and devious means, replacing them with Ganyah more amenable to their wishes.

Of those kingdoms most coveted by the Vyresh, some there were that remained untamed, for their spirit drove them to gnaw at the yoke and to bite at the hand that sought to wield it. Of these, all were Promethean or rich in their spirit, though not all Promethean kingdoms were as valiant or steadfast, for some had fallen to the Saipist screed, becoming its most fervent supporters.

And yet, the Prometheans proved the most difficult to tame. Indeed, often were they driven by their spirit to pursue an ideal they had long forgotten, to ascend to a peak they no longer could see, to reclaim a destiny that had vanished in the twilight of the ages.

Thus, it came into the minds of the Vyresh that first among the Nations and peoples of man, the Promethean Nation must be unmade, for they saw in the Prometheans, even those fervent in the worship of Vyreshian screeds, the greatest threat to their growing dominion.

As the Saipist contagion brought realm after realm into the prison of the Vyreshian empire, Promethean kingdoms that stood as islands of freedom were beset from many sides. As stars from the heavens, the free kingdoms fell to the Vyresh: victims of vast coalitions; gored by horns dispatched by the *specials*.

Few were the free kingdoms to witness the vast pilgrimages of Saipists that swept across the lands, for a new season in the growing might of the Vyreshian empire had come with the dwindling of the Ganyah; a terrible work was under way, a vast fortress and city rising upon the strong bones of a conquered Promethean country—a land renamed by the Vyresh, "Harlutt."

In these labors was seen the approaching hour of Vyreshian prophecy, the summation of Vyreshian purpose: a capital city for the Earth; Sargorthang it was called, in reverence of their God, a seat for their Lord—King of Men and Master of the World.

Followers there were of other Vyreshian doctrines that trod also the long roads to Harlutt. Not the least of these were the Essiyah: a cult of childlike fanatics that lived as though the eyes of Gorthang were always upon them, supplicants of Gorthang's favor by service to his *specials*. Chastising those who opposed the Vyresh, though indifferent in the question of their own wellbeing, they adopted Vyreshian interests, becoming zealous in their adoration—profligate in their support.

As one who yearns for rain when adrift on flotsam on a borderless sea, the Essiyah fervently yearned for the completion of Sargorthang, for they esteemed the Vyresh above all others, heeding their words as though the mouth of God were upon their faces, the will of God in their every act. Of greatest import to the

Essiyah was the Vyreshian prophecy that God would come again when his capital was made ready. Evil and suffering they said would cease—for thousands of years, bliss would reign.

When at last the city was complete, and the long Vyreshian march of the ages had come to its victory, the Vyresh stepped from behind the shadows, ordering the slaying of all Ganyah who had played as court men and puppet leaders for the masses. Then it was that they declared to the world their divine right to govern all to their liking.

Gods among men they called themselves, and the reign of their terror was truly begun.

13.4

As a black disease devours the flesh, making numb and useless its tissues, killing both victim and self as it spreads, so too did the Vyresh rule all to their liking from the seat of a vast and growing empire. Few and distant were the kingdoms that remained beyond their grasp, and of these, only the Prometheans and those rich in their spirit aroused the lust and hatred of the *specials*.

Upon their unmasking, the Vyresh stripped the Ganyah of all rights and privileges; only those who commanded the Ganyah soldiers, or who served administrative roles for their Vyresh masters, were permitted a shadow of their former liberties. Even was outlawed—by pain of death—criticism of the Vyresh and all that bolstered their power. Behind these decrees followed more decrees—each more oppressive and sinister, each more draconian and destructive for the Ganyah, for the Vyresh were now free to do as they liked with the *talking beasts*.

Late did many Prometheans come to the light of truth. Too late were their rebellions, for even Thowwister, a Promethean of genius and tireless courage, brightest of all Ganyah commanders in the service of the Vyresh, for even he in insurrection could not reclaim what the Prometheans had surrendered in their madness.

Though it must be said that Thowwister's deeds were not in vain, for he is yet remembered in song and tale: and of him those words tell of his courage and sacrifice, and of the rebellions of sabotage that troubled the Vyresh in the wake of his glory. For by these efforts, the Vyresh were forestalled, their designs of conquest embroiled while plagued by unrest.

As a distant rumor, tales of Thowwister's bravery came to the beleaguered Promethean kingdoms, giving them hope that the Vyreshian Empire might crumble from within. For Thowwister, it was said, stirred the hearts of many men, and he came at the Vyresh citadel with great force of number. Had it been not for several traitors in his midst, he might have spared the world much misery and regret. In the seasons after Thowwister's fall, the acts of revolt ebbed into a frigid winter of despair, and with that frost all hope was lost for those who had repented of Vyreshian screeds.

The diversity of Nations and peoples bred in the population a dearth of loyalty, one for the other, a lack of commonality, an absence of a fixed identity round which to rally and resist the oppressor. Moreover, the Vyreshian efforts to break Ganyah traditions and loyalties, to sever them from the accumulated discernment of their elders and leaders, had so unnamed and unfaced the Ganyah that many were like unto beasts, serving only their impulses of pleasure and pain.

Even then, the Vyresh enlisted the masses to keep watch on their neighbors, that none could speak of rebellion lest he be discovered and tortured unto death. As the beaten cur that yet longs for his master's approval, eager and ready were the masses to serve the Vyresh in this matter, for gladly they betrayed those with whom they felt little kinship or bond.

In the horror of the mounting years, the masses were become vulgarians, giving themselves to debauchery and the *pleasures* of pain; for the hope of freedom had fled like a light into darkness, leaving the cold, heavy chains of servitude behind, fostering a wanton self-abuse—the marring of flesh and mind.

It was in that wretched hour that the prophecy was made true, for Lord Gorthang forsook his lair, and coming upon the city as a deadly mist, took form in the lamplit royal court the Vyresh had long prepared for him.

At first, the Vyresh elders were puzzled by his countenance, for their ancient scrolls told of a God that when in the shape of a man was like to a Promethean: beautiful, tall, and terrible, though stern or even hard of face, and crippled, for his right foot was missing. Yet before them, the God that towered twelve feet was none of these things, for his skin was ebon—black as the hole whence he crawled—and the sheen of the blackness rippled with crimson.

Great leathern wings sprung from his back; hooked barbs rose from the upmost pinions, and throbbing veins—thick as branches—crisscrossed the membrane that hung as black curtains. Sable horns, as those akin to a ram's, grew from the crown of his head and curled round his ears to bitter points. Cruel were the black lips that glistened beneath the ceaseless lapping of his forked tongue, and framing his gaunt face was hair like unto seaweed, dark, thin, and straggling.

His lidless eyes grinned with the malevolent lust of a predator for prey, and they pooled in his head like rotting fish in stagnant meres. An odor there also was: a reek as of decaying flesh that rose from his skin and doused the air with its stench. And where once he had stumbled, his right foot missing, he walked now with a click upon the floors, for grown from his mangled leg was the hoof of a goat.

Seeing their Lord, the Vyresh elders fell upon their faces, and they cried out in fear and joy, for Gorthang now mirrored their secret thoughts—thoughts he had sown in them in ages lost and dungeons dark. But this was no artifice of Gorthang's design, be it gift or trick. This was his true being come to the surface; for though the Gods appear to die not, living forever by the reckoning of man, they wither indeed, so that death finds them as surely as it finds man. Yet Gorthang had aged little in the passage of eons, for he had discovered a terrible magick by which to prolong his life— though in the prolonging he paid a dreadful price.

At once, Gorthang ordered the Vyresh to bring him slaves on which to feed: both Ganyah and beasts. But in the feeding, he consumed the flesh not, rather he rent the flesh with terrible speed, tearing his victims to pieces with the strength of his hands and the power of his jaws. Fangs dripping over a mouth full of blood, he thickly muttered a fell curse, and coming to the Flame of Life before its escape, drew its fires between his lips.

In the wake of the prophecy made true, fear flowed across the city upon leaden vapors that rose from blackened stacks, their many fires lining Gorthang's great hall; at their bases, sweat-soaked Masule-azai fed the mangled corpses to the coals, feasting as they worked.

Gorthang named his demonic palace, calling it, "Ashgar"—that is, Hell. And thus his great hall, his ruling chamber, was become the Seat of Hell. And therefrom wild screaming, bloodcurdling baying, and his crazed laughing soared beyond the citadel—and the gore, and the rending of flesh swathed the hall in horror.

Though a mask he could don, an artifice as a shroud he could wear, never again was Gorthang able to change that dreadful form, never again could he assume a fair semblance, for he had lost that power forever, coming at the last to be naught but evil.

This was the terrible price he paid for the desires of his black heart, for his theft of the Flames of Life, for his hatred of the Promethean Nation, and his lust to see it unmade; he had come indeed to sit upon the throne of the Earth as King of Men and Master of the World, but to do so, he had made of it a rotting corpse.

A lord he was, a lord of parasites, a king of thralls and master of decay. But even as Lord Gorthang brooded darkly on his throne, even as the power of the Vyresh was come to its noontide, the might of the putrefying kingdom waned, and the fall of the Vyresh, which seemed so remote and unthinkable, came hastening with sateless vengeance across the pages of history.

The Odyssey of the King

14.1

As has elsewhere been told, numerous though dwindling and far sundered Promethean kingdoms endured as islands of freedom, the horizon of their azure skies blackened by the groping fingers of Vyreshian power, their stainless shores receding before the growing sea of tyranny, waters that issued with swart spray from the Vyreshian Empire—a dominion rotting as a decaying body, strong as with the odor decay emits.

Too sundered were these kingdoms to render aid, one to the other; too disjointed to form league by which they might resist the Vyresh, yet one there was that kept fellowship with the others, aiding with information when arms they could not spare, reporting on the movements and strength of the enemy.

This was the proud Promethean kingdom of Ananoël, and their lord was King Lason, patriarch of the house of Ettahkarina—most hated and assailed by the enemy; for the king and his Nation shone in glorious contrast to the Vyreshian Empire, a glaring alternative to Vyreshian leadership, statecraft, and culture, a light to all those with the power to choose. And more, for King Lason and his Kingdom were a galling refutation of Vyreshian superiority, a refutation that enraged the *specials*, for they fervidly believed in their own eminence, though long they hid this and other thoughts from the Ganyah—victims who knew naught of their true beliefs, not until caught in the fastness of their webs.

For webs they were, or believed to be by those who owned King Lason as lord; there, in that fair kingdom, they called the Vyresh by the name of their taking, but also they called them Web-weavers, and Orb-weavers, and Harvestmen, and they spoke of them as Vamp Spiders, and Siren Spiders for the bewitching music of subtle words whereby they ensnared the unwary. And they avowed that fools most readily they caught in their nets, though even unfools, if heedless, could find themselves in the company of fools: ensnared, poisoned, and drained of their wills.

It was held by this regal people that those whom were thus ensnared were poisoned indeed, and verily, their wills were drained, losing the power to think for themselves or to come to any thought at variance with the wishes of the Web-weavers. For in truth, the Ananoëlians held that though Gorthang be their father, a monstrous black spider, with which he and countless others had fornicated, had been their mother: Queen Whore, Empress Ewer of the black seed, Root Mother of the Vyresh.

Of her, they declared that she was an enemy of all that is high and resplendent, loathing beauty yet ever hungering for it, lusting for it, devouring it and spinning it forth in the wretchedness of her own image, driven as by a madness that would consume all that is lofty and lovely in the world, though the filling of her belly foredoom her demise.

Her destructive spirit, they avowed, was ever at work in the Vyresh. Moreover, it was held that in their countenance one could yet see the face of their odious mother, though long she be gone, for the Vyresh had her glance—and other salient features.

Poems and stories, songs and rhymes the Ananoëlians made by which ever to recall the duty of vigilance toward all enemies, and the Vyresh not least:

Webs they weave with words not silk,
But soft to touch and fair as milk.
Crawling, clinging, strangling gloom;
The fool is drawn toward his doom.
Caught therein the spider's web,
Poisoned kiss, and life there ebb,
Blackest beak, and will is gone.
Not from there another dawn.
To slay the lofty and the beauty;
Must consume to fill thy belly.
So be thou wary, sleepless eyes,
For he who blinks is he who dies.

14.2

Unbroken and undaunted by the incessant onslaught and crazed hatred of the enemy, undiminished in spirit and zeal, so were the Ananoëlians under the lordship of King Lason. For they were a people given to high culture: wise in lore; fond of fair music and poetry, fine art and architecture; skilled in prose and crafts of high learning.

They were masters of the wood, the dale, the mountain, and captains of the sea—a rugged, thriving, and valiant people, a Nation in harmony with the Earth and its beasts. Subtle and gentle of mind were the Ananoëlians, considerate and respectful, yet terrible and deadly in their wrath, for the light of Prometheus was undimmed in their eyes.

They were a people that esteemed the Lore Master and the warrior above all others, for by the wisdom of the wise and the strength of the soldier they endured; and from that sturdy base they ever served the purpose sewn into the fabric of their being: the onward and upward march to mastery. Many fair and wonderful things they made, though the age was become dark and oppressive; and while beauty climbed behind their high walls, red ran their long swords with the blood of the enemy.

Theirs was the kingdom that recalled the splendor and bliss of the legends of yore: faint recollections of ages past, a limb of a hallowed tree whose trunk was carven from the souls of Sentilleena and Qwindellin. Yea, fair indeed was Ananoël, the noble city through which many rills of limpid waters mirthfully played their sweet music, and glorious was the palace Rhovannion, for against the growing darkness its towers glimmered like silver spikes in the pale beams of dawn.

Tall and fair, and glittering as if wrought of flawless crystal, rose the palace from the midst of the city, and to it the city was as the Sun, igniting Rhovannion and filling the lands with its light and beauty. Here, beyond the walls of Ananoël, was a wide plain of rich soil, steeped in lush grasses and merry downs, painted and flecked with fields of wild flowers and rustic farms. Here was a kingdom of natural defenses, for it was bordered by the shoulder of a mountain exceedingly steep, a forest dark and pensive, and a river wide and deep; "Shantellise" that river was named: swift as the current of thought, flowing untroubled to the mouth of the sea.

This was a country set as it were a glade amidst breathtaking beauty, a Sun-filled meadowland that only Prometheus could have caused to be. Briskly, fluttered the Promethean standards from the battlements of the city; burnished were the stately domes that gleamed like birdsong in the Sun's golden light, yet glowed like opal in the stars of the night. High, climbed the white walls round Ananoël; and clear, rang the music of silver trumpets in defiance of the Vyreshian scourge.

Lason's kingdom, like the other citadels of freedom, had preserved itself from the Vyreshian yoke by ever harboring a wariness for the outsider, a sleepless eye, a deathless vigilance for the *Other*. It came to pass that to each of these kingdoms the Vyresh came as pitiable friends and distinguished emissaries, promising fortunes, pleasures, powers and secrets to all those who would but let them in—who would but have compassion on those who had claimed to know only hardship and *persecution*.

Those of wiser counsel and deeper minds barred the doors, pleading the travelers be entered not upon the body of their kingdoms, yet the desires and counsels of those with childlike minds prevailed, for they were unwary and trustful of words, and they invoked honored customs, welcoming the Other with amity no less warm than sunsets on island waters.

Those who shared with children the debilitating trait of naiveté, though their years be beyond the years of children, the wise named, "Heelaw," signifying the childlike or the stunted: those whose bodies grew, but whose discernment grew not.

Thus, wisdom ripened not in the Heelaw, but a proudly contrarian, dimwitted, gullible nature, a diseased nature that saw evil in good and good in evil, an air that rendered itself as pompous self-righteousness, unmistakable as the priggish Heelaw shuffled with their noses high, puffed-up with affected dignity as if bearing superior truth rather than debilitating sickness.

It was often observed that when the policies of the Heelaw brought ruin and misery rather than their promise of refinement and felicity, they were yet unfazed, and all the more determined to advance their illogical notions. Yet the Heelaw, credulous as the blind and naïve as children, were not alone as useful to the Vyresh, for opportunists of criminal nature, ever lusting for power without regard for the consequences of their actions, swarmed round the *specials*, eager to serve and thereby obtain the promise of power and riches.

Those of criminal nature in service to the Vyresh, the wise gave names like unto colluder and betrayer, calling them Villam, and Dred Villam; ever were the wise wary of their deceptive smiles, their unctuous tongues and duplicitous arguments. And yea, more, for the wise held that like to the ancient minglings that caused Promethean Spirits to wear foreign masks, so too had ancient minglings caused in these a Promethean mask, but a foreign spirit.

In no kingdom would truth and freedom prevail against the insidious efforts of this trine—the Vyresh, the Heelaw, and the Villam—had it been not for the efforts of the Arvanyenne—the Order of Air and Fire.

It has long been held that Lason, ere he was become king, founded the order, which ever strove to inform the people of the Vyreshian danger, to observe and study the Vyresh, to undermine their efforts, and to expel them, lifting the pall of sickness from their kingdoms.

Though women were counted among the Order of Air and Fire, most were men, and of these a great part had the ability to reject the passions of women; while most men satisfied their desires and built families, women and children who consumed their energy, obligated their protection, and clouded their judgment with voices near and persistent, these were men who married themselves to the body of the people and the love of their resplendent king. Theirs was a cloudless judgment because the impetus of their love and desire found its fulfillment in the ideal of the Nation—the unwavering will of Prometheus Ethelleyah.

Thus, though many members had wives or husbands and children, the Order of Air and Fire was a higher calling than that of the single family; it was an obligation to the protection of the greater family—the Promethean Nation.

In addition to the Order of Air and Fire, King Lason established the Airasayah Arvanyenne, the Knights of Prometheus: soldiers of both the shadows and the battlefield. Amongst those who won greatest renown throughout the free kingdoms of the world, not few were of this glorious order, and some of their most heroic were found also among the king's guard, the Arganantum.

In every Promethean kingdom that resisted the Vyresh, and in some that failed, the Arvanyenne contended with the

Vyresh—both before and behind the curtain. In this contest, the Heelaw and Villam were ever useful to the Vyresh, for the Vyresh waged their war through these puppets as often as they might, vexing the Arvanyenne in all their efforts. Yet, in those kingdoms that rid themselves of the Vyreshian affliction, the trine was unable to curb the endeavors of the wise, and had not the power to stay their hands—when the wise would move them.

Thus, the Vyresh escaped not the watchful eyes of the Arvanyenne, though they feigned great and grievous injury. Cringing in misfortune and insolent in prosperity, they complained vehemently and with much theater that the suspicion of their intentions was a bitter thanks for the *selfless service* they rendered the Prometheans, an egregious act against historical victims, an unwarranted slight for those who came bearing gifts and promises of more gifts, and promises of gifts yet to be named, playing like lambs beaten for nuzzling the shepherd.

The Heelaw heeded the Vyreshian arguments and came like witless birds chattering to their defense, decrying the watchfulness as foul and unbecoming of their people, an insult the watchers would have done not unto themselves, a crime beyond measure because it was a crime against *victims*. Yet, despite the protests and the wringing of hands by Heelaw and Villam, and the strident complaints of innocence injured brought by the Vyresh, no end was there to the sleepless watch. And thus, in time, the

Vyresh were discovered to be not what they claimed, their plans revealed as other than averred.

And so it was that the Vyresh, and their allies in the Heelaw and Villam, were cast out of these kingdoms, the strong walls and tall towers—garrisoned with ceaseless vigilance—set against them. But the Vyresh were unrepentant and undismayed by the discovery of their plans, for they hastened to kingdoms mortally infected by their kind, and there bade their brethren to crush in all haste the insolent kings. So it came to pass that where the tongue and the conspiracy had failed, the sword and the onslaught they hoped would avail.

Thus carrying on their black lusts, they endeavored by sanguinary means to come to the crowns of these kingdoms, and indeed many kings were toppled by vast alliances summoned by the Vyresh, who were ever willing to fight to the last of their Ganyah thralls to satisfy their desires. Yet some kingdoms there were that fell not, for they had strength enough to defend their borders. Whether by the genius of their captains and the courage of their knights, or the harshness of the terrain by which they were preserved, they had come to witness the day when the shadow of their enemy had grown tall and ghastly, a menace become too powerful to resist forever.

Of those kings and kingdoms, it was King Lason of Ananoël that suffered the Vyresh least, for he was more cunning than they, keener of eye and wit. Ever could his mind pierce the fair attire of words and probe the naked secrets of thought therein; ever was his a voice that had power to move those who harkened, to transform those who opposed, to set their minds—as his— upon the victory of the Promethean Nation. Verily, wise grew the hearts of those who lent ear to his words.

To his kingdom had come the sacred truths of the ancient past; for his Lore Masters preserved the memory and many forgotten scrolls of ages remote and lost beyond time. Yet even here, many of the laity worshiped gods of their imaginings with as much vigor as they worshiped Lord Prometheus, so that he was become not more than a face in a host of deities, a set of *opinions* not more important than those of their own devices.

Oft, the Lore Masters said that if only heeded had been the wise counsel and sage warnings Prometheus had given from the high seat of Qwindellin, naught of the sickness that had afflicted the Prometheans would have come to pass. Indeed, despite the efforts of the *Other* to pull them down, many beautiful and wondrous things would have come to their springtide.

"But heed this above all else—" said Lord Prometheus in ancient days, "heed *this* or decay: for all your strengths can be turned against you; all that might carry you to the stars can be made to bind you.

"This you must guard against with all vigor and sleepless diligence: for your innocence and trust could fall prey to forked tongues—your intelligence and creativity become engines of interests other than your own—your compassion, selflessness, and charity, a means to your waning and the waxing of others—your imagination, a tool by which your life conforms to false and harmful beliefs—your lofty thoughts that seek objective truths become bound to notions that make a sacrifice of the *spirit* on the altar of an *idea*.

"These are warnings that know not a winter, for they are evergreen—*ever* must they be reckoned!"

14.3

In the long pages of the *Finloth Aëta*, much is told of the efforts of the Vyresh to corrupt and undermine Ananoël, to come to power and supplant King Lason as ruler. There, it is told how the Vyresh sought to convert the masses: some saying that Prometheus Ethelleyah and the Valaroma existed not; others saying that Prometheus was a byname for Gorthang, and that they were his *specials*; all saying that only through them and their ideas could grace and happiness be found.

In that sacred book, it is told how the Vyresh—and their collaborators in the Heelaw and Villam—spread the Saipist and Essiyah screeds like a sickness that passes on the breath. And there, detailed in darkest ink, are the efforts the Vyresh made to turn group against group, neighbor against neighbor, wife against husband, and youth against age—and this by way of spreading discontent through propagated falsehoods. There, it is told how the Vyresh furtively worked as agents of foreign loyalties: revealing secrets, plotting assassinations, troubling the machinery of finance and education, and more and yet more.

Where this tale says little of Lason's desperate quest to save both Nation and kingdom, all is told on the tear-and-blood-wet pages of the *Finloth Aëta*—of Lason's heroic efforts, of the three hundred Arganantum who bravely joined him, and of the selfless sacrifice they made upon that merciless road; for King Lason, having long defended his realm by might of arms and cunning of mind, foresaw that victory would lie not in defense alone, nor in the strength of men, but that aid had to be sought beyond all hope in the legends of yore.

The ancient tales spoke of mystifying and wondrous things, things that housed hope, mysteries locked in the dusky legends and tattered pages of aged lore. Victory, Lason surmised, might lie hidden in the haunted dwellings of the past.

Of these ancient tales, some there were that spoke of Valaroma and of Accalobain-Iedolin, saying that all Valaroma were slain not, and that having survived the conflict, they had lain hidden since those ancient days. Rumors, survived by oral traditions, spoke of the likely haunts wherein the survivors might dwell; moreover, King Lason had been an adventurer, waging many battles and crossing many lands, and oft he felt a calling as though the land or some ineffable force spoke to him, or rather on which his thoughts intruded.

Perhaps, Lason opined, as his Lore Masters and the chiefs of the Arganantum sat in audience, perhaps the Valaroma awaited a summons, eager to rejoin the conflict.

Swift and many were the voices in protest: The legends might be naught but legends. And if real, the Gods may be dead. And even if living, the king was unlikely to find them. More valuable was he to his people if he remained—no value if he perished on the long and trackless road.

But he stayed their objections, remained firm before their tears, for he knew if he stayed, even he—in time—would fall to the foe. The hour was come, he said, a king knows when destiny is upon him.

The Gods—they were things of an older world, yet they were powers that, once resurrected, offered new and perhaps indomitable hope. So it was that King Lason, undeterred by the immensity of the challenge, undaunted by the slim hope of success, entrusted the lordship of his kingdom to the able hands of his eldest son, Anairyan, a captain of great acclaim.

Choked with sadness so that words he could not find, or in the finding he could not voice, he smiled farewell to family and hearth; for he knew his return unlikely should his quest come to naught, he knew he might look never again upon kin and kingdom.

Turning, he set forth with the Arganantum, and thus began a journey of desperation, an odyssey that sought to marshal the legends and power of the Gods.

14.4

Here is told but a portion of the quest on which King Lason and his Arganantum embarked, for their journey was trackless and they were mercilessly pursued.

When to the Vyresh came the tale that King Lason had left the protection of the city in pursuit of the fables of the past, they laughed, believing not the legends, though welcoming the chance to slay those they so dearly despised.

From numerous kingdoms, countless riders were dispatched so that Lason and his company fell under the watch of the Vyresh, for the haste of their journey lent not to furtive passage—less still to secrecy. Setting no pavilions and traveling light, they were continually assailed by an enemy who knew naught but to defile and debase all that was lofty.

Without reprieve were the months of conflict for the king and his men, for the Vyresh sent endless sorties of Ganyah to waylay their hated foe, hoping to prevail with numbers where outmatched in valor, in brilliance, in courage, skill and strength, and in matchless glory by the proud Arganantum and their warrior king.

Few are the tales of old that in their telling draw nigh the notes of tearful sadness and the crescendos of triumphant splendor that laced their long and desperate road, for many valiant battles were waged, victories secured by acts of heroism unrivaled, and Promethean lives given gladly as they fought by the side of their lord.

Numerous were the occasions when Lason and his men were entrapped and encircled, outnumbered and overborne, yet time and again, though the odds against them, they overcame and broke through the Vyreshian armies—even as the Vyresh wrapped crooked fingers around them.

But their long road appeared to have no end, their sacrifices a loss without profit. Yet, when failure stalked them most feverishly, they came to a deep, dark wood amid the long shadows of a glowering forest; thicker it was and more menacing even than the encircling woodland, a place where turbid mists trailed along the earth and lurked ominously in the hollows.

Though hotly pursued, coldly they poured their arrows into the faces of the enemy, seeking—if they might—to yield their king as much time as could be dearly bought. In this, there would be no escape, nor was there hope of victory in battle, for the enemy was too numerous, the Prometheans too exhausted.

Into the deeps of that dank and ominous forest strode King Lason, as a scintillating star on a winter's night—proud lord of the Promethean Nation and banner bearer of a New Dawn. Guided by no map and having no compass to lead him to the legends of yore, he had followed the wisdom of his spirit and the tattered descriptions of lands wracked and ruined. But now a dread it was that gripped him, a dread issuing with great horror from the deeps of the darkness, and he realized on the sudden that the path he was made to hate and fear most was the path he had to walk for salvation.

Such was the fear lain in horror that naught of the living save for the trees endured its menace, for it was a blackness as a vapor wrought with venom, bringing confusion and blindness to the mind no less impenetrable than to the sight. As down the forbidden lane the king courageously strode, so grew the sensation of a presence, a lurking malevolence, a hostile will drawing in upon him, drawing in as much from the shadows of his thought as from the shadows that enmeshed him.

And the king halted, for he knew that one step more would carry him beyond return. His legs had grown numb, his mouth dry, and his breathing unsteady. Now, in his mind's eye, a great pale cowardice arose within him. He longed to flee, to be rid of the malice bent upon him, to live his life as a craven without duty or honor.

But even as the wan specter of cowardice arose, even then an arrow of fire sped, an arrow singing from the darkness of thought, and piercing the heart of fear, it wavered and staggered—and fell. There in his mind, a new figure stood, bow in hand and clad in flame—the courage of the king had prevailed.

Setting his jaw, he rushed down the forbidden lane, clambering, groping, and stumbling in the dark until he came to a narrow glade. Roofed by the heavy boughs of tall trees, the glade was lit as if by an unholy magick that fell upon the forest as a frigid blue, cold as the depths of winter, fogging the king's breath as a fountain of smoke.

And there, against the side of a low climbing hill, was a house of horror, a chilling sight such as stops the heart and looses ice through the veins, for looming up out of its slope was the den of a beast. Ghastly was the black portal from which the coals of its eyes peered out upon a world made helpless before it.

"Who—are—you—insolent rebel, disregarder of my threats, conqueror of my snares?" said a snarling voice from within the pit, the clap of teeth ringing every word.

"I am Lason, King of Ananoël, Emperor of the Promethean Nation and ardent servant of the High Lord, Prometheus Ethelleyah," said the king with great pride and majesty, though against the power of the beast his words fell sickly from his lips, collapsing as having neither breath nor sound.

Upon hearing the name Prometheus, the beast's eyes flared so that its den was become alight as though filled with amber fire, and stepping forth from its lair, the menace was finally unmasked. A dread wolf it was, larger than a horse, its coat matted and tangled, its joints popping from ages of disuse.

"Long ago—I climbed into this forsaken hole, ringing it with my enchantments; here I have rested, and now you, a stranger, unlooked for, come speaking of Lord Prometheus—he is dead.... What brings you, then, to my den—long descendant of a once-glorious Nation?" said the great wolf, a wrath stirring in his snarling words, his breath hissing through clinched teeth.

"I seek Valaroma, for war is waged upon the Promethean Nation by a relentless foe. We have endured for many years, yet the tide is against us, and thus the cause of our survival teeters upon a sword's edge.

"My people are my life, dread wolf, and so I give my life freely for theirs. If in my efforts to save my Nation, I have fallen to folly, if at the door of a foe I am come, then I am to be forgiven," said Lason, his features hardening, "yet I do not beg your pardon, for I will not allow an enemy of my Nation to live— once my path and his, or hers, or its, have crossed."

Lason threw back his cloak, and then it was that, though wayworn and marred, he seemed to grow taller and more glorious in the eyes of the wolf, a burnished statue, dazzling in its glory as though lit by a cataract of the Sun.

Widening his stance, Lason avowed, "I have little doubt, dread wolf, that in you is the power to slay me, but I shall make of ours a fight you shall not soon forget. And if fortune is with me this day, I shall add more than one scar to your thick hide!" he roared, a mist of weariness glowing in his eyes.

Setting his hand upon the hilt of his sword, Lason prepared to fight to the death; it was then he noticed that the fell wolf was injured, for thick blood sluggishly dripped from both hip and rib.

"Yes...my wounds," snarled the wolf, his eyes tilting toward his injuries. "I have not the power to mend them, for they were made by those with might greater than my own.

"I can slay you, indeed, Emperor of the Prometheans, and I doubt not that you could do me grave hurt, yet you need not fight to the death, for I can read in your mind all that you would reveal in words, and there now I see the truth of who and what you are, and of the noble mission that is yours.

"Draw not your sword, beloved king, for I am Balarre, Gorthang's bane, his foot I devoured—Balarre—great wolf of the Valaroma!"

14.5

Then it was—as though dawn tore through a wrack of dark clouds—that the menace of the wolf was withdrawn, and Lason saw clearly that he was indeed in the presence of a God, a God immortalized in the ancient texts as a warrior of great acclaim, a soldier who had laid waste to the enemy; yea, in great heaps he had gathered his harvest.

Turning his head to the heavens, Lason gave thanks to Lord Prometheus. It was then that the clash of battle returned to his ears, the cries of men in anguish and the throes of death, and knowing not whether it was his men or the enemy who fell, he pleaded with Balarre to join his cause and come to their aid—but Balarre refused.

"I cannot do what you ask of me. I loved Prometheus— but he is gone, and our cause...it is lost," lamented Balarre, lowering his gaze. "More harm will I do you than good, for if I extend power greater—if I set forth into war—I will awake Zeushin's wrath. And I have not the strength to contend with him.

"A burden I would be to you and your men, not a boon, for when Zeushin would come—not one would survive. But this I can share," he added, raising his head, "there are other Valaroma—some more powerful than I—to them you may turn...perhaps they can aid you."

At that moment, a stream of images raced through Lason's mind so that in him there was an instant knowing, an awareness of the regions wherein these lonesome Valaroma might be found.

"I am grateful for your aid, Lord Balarre, but if from you I glean naught but a direction and a hope, they will be of little use to me, for my men and I will perish this day," said the king flatly.

"Stretch forth your thoughts, if but for an instant, and see the odds set against us. We are but seventy, and they are some three thousands."

The great wolf lifted his chin, and then looked again—gravely—at the king, "Your men are but fifty, and your enemy is some four thousands. So it is that you have come to me at the end of your long road—desperate and beyond all hope."

"It need not be the end, Lord Balarre…," said Lason eagerly, his words swelling with power.

"Join us; fight now as you once fought by the side of Promethean warriors, as you once fought the enemy of our Nation; fight now for Lord Prometheus!

"Die not like this—in a wretched hole in the earth, cravenly licking old wounds, shadow haunting in the coward's hope that his tormentor will leave him to languish. Die a glorious death—a hero's death!

"Let Zeushin come, and we shall meet him in open combat—there to slay him with mortal wound or to die as brothers in the name of our Lord!"

The great wolf growled and bared his teeth, fangs as long as a man's forearm, eyes gleaming and growing bright with a God's fire.

"I doubt not that alone you would wield sword and shield against Zeushin for our cause," said Balarre, a deep reverence coloring his words and features.

"Know this—though far his Nation has fallen, your Maker would have called you—son."

Rising to his full height and narrowing his eyes, Balarre declared, "Today, Lason, King of Ananoël, Emperor of the Promethean Nation, today I die a hero's death!

"Onto my back, dear king," urged Balarre as he crouched.

Through the king surged a great thrill of power—Balarre's power, filling his veins as they leapt forth from the glade with a gale's ferocity.

"Fall back! Fall back!" shouted Attalass of the Arganantum, driving his sword into the throat of a Sarraneem, arrows thick as flies hissing all about him.

In full flight, the Prometheans sped for their lives, sending arrows on high arcs, hoping the wayward shafts would bite like vipers the flesh of the foe. But against the hastening enemy came a force sudden and unexpected, a collision like to the anvil that cracks under hammer, throwing winged sparks and ringing in the ears.

Then it was that the Arganantum saw their king atop a lupine steed, his sword naked and flaming in the wooded twilight, his body aglow with a silvery sheen, as if in him was the light of the stars.

Loud as thunder, hard as steel came Balarre—great wolf of the Valaroma; against his wrath, the enemy withered and broke as dried reeds swept to flame by a scorching wind. Together, he and the king plowed a deep, sanguinary swath through the enemy's lines. Those who yielded not to flight forsook their pursuit of the Arganantum, and turned instead their fury on wolf and rider. Seeing this, the Arganantum wheeled and regrouped. Sounding the Horn of Sarpidon, they advanced on the unguarded rear of the enemy, hewing them where rooted they stood.

Like a falling star streaking through a night-menace of glowering clouds, so too did Balarre and King Lason streak through the body of the foe, cleaving them to the death with sword, fang, and claw. Again and again, Balarre dashed from contest to contest, blood-splattered and menacing, the gore coating his hide, yet Balarre was not without hurt, for as he and the king gathered their harvest, Balarre suffered from countless wounds.

Long were their efforts and deep into the enemy had they plowed when a gully, hidden amidst the underwood, snared Lord Balarre, and he stumbled—and the king was thrown. Crashing to the earth, Lason sprang to his feet with sword in hand. And he assailed the enemy as a man no longer desiring life, but possessed by an undying wrath and a glorious destiny.

Bright gleamed his sword as a spire of glittering ice, veined with the blood of the enemy. Four, then six, and then ten, and now twenty piled high round the king, a wild gleam in his eyes, a madness of purpose and a fearlessness now overcoming him, for he began to chant as he slew the enemy:

"The darkness is dying

The climbing Sun

The dawn is rising

The night is done!"

Thirty-three times King Lason chanted thus, hewing the enemy in such heaps that he strode across their writhing mounds; now seventy lay dying round his wrath, now eighty, then ninety, until at last his strength began to wane and wounds he took from sword, dart, and spear.

Putting his back to a dead and twisted tree, cursing the enemy, Lason made his final defense, but as the leering foe pressed in upon him, there was a sudden shattering of their force. Enemy soldiers were tossed through the air, screams of men from bodies hurled and severed in twain, for Balarre had come to the aid of the king!

As Lason fell to his knees, his breathing hollow and labored, he watched with slackening eyes as Balarre, mortally wounded, tore through the armor and flesh of the foe until not one remained to challenge his might.

Save for the distant sounds of the Arganantum pursuing and slaying the fleeing enemy, all succumbed to silence. Still gasping for air, Lason fell and lay as a man in a swoon, half in the world of the living—half in the dead. To his side came Balarre, dragging his wounded and broken body. Uneven was his breathing, halting were his words.

"…Dear king…to you…I give thanks no less than to Prometheus himself…for where he gave me power and life beyond my making, you have given me an end as glorious as my beginning."

Struggling, unable to speak, Lason extended his shattered arm, setting his bloodied hand upon Balarre's cheek. The wolf's hard eyes softened, and they filled with warm tears.

As Balarre and King Lason lay dying together, their wills climbing from their broken forms, a rush of light sped into Lason, a faint glow as the world receded to darkness and memory took wing, for Balarre had sacrificed his final strength to heal the wounds of the king.

14.6

Succumbing to the darkness, Balarre was become a glittering ash that leapt into the winds and fled from sight—though not from knowledge or tale.

Made hale by Balarre's touch, King Lason and his surviving Arganantum, some forty-six men, set forth in all haste for the regions wherein the Valaroma lay hidden.

Enemy Gods, and mercenaries in league with the Vyresh, and soldiers marching at the will of Vyreshian masters they encountered, and battles were fought, and men fell and men triumphed, and the king and his Arganantum marched on.

Help they were rendered by friends and by strangers, aid they were delivered when aid they sorely needed, for the lands they trod were grim and unpitying. Over angry seas and under noxious fogs, over Sun-withered wastes and under tree-clad slopes, through forests that rolled up mountains, through rivers that fumed on stones, by din of arms and by gore-slicked earth, the king and his men unearthed the Gods of legend.

Mournful at times were their journeys, for they were reluctant observers of Vyreshian atrocities, reluctant witnesses of deserted towns and ruined cities, reluctant wayfarers through lands that belched flags of smoke. But so too were they lifted by the works of Prometheus, by mountains in gowns of glistening snow, by skies that rippled like pristine waters, and pristine waters that wrapped arms round supple headlands, for the ugly made stark the beautiful, and weary roads joined roads that were glad.

As much was theirs a conquering of self as of enemy, for with every joy there was a hurt—and with every victory, another struggle. The desperate flight of the king and his men, though grievous and woefully endured, brought them time and again to the audience of Valaroma, yet each would proffer no more than knowledge: truths of the past they shared, predictions of the future, but for the present, no more than locations they revealed— haunts where others of their order might dwell.

Times there were, however, when Valaroma came to the aid of the king as Balarre had done, for the dispersion of enemy Gods and the use of their powers cloaked somewhat the doings of the Valaroma. Yet more aid they rendered not, for were Zeushin to discover them, a swift and brutal end—they knew—would be made of the king.

This is the fashion whereby King Lason and his Arganantum came to the entrance of the underworld, the labyrinthian grottos delved deep in the Earth wherein dwelt an enchantress of inimitable beauty—Airehdelle, the Goddess Mother of the Promethean Nation.

The king well knew that Prometheus had hidden her in the depths of the Earth, a haven for the mending of her wounds after the Battle of Arn-gelwain. With great hardship and trackless journey in the deeps of caverns lost and forgotten, the king and his men found the maw to the belly of the world. Chilled with fear, they trod through the darkness, for shadow-shapes lurked therein, ever nigh but ever beyond the limb of their torchlight—flames as red flowers afloat dark currents: skulking nightmares, both drawn and repelled.

Even here did the enemy pursue the king and his men, for their Vyresh masters drove them without pity or regard for their lives. Creatures there were in the caverns, beasts of forgotten ages that waylaid the Prometheans and their pursuers: battles below the surface of the world that rang with the screams of men and the cries of monsters.

Nonetheless, after a long and grueling journey, Lason and the Arganantum came to the leviathan chamber wherein the Goddess made her abode. Little is told in these pages of that meeting, of the dreamlike palace that shone like the Moon in the depths of the Earth, of the Goddess's memories that swept like ghosts through its hallowed halls—of the dark, placid waters and dancing fountains, of the flying bridges over prancing streams, and the night songs, and the music of birds, and the fresh air that sighed through the leaves of green and silvered trees; nor is there told of the exodus, of the days without count and the dangers without measure that followed the enchantments of the Mother. Yet the tale has been told, first in the Lay of Farr

Rohthemebrienne—taking its name from the Mother's palace—and later lain down in the sacred pages of the Finloth Aëta.

Here is recounted naught but *the secret* she revealed to her children: The Goddess would come not to their aid, for, like the others, she knew her presence would work their undoing, yet her revelation spoke of something far greater than the aid of Valaroma.

A new hope she gave them, a new direction to fly: a region atop a towering wave of rock on the banks of a mountain—once enshrined, yet now forgotten; for she revealed that there the king and his men would find the greatest of treasures, for, if salvation yet lived—there they would find Prometheus the Lord.

14.7

Now there was a cold predawn on which the king and his men ascended the rugged slope of a mountain, chased by the foe as the taut sail is carried by a hard wind.

Adamant purpose drove King Lason and the proud Arganantum; for the survival of the Promethean Nation depended upon rekindling the untended fire of the Promethean Spirit: Prometheus would rise or the Prometheans would fall.

Alas, peering down upon the two thousands in pursuit, the king and his three Arganantum grimly established their final defense. Here was an inviolable cleft, a natural feature where three could bring death to scores, waylaying the enemy so the king might reach their journey's end.

Surrendering his bow and quiver, King Lason warmly embraced each of his men before climbing a perch; dry tears welling as oases upon deserts of lamentation. Each, he knew, would see not another sunrise nor their families again, for though impeded, the foe could not be resisted.

As the Sun broke through the night's sable curtain, globing the king so that he gleamed like a winged God, gilding his words so that they rose from his lips with unnatural majesty, he bade them farewell: "This day—is our last, but our lives are given not in vain—they have been squandered not on the crimes of self-worship and idleness, they have been forfeited not on the crime of servitude to dangerous ideas," said the king solemnly.

"Our lives are given to the only cause that bears the right to claim life, for ours are given to the Fount from which we came—and to which we owe *everything*.

"Decadent has our age become under the Vyresh. Many of our people worship themselves, dedicating their lives to the pursuit of that which ever fails to fulfill, ever beckoning, ever snatching away its promise. Others squander their lives in torpor, spectators of life rather than participants. And still others of our Nation," added the king, deliberately gesturing to the kingdoms in the valleys below, "embrace meretricious doctrines; zealous do these become, disciples of insidious ideas, vassals of disfigured afterthoughts, slaves of diseased notions.

"Creeds they worship—creeds that would live not in the body of a Promethean had there been no Prometheans, yet insolently they declare these creeds more worthy of fealty and sacrifice than the spirit that brings forth the Promethean.

"How impudent for *ideas* to march upon streets, demanding obedience from the masses," said the king, lifting his eyes as though seeing the thought-diseased marchers.

"Ideas ride upon the currents of our thoughts, and yet our thoughts are not but a reflection: waters that owe their insignificant shine to the Sun's radiance in our Promethean Spirit…how black the crime when the idea takes precedence, and how much blacker when the idea repudiates the authority of the heavens?

"Can a doctrine give you life?" demanded Lason of the distant kingdoms beyond his audience. "Have fantasies ever conquered the real? Have ever the ideas of man overturned the will of the Fount? Nay! There is only one who is worthy of allegiance, one who can justly demand the obedience of our Nation—and he," derisively laughed the king, "is no afterthought of man—for he is the Source of our Nation.

"To us is given naught but the choice of duty or disgrace. The best choose service to our spirit—to the Fount—to repay their debt. The worst turn their backs on our Nation…thankless squanderers…ungrateful inheritors…betrayers of our progeny."

As the foe's approaching shouts galloped over the hills in wandering echoes, the king continued, "We are pledged to a purpose crafted by no man, but a mystery beyond us, a Maker who cannot be gainsaid; for here we are, in our talents and limits: lives of infinite value, but possessing neither value nor purpose without our Source.

"Both will die, the best and the worst, the heroes and the traitors, but where theirs is a death like unto a cur whose memory and flesh are joined in decay, ours is a rebirth, an undeath and destiny written in the stars.

"We die for a cause far greater than the cause of our lives or the caprice of man," breathed the king, stepping down from his perch and laying hands on his men's shoulders.

"Ours is not regret, but gratitude, for in our commitment, our resolve, our sacrifice—in *us*—the Promethean Nation conquers even as the rising Sun conquers the night.

"Your flesh—no matter your effort to preserve it—will wither and perish; by your deeds and deeds alone are you remembered. Verily, only by your deeds can you live forever," he smiled, the warmth of his love mirrored in the faces of his men.

"Now," Lason ordered, a hard note in his voice, "take your positions. Have no mercy, as none has been shown you. Make use of treachery as treachery is used against you. Master deception as deception has blinded you; put your mind and your efforts upon this course and no power can resist you. Let no principle of decorum bind that which weakens the enemy, but meet fire with inferno, trump cunning with guile. Feign what you must, but give misery to the foe, yea, as cruelly as he has given it to you.

"Let this be a red day; let your wrath and your vengeance spread like a chilled wind of terror from the fields of conflict; let there howl a dreadful gale so that even the Vyresh—*yea, even they* atop their hillocks of stolen gold are kissed by its horror!

"This day," said the king, looking into the eyes of his men—"we become immortal." And turning, he looked not back, but put forth his final strength for the last leg of the ascent.

It was not more than an hour into his climb that the distant clamor of battle, wafting upon the lofty winds curling skyward, brought report of the conflict below. At length, silence followed, and the king knew his men were gone—become now, eternal in the legends of all who are worthy of their sacrifice.

14.8

Exhausted, and days without food or drink, King Lason climbed with the knowledge that his pursuers were fresh, well fed, and moving more quickly than he. He had not the time to rest or tend to his numerous injuries, to pity his plight or to assuage the grief that like unto a living death, threatened to drown him in sadness.

At long last, bereft of the splendor that haloed the king and his proud men as from Ananoël they marched, all that was left him was the love he held for his people, and the knowledge that the lives and safety of Promethean families lay no place other than in the victory of the Promethean Nation. It was this love that fueled him when all else had come to its dregs.

His body broken, his limbs inert, heavy and thick with numbness, his heart straining even as it began to fail, King Lason conquered the mountain.

Nigh the end of his strength, he heaved his tired frame onto a shelf—expansive upon the mountain's shoulder. Smooth and level was its surface, and there, prostrate upon its lip he lay, feebly watching the enemy as they climbed from the mouth of the swallowing dusk that pursued them: the rolling boil of their black forms, blacker against the blackness of night.

Adrift on a violet sea, deepening to darkness and rising with the cries of nocturnal hunters, Lason's life was no more than a sputtering flame. Straightening painfully to his feet, the once-proud king strode with great difficulty toward a shapeless boulder that leered from the middle of the shelf. Alone, it disturbed the flawless expanse—torn loose from some distant cliff, perhaps: a colossal interloper against which he leaned his trembling body.

Scanning the shelf, peering blearily from rim to rim with squinted eyes, he searched for sign or clue to Prometheus in vain.

Surely, if here were a power to deliver his Nation from hastening oblivion, it would need not the suppliant's faith and discernment, but would glow like Sun and Moon, and roar like bolt and thunder. But here, there was nothing. In the sinking awareness of failure, of defeat, a darkness of grief invaded him from within.

He longed to scream his anger into the night, to beat his fists into the dirt, but his thoughts spun loose from his grasp, careening through his weakened mind like withering ghosts on a winter's gale. Shivering with the horror of failure, his mind flitted into darkness and back, the world tilting under his feet. Twice, his knees buckled, and twice he caught himself, his bloody fingers clutching the ugly stone.

Grief, like a rising tide, swelled with a quenchless furor from the deeps, but in grief he would not drown. For even as the stars winked into flame across heaven's canopy, his troubled thoughts were broken by the sounds of the lurching enemy, and turning as one driven by instinct, he prepared for his final battle.

Probing the night shadows as tragic fears chased one another through his slackening mind, Lason saw no bulwark or blind behind which he might contend with the enemy, save for the dark side of the boulder. Doubtfully, he unsheathed his riven and pitted sword, and using the ugly rock for support, made his way around its girth.

He would not survive. His kingdom would fall. His Nation would be unmade by the cunning words of the Vyresh. Many he had sought—in the Valaroma—to come to his people's aid, but at the last, he discerned that in one alone could the flower of hope come to full bloom.

Neither weapon, nor logic, nor argument, nor genius, nor glittering standard, nor Gods' might of Valaroma could save his people. For from the beginning to the end of time there had been only one from whom salvation could come, one who could deliver them—*"Prometheus,"* uttered the king through cracked lips as he rounded the boulder, startled by the sight of an emaciated man chained to the rock, his belly torn open, his glistening entrails coiled at his feet.

Prometheus Rising

15.1

"Yes…Lason. I am Prometheus," said the Lord, his head feebly rising from where it hung over his shoulder.

The king stood as one struck with horror, a confusion wrought of a vision both miraculous and terrible: a treasure long sought, and yet in the finding, unexpected and unlike to what could have been imagined. For distinct from the Valaroma, Prometheus was no more than a man, cruelly chained and nigh upon death.

His body, clothed in dirt and lividly marred, hung from shackles as though no strength were left him; a wound, gaping and raw, bespeckled him in gore and pooled at his feet.

"Lord…but how do you know me?" faltered the king.

"Often, to you I have turned in my thoughts, and in you I harbored my greatest hope. Though longer far have I endured my prison, long have I hoped for this moment, for though here I have been chained for ages now distant and lost, untroubled is my vision…."

Limping forward, his eyes darting over Prometheus and his bonds, "Then you know, Lord, your children are nigh their unmaking—though not from dearth of spirit or strength do we wane…it is our identity for which we want."

"This, too—I know," sighed Prometheus.

"Then of the Vyresh and their deeds you must also know," added the king hopefully. "You must know that your children…they are trusting of words…easily deceived…conquered by the agile tongues of their enemies."

The king swayed light-headedly, took his face in his hand and used his sword as a cane. "Masters of the lie!" he spat, rubbing his temples. "Your children are ensnared by ideas that work their undoing. Too long have my people harkened to crooked promptings.

"The Vyresh…they mingle truth with lies, and mercy with deception to sweeten the poison. Our glory is blackened by their cunning mendacity…thieves in the night…treacherous friends…foes without honor…corruptors of letter, word, and meaning…in all ways the Vyresh have recast your children as flawed and evil—only then to supply them with baleful ideas they swill as a liquor, crippling their minds…. And once besotted," choked the king, coughing violently, blood moistening his cracked lips, "once besotted, the Vyresh bring them willingly under the yoke, cursing them with doctrines that disfigure their will to survive, reshaping it into a desire for unmaking…the fruits of this evil the bewitched call atonement and just."

The Lord closed his eyes as memory swept him over the suffering of his children. "I have seen the Vyresh, Lason, so poison the people that like unto swine they follow their swineherd. And I have witnessed them goad their herds into great works of evil: corrupting the minds of Promethean children, coming with force of arms against Promethean champions…."

The chains binding Prometheus clanked as he shifted weight to his tired legs, the cuffs backing slowly from deep, bleeding gouges in the purple flesh of his wrists.

"I have kept your teachings," proudly declared the king, his fist held before his chest, "but too often and too easily have many submitted to the will of the enemy. Pompous, they hold their views, arrogant and disdainful in their condemnation of others, but not with reasoned judgment or wise council are they alight, for they are contradictions to nature…blights upon the body of our Nation…and when into wickedness their ideas lured them, I threw them down—gladly."

Silence gathered as the Lord struggled to remain conscious; his lids fluttered and his eyes rolled before refocusing on the king amid the darkness.

"In battle we thought you fell…," Lason whispered anxiously, pained by the Lord's suffering, "yet here you have been chained from that time to this…a grievous fate beyond words. By Airehdelle we learned that here you might be found, though dead or living she could not say, yet this I did not expect."

"In victory the enemy had not the power to slay me," said Prometheus, a faint grin curling through a wince, "yet in league, they had the strength to bind me. So perfectly they set my bonds that nothing save great effort and toil could break. But the chains assuaged their fears not, for they doubted their work and feared exceedingly the wrath of vengeance that, loosed, would find them—they feared justice, Lason—and thus they set upon me a Viciant, a devourer of my strength, a diverting of my attention, a wasting of my powers so that against them—I could not rise.

"Daily, it spills my life—and daily…time and effort I squander repairing the damage. If here I remain, shackled and burdened by the devourer of my strength…I will diminish…and death will take me as naught but a whisper."

"Viciants the Vyresh set also against your children," said the king, "enfeeblers that make difficult our resistance…many forms they take…many forms…," his words trailed as he drifted in thought to the brazen effrontery of Vyreshian duplicity.

"Gladly would I slay your Viciant, Lord, but the enemy is nigh. To conjure the Promethean Nation, to kindle its death shroud, I must free you, but I fear I have not the knowledge nor the strength. I know not the way, Lord. If these bonds you cannot break, your children you cannot aid; what chance have I of cleaving links that bind one so lofty?" asked the king, a note of rising desperation in his voice. "The enemy is upon us, and death wraps cold arms around me. Is there nothing that can set you free?"

"Strong are these chains, Lason, yet they are not unbreakable."

The king, suddenly overcome with quiet hope, his wayworn features filling with life, spoke eagerly against the growing urgency.

"If in me is this power, I shall grant it. To what will your bonds yield?"

"A key—I need—to unlock the chains," answered Prometheus.

"Where shall I find such a key?"

Mute was the Lord, as though the answer he wished not to speak, yet, sullenly, he raised his voice, "It cannot be found, Lason—for I must make it."

Joy fled before bewilderment on the king's face; his eyes narrowed, seeing not the stones on which they landed. "Long ago you would have fashioned this key…." said Lason, shaking his head.

In the silence that followed, a truth of unimaginable weight settled upon the king's weary mind, and he cast a tired glance at his grime- and blood-covered hands. Slowly and deeply he sighed, doubting himself and yet nonetheless reconciling himself to an impossible feat. Meeting the Lord's eyes, the king spoke with faltering poise and wishful confidence, "By what path shall I escape? What shall I retrieve you?"

"Clay…and Fire I also need."

"You speak of the Cosmic Clay…and the Fire of Life, Lord?"

Shifting weight to his shackled wrists, wincing as the cuffs dug into his flesh, Prometheus nodded.

"Where can they be found?" asked the king, confusion pinching his brow.

"They—cannot be found," answered the Lord, regret tinging his voice, "for long ago the last of each was joined in creation."

Now hopelessness ran like a winter's storm, a slanting rain of ice over the last hope in Lason's heart. As doubt yielded to confusion and confusion to fear, the distant scrabble of the enemy crawling over the precipice like a brood of swift-legged spiders, grey-shadowed by the starlight, woke the king to the approaching nightmare.

Presently, though they came not, waiting for their captain and the swelling of their numbers, the foe profanely taunted the king, demanding that he come from his hovel to see what they had done to the bodies of his men, describing the lecherous savagery they had inflicted upon Promethean women and children, detailing how they would torture him, letting him die not, prolonging his anguish as long as they might.

The number of their voices grew, and foul things about his Nation they cried: iniquitous allegations, horrid descriptions, and here, to the regret of the king, Promethean voices were not least among the barbarous choirs.

Too tired was the king to wield his sword, too weak was he to fight, for even his mind had faltered amid the shouts of the enemy. And yet, in that moment of deepest despair, a faint and distant thought occurred to him, a question that filled his darkening mind as the voice of a silver trumpet with the final summons of valor.

"Lord…is not all but the Gods made of the Clay?" he asked breathlessly, "and is not all that lives infused with the Fire?"

"Yes. All is of the Clay, and all that lives is infused with the Fire," said Prometheus, a knowing both of sympathy and grief softening the hard lines that long misery had carved on his face.

"Then in me is the salvation of my people," declared Lason, strength creeping once more into his weary body. "Am I not of the Clay? Is my life not of the Fire? Take from me to fashion the key—let my life unlock the chains that bind the Promethean Nation!"

In that hour, there was an undying change in the eyes of the Lord, a compassion and gratitude eternally joined, for though he was Prometheus Ethelleyah, the First and the Last, never had he witnessed a life so faithful, an act so noble, an end so beautiful.

"Place your hand in mine, and your will—shall be done."

Reaching, Lason paused, "Lord…my family…."

"Know this, King of the Prometheans—they will learn that for them you made this sacrifice, and of them were your final thoughts. To King Lason and the Arganantum, they and the Promethean Nation will sing dirge and praise, honoring your sacrifice and celebrating your victory—for your herald shall be none other than Prometheus Ethelleyah, and to the world he will bring the message of your glory."

Even as enemy soldiers amassed upon the shelf, even as their Vyresh captain crossed the precipice and signaled the order to advance, even as the deadly ring of drawn swords mingled with the taunting insults of the enemy, so too did Lason, King of Ananoël, Emperor of the Promethean Nation, set his hand in the hand of the Lord.

15.2

Lightning seared the midnight sky with such ferocity that its ghost throbbed as an angry vein across its dark waters. From the Lord fell the heavy chains that bound him, shattering like glass as they struck the rocky earth—a vision of victory to the departing king, a smile in his final thought as it winged away.

And behold! As a clear note that pierces the chill of night, sounding over sleeping hills and forgotten ways, Prometheus Ethelleyah rose from his prison.

Round his neck hung the *key*; gleaming and silvered, it gathered and rejoiced in the starlight and gave it back with a fire and pulse of its own, brilliant in its radiance. Extending his powers to conceal his freedom from the enemy Gods, Prometheus healed himself, and donning the threadbare raiment, sword, and shield of the king, he evinced his glory not, but kept the countenance of a man.

Stepping from the shadows, he strode toward the enemy. His sudden appearance was greeted with snide gaiety, for the foe mistook him for King Lason, a man nigh death and alone against the bristling weapons arrayed against him.

Threats and taunts pierced the enemy's raucous laughter. Their advancing line, now twenty feet from the Lord, slowed as their Vyresh captain pushed his way through their ranks: a sneer twisting his face, his lips curling in a boastful grin.

"King of *exploitation*, emperor of *oppression*," he bellowed, revealing crooked yellow teeth. "Crawl to me."

Prometheus responded not, but halted and stared at the Prometheans and those rich in their spirit.

"These, I will kill first—" he uttered, but the Vyresh captain, his mismatched features alight with invidious delight, scathingly cut over him, "Shut your mouth, *oppressor!*"

Catching sight of the key on a silver chain round the Lord's neck, gleaming amidst the forlorn visage, the captain barked with mirth, and then raised his graveled voice in covetous disdain, "That treasure *I* will have when we are through with you."

The enemy cackled and beat their shields with their swords, grinning wickedly at the Lord, but silence swept over their number when the stars gleamed suddenly the brighter, and Prometheus disdainfully answered their captain.

"This key you will not touch with your filthy hands, for it is the key to the hearts and minds of a people. Against it, no shackle may bind, no door remain shut, no hope withheld, for *it* is the deliverer of the Promethean Nation."

And lo! His shield he withdrew from under his cape, and it shone like the noontide Sun. So bright was the unveiling of the king's shield on the arm of the Lord, shadows leapt from the enemy as blackened cliffs laced by swift fjords of gold.

His sword he then withdrew, and like unto his shield, it gleamed fiercely in the chill of the night: a pale blue it seemed, in silver mist, as of crystal withdrawn from frigid waters, hissing with a voice shrill and menacing.

Recoiling and retreating through the ranks of Ganyah soldiers, condemning the Lord's unnatural blaze as the work of a bewitcher, the Vyresh captain ordered his men to kill the king.

As a man, Prometheus wielded sword and shield, but as a God, he slew the enemy. Heaving was their ruin, for like shorn wool the enemy fell in scattered heaps. Ere long, the soldiers followed their captain in haste down the mountain's face, for already was Prometheus in pursuit, and fear of his wrath, and shock of the king's sudden prowess turned the bloodthirsty foe into a flight of cravens.

As a red Sun lolled in the eastern sky, scores of carrion birds descended in great wheeling flocks upon the enemy dead, thousands in their number. So complete was the rout that naught but a howling wind, laced with the cries of the slain, returned to the kingdoms whence the enemy marched—a chilling omen to their Vyresh masters.

15.3

Prometheus looked upon freedom's first rising Sun, and there, against the backdrop of a pink-violet sky, he marked the approach of a great black vulture.

Heeding not the feeding frenzy, the bird closed with outstretched wings, and nigh Prometheus came to rest on the heavy bough of a dead tree. Queer was the glance of the dreadful beast, cocking its head to better see the Lord.

"I know not how to this place you came," it croaked in a coarse voice, "but I have come to burden you."

"Hear me, vulture," blazed Prometheus. "No longer will you devour my life, for chains no longer restrain me. Attempt it— and you will have earned your death. But force me not to take your life, for you are no Viciant.

"Once it was that you were a loyal friend and courageous warrior of the Valaroma, yet long ago you were bewitched by the enemy. Upon you was lain a veil of menace, so that friend you called foe and foe you called friend.

"And now, from you I shall take this veil, so that you may see all the days from that day to this, and to your mind will return the good that was eclipsed."

And even as Prometheus spoke these words, a coal black feather fell from the vulture's head, revealing a snow white feather below; watching it float earthward with a bemused curiosity, the vulture looked suddenly to the Lord, and tears unnumbered on waves of knowing swam in his sharp eyes.

"Once it was that you were called 'Aditon,' and by that name you are known again. But time is short, and we have much work before us, dear friend. In token of your sorrow, you may atone for your crimes with a faith and fanaticism unknown to the world, and though regret you shall ever feel, by such deeds your debt shall be repaid."

At once, and in secrecy, Prometheus and Aditon set forth to recapture the destiny of the Promethean Nation. It is thus recalled by the wise, that while all that was good and lofty in the world was succumbing to disease, a new and unexpected seed stirred in the Earth's womb, and leaping from the soil, gathered its father's light. Resistant to the contagions of the past, it flung leaf and branch and bough, and its trunk grew tall and strong and soon there were blooms, and cones of seeds there formed—and where those seeds when they fell, naught but time and growth would tell.

15.4

The sheer walls and garrisoned turrets of Ananoël eased not Anairyan's unquiet. For in the absence of his father, the Vyresh had assembled an alliance greater far than faded ink on tattered pages could recall.

Far seeing was Anairyan, however, for he let assemble a swift vessel, swiftest of the vessels of yore, fairest of the ancient songs, and most dear to those she bore to safe harbor. *Helain* was she called—that is, rill song: a white bird atop sunrise surf, a gem of matchless fire that sailed upon the glimmering waters as though borne aloft by lissome wings.

In the Epic of Ringelshum, it is told that Anairyan and the army of Ananoël vexed the enemy for many seasons: beleaguering the armies marching from distant lands to join the main Vyreshian host, seeking if they might to forestall the union of the enemy's forces.

Many battles were fought, and great victories were had, though the enemy was vast and the defenders were few. Nonetheless, the foe's preparations were brought to a close, and so marched the Vyreshian horde like the angry roots of a dark tree: knotted and wrinkled, blindly twisting and curling along the surface of the earth—cleaving soil, splintering rock, groping toward its feast.

No hope was there of victory, no hope was there of withstanding the tide that surged with pluming froth toward the city. And thus, Anairyan ordered the flight of the population, saying, "Look not too lovingly upon the works of your hands and minds, for these are but blossoms on the stalk that in you leaps for the Sun. I say unto you, this winter will pass—and spring shall come again! Look then beyond your tears and your grief; look to the first flowers of spring and the blooming of the white rose— for then you shall know our time is come."

As forty-three clans, besotted with grief and stained with numberless tears, the Ananoëlians fled before the enemy, sundered thus so that hope would lie with many. Ettahkarina, the forty-fourth clan, however, departed not; for at its helm, in the absence of the king, stood Anairyan, bravest of the elder days, wise as the serpent, cunning as the fox. With him remained the knights of his house, the Lore Masters, and as many knights as could be sundered from the departing clans.

The city Anairyan's family would not abandon until all hope was lost; for as the caretakers of the Promethean Nation, as the royal house, a duty far greater lay upon them, a duty that in the taking warrants the crown.

Few were the days to prepare for the foe, for even as the twenty-first day of the exodus waned, so came the Vyreshian hordes. In a guarded sleep the city lay, yet in her belly turned the gears of war. Aglow in the night's lightfall, Anairyan and his captains massed on a lofty terrace.

"Pity…the Vyresh should come on the moonrise," said Anairyan as he surveyed the enemy; Erson, a friend and war-hardened captain of the cavalry, standing by his side.

Turning his gaze to the hills that rose as a monstrous spine upon the somber sky, the enemy's countless torches filling the blackened plains at their base like swarming wasps—their wings afire, Anairyan whispered, "Where are you, father?"

"Perhaps he'll ride to our aid—with Valaroma at his back," bolstered Erson in his sonorous voice, smiling as one that fears not the throes of battle, but ever laughing in the face of danger.

A fierce grin leapt across Anairyan's young face, and dismissing his lingering doubts, he pivoted toward his assembled captains and ordered, "Then let us look to the skies in hope for

261

the king, but let us ready ourselves to meet the invader. And if death the Vyresh bring, then death they too shall find!"

Unsheathing his sword, Anairyan set upon the Moon a sacred mission: "Hear me, Night's Eye—long have we honored you as a work of our Lord, but I call you now to a greater purpose, for tonight you sit upon the vault as an observer of our valor.

"Sit not there a passive witness, but carry forward the memory of these valiants—their courage, their sacrifice, their love for the Promethean Nation. Whether wide your view or narrow your gaze, go to the Promethean on your wandering ways; remind him of our glory—be ever to him a divine scale, a weighing of *his* deeds against *ours*. Call him to his duty as we have answered the call; summon him to live for the Promethean Nation as gladly *we* have fulfilled that summons!"

Departing the palace, Anairyan and his men went forth to battle, and though a hope yet slim they held for the return of their king, never would they see him again, for even as they valiantly strove with the invader, the king and his Arganantum sped in all haste toward a lofty precipice—and a final hope.

15.5

All is said of the Battle of Ananoël and the Promethean exodus in *Arkalanta: The Fight of the Ananoëlians*. There, the histories of the forty-three clans are told, and there can be traced the seeds from which the Ananoëlian kingdom sprouted from the ruin of its fall.

Here is recounted naught but a sketch of the battle, for by cunning design and feats of courage that in ages thenceforth were exalted in song, Anairyan and his men brought ruin and death to the enemy.

Abandoning the outer walls when they could be held no longer, they lured the foe again and again, channeling them through infernos, districts of the city become prisons laced with leaping bars of fire. And when, at the last, no more could be done to save the city, a lofty dam was broken—a lake skinned with oil— and thus Ananoël sank under combers of fire, its proud spires toppling like white candles into the abyss.

So few were the Promethean defenders that the Lore Masters put down their quills and took up the sword, heroically aiding in all manner in the defense of the city and the evacuation of the women and children; by secret ways, these were brought to *Helain*, and there stowed in the deepest recesses amid great stores of goods, heirlooms, and the precious scrolls of the past.

In grave peril, though cloaked by the wrack of the city and the confusion and carnage inflicted on the enemy, Anairyan and his remaining knights came at length to the hidden ship. Loosing *Helain* from her moorings, they put off from her berth and sped for the mouth of Shantellise.

So sudden was the appearance of that swift and glorious ship—radiant as though a star set amid a sparkling stone burned in her breast—that the enemy was taken at unawares, reacting not in concert until *Helain* was beyond their reach. Yet danger the refugees had not escaped, for five enemy ships waylaid them beyond the coast, and there they would have joined the cold silence beneath the waves had it been not for the gallantry of *Helain's* sailors.

As two enemy vessels groaned and splintered under the pressure of the sea, and one lit red the low-slung mists, *Helain* sped beyond the pursuing grasp of enemy reinforcements. So marvelous was that vessel made, so great a mariner was Anairyan, and so timely was the providential wind that blew as a blessing from the Gods, that *Helain* outstripped all pursuit and was soon alone upon placid waters.

15.6

Now there came an evening on the fortnight following the rising of the full Moon while Anairyan stood upon *Helain's* prow, contemplating their course, plotting their doubtful future as exiles amid the tumults of the world, when he caught sight of a great molting bird wheeling athwart the heavens. And following with his gaze the raptor's path toward landfall, he espied a tall, hooded man in the wayworn raiment and cloak of a traveler; alone he stood, impossibly prominent atop the great white cliffs, sternly regarding the ship from the heights.

As a resonant music borne upon the winds, there issued the voice of the traveler, "Hail, son of the king—hail Anairyan; I am King Lason's herald, and to you I bring his message."

Therewith, as though he walked in a dream, Anairyan sent for this stranger, questioning not the eerie power of the herald's voice, or the unlikely chance that here they should meet. Manned by four marines, an agile craft he dispatched that landed upon the shore. There, the marines found the herald, hooded and giving not his name; nonetheless, cordially they retrieved their guest, and swiftly they returned to *Helain*.

For those who waited upon the ship, the Sun seemed to sicken, the music of the waters seemed to fail, for long they yearned for news of their king and his men, and yet they feared the arrival of a dark messenger, an omen of despair.

With a shower of chills washing over his body as though it were Death himself on whom he waited, Anairyan received the herald in the company of his closest kin, remaining captains and Lore Masters. Though they perceived not that the herald was indeed the Lord, a strange power globed and went before him as the winds that portend the storm.

Slate as an ominous statue, still as a pillar of marble, the gruff voice of Herald Prometheus spoke from the low hanging darkness of the hood. Yielding not his name but calling himself the *voice of the king*, he delivered the king's message amid the tears and wailing of the court.

As though from the gates of the city with the king he rode, the *voice of the king* a tale he told:

Of great battles and long weary ways…

And cold nights and blistering days…

Of the panicked flights and the wrathful pursuits…

And the combat of swordplay and winged-dart disputes…

His hearers swelled with pride and sank with sadness, tears of sorrow and tears of gladness. There were women who crumpled and men who frowned, but rapt by the tale they made no sound…

Of the deep bonds of their unending love…

And of the matchless deeds of fealty thereof…

Of the glories, the triumphs, and the renown…

And of the loss, the death, and the misery of the crown…

Of the musings of the men and their king…

And of their unbreakable oaths that knew naught but a spring…

And some as they listened to the floor they assembled, and others embraced, and others trembled, but Anairyan sat as though made of stone, though his high cheeks glistened and his keen eyes shone.

And the herald dazzled with tales Valaroma…

How victory with them was bittersweet aroma…

How against Gods of the enemy they drew sword and spear…

How narrow escapes, how purpose was clear…

And he spoke of the final hope to which they sped, though pursued by death and haunted by dread…

Of the end he told—of the end of their quest, bold though they were, so too were they blessed.

And here, the herald shared the final threads of his tale, for the king alone, last of that noble mission, came beyond all hope to the aid of the Lord. Pausing as the faces of his audience now beamed ever brighter with reverence and awe, wonder and joy mingling in eyes that glistened with tears and sadness, he told of the king's choice: a gift of his life to unlock the hearts and minds of the Promethean Nation—an act that broke unbreakable bonds, echoed the herald's voice eerily in the cabin, and the rising of Prometheus Ethelleyah!

At once, Anairyan leapt to his feet, pride and tears alight like the stars of heaven in his glance; from him had passed the pall of sadness as a cloud before the face of the Sun, joy in the cords of light as a music that dispels the mien of sorrow.

"My father!" cried Anairyan. "He died even as he lived! By his deeds, he has delivered us! Glory to the king! Glory to Prometheus Ethelleyah!" he shouted to the room as renewed tears

267

gathered in his tired eyes. And lo! All cried in a single voice: "Glory to the king! Glory to Prometheus Ethelleyah!"

Even as Anairyan's heart swelled with pride and gratitude, seeing in his mind all the memories of his father's days, even then the herald held aloft the king's gleaming crown—sparkspray adance in its radiance—and setting it upon Anairyan's head, bellowed, "All hail King Anairyan, King of Ananoël, Emperor of the Promethean Nation!"

With the crown were gifted Lason's raiment, shield, and sword as a legacy to his son, an honor so moving as nearly to bring Anairyan to his knees. All then bowed to the new king—save one only; for the herald bowed not, saying as one that speaks just beyond the breath of a whisper, "To one alone do I bow, for he was *my* deliverer."

And dropping the hood from his head, Prometheus evinced the glory of his divinity, filling the ship with a light as pure and radiant as creation.

"Yes," said the Lord in a voice as wide as the heavens and as deep as the seas, "I am Prometheus, bearer of King Lason's gift. In it is housed the healing and the hope of the Promethean Nation; in it resides a power that the enemy cannot surmount, for there is no darkness that can smother its flame, no night that can withstand its dawn!"

Helain glowed thenceforth, hallowed as it were by the touch of the Lord, a light upon the seas as if she were the Moon setting on mirrored waters, her sails as silvern clouds rippling against the breeze. On that blessed vessel, those of the forty-fourth house arose from the winter of grief, and turning again their proud faces toward the struggle of the living, sailed with purpose upon a journey set by the Lord, a course that would take them to the Bay of Aelumé, for there was harbored a new hope, a cryptic land, and a deep mystery whose hour had come.

The Waking of the Swans

16.1

This is the fashion whereby was made the habitation of Promethiea, the royal seat of the Promethean Nation—to which the Earth is the antechamber, and Vedyah its domain.

As Prometheus steered *Helain* toward the Bay of Aelumé, foam flying from her prow like the spray of snow before a mighty wind, the enchanted lands drew into view, a vision of bliss and mystery as though it were a divine music that had taken to itself form and profundity, wreathed by a crystalline light that had dawned before the ages of man, mantled by a beauty incorrupt and inviolable.

In the outlands dwelt Prometheans in various townships and petty kingdoms: descendants of earlier exiles—survivors of Vyreshian wars, infected with Vyreshian ideas. These folk rarely ventured into the enchanted lands, for to that place was connected strange tales, stories that spoke of bewitchments and snares. And they said the forests and waters therein *lived* as though spirits moved within them, and others spoke of haunting songs that laced the wood, revealing neither source nor purpose in their strains.

Their legends spoke of its magick, and their ghostlore of its riddles. Common was the saying, "Seven rivers mighty, and seven lofty peaks, seven bays aglitter, a land that lives and speaks." And many more peculiar stories were told by those who challenged the daunting mysteries, yet these intrepid few returned never to themselves, lending yet more credence to the eerie claims and frightful suspicions.

Into the Bay of Aelumé, the largest of the seven bays, sailed *Helain*, Prometheus and King Anairyan at her helm. Their voyage at its end, they anchored and put off in agile crafts, landing themselves upon the pristine beaches. It was then that Prometheus revealed to the king that the land had once served as his haunt— and that here he had veiled the most precious of treasures ere its light could be sullied by the enemy.

No longer the black vulture of his dark days as a tool of the enemy, the eagle Aditon, now as glorious as he had been when into battle he sped as one of the Valaroma, aided the royal house as they laid the stones of their first settlement by the shore. Prometheus and the king, however, set forth into the forest to seek the treasure that hidden in ages past had remained inviolate.

As a man, the Lord traveled on foot with the king, and to him he spoke of many things, both of the past and of what might yet come to be. Twenty-one days they journeyed into the forest, dressed in the wood's enchantment, a magick tangible as a heavy fog, yet utterly beyond the grasp of sight.

At length, on a night of brilliant starshine, the Lord and King Anairyan drew in upon a deep, dark lake: still as though shrouded by an unearthly peace, slumbering as though in the euphony of a dream.

16.2

So distant was the far shore that it receded beyond reckoning as the foggy limb on a vision inspired by the Gods, and so tranquil were the bewitched waters that the stars reflected not therein, appearing rather to glow in the depths as though the sky were a reflection of the water's beauty.

Spines of a verdant mountain, sinuous and tall, cleaved portions of the lake so that many inlets and bays lay hidden: night shadows draped as curtains over their mysteries. As threads of glimmering glass, lit silver by the night's fires, distant cataracts hurtled from the heights, piercing glistening clouds at their bases. Trees, silent and watching, foreboding and tall, crowded near much of the shore like aged sentinels.

Confusion gathered on the king's face as they approached the lake's edge, and in a hushed voice he said, "My Lord, why have you brought me to this slumbering place?"

Prometheus returned not the glance of the king, but stared fixedly over the waters.

"Before you is the Lake of the Swans; and beyond is Swan Haven—therein, the treasure resides."

No more did he say, nor would he say, as into the darkness he gazed.

The king, alone in his thoughts, gave first his attention to where he thought the distant shore must lie, but seeing not a purpose hidden therein, nor able to plumb the silent workings of the Lord, turned his attention to a streamlet dancing minuets by his feet.

Strange it was, for when to it he gave his thought, it drew him in, holding him, fixing him where he stood. Dark was the backdrop, though glistening was the water: astir with heaven's lights as though they too danced among the tiny ripples. A music he thought he heard, a music as a voice rising from the trickle.

"Do you hear—" he whispered when his voice failed. It was at that moment, in the slackening of his utterance as though sound itself was withdrawn from the world, that there bloomed a melody, distant as though it came across time rather than space, a song bewitching and profound, rich and glorious. And then—it was gone, gone as the sunbeam that cleaves the storm as a pillar of fire and is swallowed by darkness as quickly as it gathered.

With difficulty, he awoke from his fixation and stared into the blackness, into the abyss beyond the Lake of the Swans. A lure it seemed to him, drawing him into eternity, a mingling or a surrendering of his will, a fading as one breeze that joins another.

Greater was the song that rose against the silence, and more were the voices that sang from the darkness: an enchantment upon the air—and an echo that joined the music in rapture. As though he too climbed with the music, Anairyan felt his spirit rising with the crescendo of melodies, refrains that soared beyond hearing, gathering to their bosom profundity and fire.

Shivers as of waves of pleasure swept through the king, longing and strength twining like serpents within him; for the song grew and its power deepened, and soon the forest was alive with its life, thriving as though it were eternal and all else were caprice. And when the song he believed could grow no stronger, when no more the divine upon the air could climb, he saw them—like wraiths coming through the cloak of the night: bodies upon the water, white with an immaculacy beyond equal, grand as beyond grandeur, graceful as beyond grace. Swans upon the water, singing with the voices of gods.

16.3

And behold, hundreds of regal swans swept along the surface of the water, emerging from the shadows to greet Prometheus and the king.

"Their voices…they speak no words, but are like to the music of our lovely instruments…" breathed Anairyan, "yet—I can understand them…they sing a song of blessing and triumph…."

The king marveled at the swans as they sailed into the light, their numbers growing as they issued from the darkness. Then it was that Prometheus told Anairyan of the fall of Sentilleena, and he spoke of the houses that refused to flee, wishing rather to die with their Lord. And for the king he recounted the final moments when all was lost, how to these he gave the likeness of swans—of their flight from danger, and of their coming to Swan Haven.

All—he imparted not, yet enough he shared, for the king now understood that these were not swans, indeed, but Promethean men, women, and children who neared the shore, distant descendants of those who fled from strife on the order of the Lord.

As the waters filled with the fore of the Swans, the music ceased. Nine great Swans glided into the shallows, and they alone began a song of greeting and praise to the Lord. When at last these too fell silent, they lowered their heads as one who bows, and the king saw tremors on the surface of the lake, for tears of joy danced from their eyes.

Inclining his head, Prometheus cast a prodding glance to a vast greensward that joined the lake, and toward that shore the Nine departed. As they approached the water's edge, the woodland stirred from its slumber, a heaviness lifted from its shoulders, and there then rose the whisper of a breeze and the kiss of its touch— and eyes that finally fly open.

The forest took its first breath, its chorus rang out in clear voices, its leaves gamboled on their branches, and there stood nine Promethean men in the shallows, robed in white where nine swans had been—more majestic, more glorious than King Anairyan could have imagined Prometheans to be.

They marveled at the bodies they had long known in waking dreams, visions that saw them as truly they were: in their springs, their summers, their falls and their winters. And now they embraced and they laughed and they beckoned the others as they strode from the lake.

As to the shore more did swim, so too were they become Prometheans like none the king had ever seen, for these were Prometheans as the Lord had made them: like, but unlike— beyond in every measure.

"These are your elders; for you and yours are my younger children," said Prometheus.

"But how is it that we are sundered from them?" asked Anairyan, mystified, as he turned reluctantly from the Swans to the Lord.

"When into darkness my kingdom fell and misery devoured my children, the three Nations of man were come to be splintered: wanderers clinging to life amid the maelstrom of the world. No longer could my children ennoble themselves in the cruelty of that age, but choices they made that squandered their glory, unions that sustained life, but set their feet on gainless and guideless roads.

"Some there were—Promethean clans—that took *trophies* in their battles with Masule-azai and Sarraneem. Thus it was that small measure of their spirits entered into my creation. Over the span of many ages, these currents gave rise to you and yours—my younger children.

"A student you have been of Promethean lore. Clear are those tales when on highroads your sires walked, but difficult was the keeping of memory when into darkness their paths were plunged. Of the men wrought by Masule and Sairren—there is much that you know, for they were made in your despite, and the purpose in their making was *unmaking*—to extinguish the Promethean Nation. But these appeared not as they appear to you, for in their beginnings they were like to the Promethean. Their forms today—so different from your own—are the fruits of their choices and the fires within: a bodying forth of their spirits in flesh."

"Here lies bare the root of many questions," said the king. "Here is buried the cause—why in some we see a will to crime and a will to vice, yea, a will to self-hatred and unmaking; these appear Promethean no less than I, but in them burns a greater portion of malevolent spirit. This and our abandonment of the path to ennoblement have caused us to stumble. But we of Ananoël have

277

practiced Lambonnsie for generations. We have made virtue the choosing of mates to better our people."

"And so you should, good king—wise have you been in this decision, but never again can offspring my younger children and their elders bring forth—so great the gulf. And this too must be the mark for which my younger children need aim: an arrow that flies beyond the other Nations and peoples of man: a sundering that cannot be bridged by offspring.

"Ennoble yourselves, your spirit and your flesh. Go beyond in all things: in loyalty and in brilliance, in health and body and beauty—kindle these traits to such a fire that the unwelcomed are diminished by their glory."

Long the king waited in thoughtful silence as the Swans climbed from the lake, and long he pondered the truth now revealed. For in him and those of his like—their portion of malevolent spirit was dim; more like to the Swans were they, yet they were also distinct: Prometheans indeed, yet the younger children of Prometheus Ethelleyah.

16.4

When from the waters all had stepped and daybreak gilded the forest, Prometheus and King Anairyan led the ten thousands through the enigmatic wood, a train as it were of the sublime robed in white, musing when not singing, heedful when not mirthful:

voices as haunting as when swans they made their music, songs of enchantment as they had sung for eons.

As demigods the Promethean Swans appeared to the royal house, vessels of power and grace, as memories from before the fall of Sentilleena, bearers of intelligence, strength, and beauty rarely seen in part, never seen in whole in the younger children.

There, by the Bay of Aelumé, was built the king's pavilion, and there the Promethean Swans swore allegiance to the king. To the enchanted lands the king gave names, calling it "Promethiea" in reverence of their Lord, and he named it "Valhalanoria"—the seat of the Promethean Kingdom, "Illyshium"—the land of gift, "Aeden"—the sumptuous garden, "Azgard"—the Promethean fortress, and "Walhalumn"—the land of healing. Later, he gave it also the name, "Atavunyia-Atalanta"—the land of the secret way, and among the peoples of the world its names are manifold.

In that settlement by the shore, which later came to be called "Quinya," many of the Swans joined the Arvanyenne and Airasayah, and Lore Masters they also became, and a new king's guard the elder and younger children formed—the Arganantum, and a new army they assembled, calling it and its members the "Valhierim."

And thus, in years to come, though in ages now remote, the Promethean Kingdom rose from the enchanted lands as a mountain haloed by the eye of dawn, a music crowned by the gems of night.

The Reckoning

17.1

Blessed were the days of reunion, of elder and younger siblings united in the worship of Prometheus and the work of the Promethean Nation.

During that time, it chanced that an unnatural mist crept over a pale dawn, and a thunderhead borne upon thin cold winds was spotted by the sentries. As it passed—even beyond the long sight of the elder children—they perceived that Prometheus had gone.

None knew to what danger he sped, but by later account the truth of that errand was revealed. For while Aditon, the Swans, and those of the royal house toiled, while they carefully wrought the foundations for the harbor city of Quinya, Prometheus sought entry into Zeushin's capital.

Into such debauchery and weakness had Zeushin's kingdom fallen over the long years of its waning, slowly eclipsed by the growing might of Gorthang's empire, that Prometheus entered Natteley without concern, and passed without hindrance or detection into the royal rotunda. Unbeknownst to all, unperceived even by Zeushin of the high golden throne, strode

Prometheus as not more than the shimmer of heat atop a candle's flame.

Gathering himself behind the throne, he listened to the vulgar pleas of a belligerent—beseeching Zeushin for an indulgence. And he peered through the high-backed chair at the smug king, rendering authoritative decree as millennia before he had ordained that, in the name of *equality*, Prometheus would be masked, cloaked, deprived of his powers, imprisoned, and at last— murdered.

To his persecution, his memory stirred; his damnation as persecutor he recalled—persecution justified by the charge of persecution—and he lingered in thought on the treachery of those whose wicked intent they hid with noble façade.

The fires of vengeful anger, of righteous revenge, overflowed in his heart. And blasting into human form, armed with a spear as of glistening lightning, hissing and crackling with malice, he drove its killing shaft through the back of the golden chair, impaling Zeushin where proudly he sat.

The rotunda bawled with horror, and Zeushin howled with the voice of thunder and the shriek of infants. When the Royal Guards, suppliants, and councilors saw Prometheus step from behind the throne, and they beheld their mighty king spitting blood, eyes and mouth agape in livid horror, dying as a skewered pig, some turned to flee, others begged for their lives, but

Prometheus slew them all with naught but a thought: like raw meat hurled to the floor, their bodies thumped and slapped the polished stone—some sliding, others crumpling where they stood.

"This…is not…your way…Prometheus," panted Zeushin when he found his voice, shock contorting his blanched face as one who believes not his eyes, pinned to his gleaming throne as his gushing life stained amber its gold.

"My virtues—I gifted those who deserved them not. By those virtues I bound my hands. By those virtues I was easy to foretell. That was a weakness of which I have been cured," darkly whispered Prometheus as he took the crown from Zeushin's head, fingering it with disgust, and then willing it to dust.

Blood flowed freely from Zeushin's slack mouth as he studied Prometheus with disbelief: an unbelief born in part by Prometheus's impossible rising, a breaking of unbreakable chains and burdensome Viciant—chains and Viciant that anchored him to decay and death—but the larger part of his disbelief was given to the freedom with which Prometheus served his revenge.

"Without honor…Prometheus, you have delivered my deathblow…," gasped Zeushin, struggling to force the words over his twitching lips, his features growing wan with the quickening footsteps of death.

"Speak not that name, nor give it to my children; for to you and all enemies of my Nation—we are Vengeance!"

Prometheus positioned himself before the dying king, a hard sneer upon his face.

"You speak of dishonor—but suffering and dying for an ideal that serves not the purpose of life is the greatest dishonor. Too long for lofty principles did I needlessly suffer; too near to death did I come, yet I come today in the service of a new principle—loftier than they.

"Look now—fallen king—upon your undoing, for no greater honor is there than victory in the service of the Promethean Nation—no matter the deed." So declared Prometheus, contemptuous of the virtueless king who feigned to lecture on the acts of virtue.

And raising his arms as one who would take the throat of another, Prometheus let thoughts of angry light pierce the king, and up went Zeushin's dying cries, cries of anguish that split the dome of the Court Rotunda with the ferocity of their voice.

Stone dust trickled from the fractured vault and coated the corpse, giving it the appearance of a gruesome statue, a dire token and a deathless warning to all those who wish, or seek, or do ill to the Promethean Nation.

So it was that he who harkened to the dissembler of words and called virtue the plundering, the despoiling, the murder of Prometheus and the unmaking of his Nation, he who was the King of the Gods, he who was named Zeushin of the high golden throne—was dead, and this tale speaks of him no more.

But unfinished was the work of Prometheus, for he purposed to slay all who owned Zeushin as king—and to lay waste to the royal city. It is held that Prometheus took to himself the posture of a volcano, wreathed in smoke and crowned by fire; in that dreadful form he left not one alive, and of Natteley he made such a ruin that the mountains on which she had once reposed were become not but wrinkled shadows of their former majesty.

17.2

When to Quinya Prometheus returned, he told of all that had come to pass: of the razing of Natteley, the toppling of its king, and the slaying of those who to him were loyal. Yet he spoke also of the need to hunt and to slay all those of divine race who fought not for the Promethean Nation—be they sycophants of Gorthang, or chieftains of men, or misshapen monsters of desolate wastes.

Therefore, he awakened in Aditon the want to rouse the Valaroma, to bring them the news of the downfall of Natteley, and to kindle them to the work of killing the enemy. Therewith, Aditon took to the airs, and the beating of his mighty wings, and the upward rush of his going was like to the tempest upon the shore. And his cry, clean and strident, rang through the airs as a hastening doom unto the foe.

It was then that Prometheus urged the king to speed the Arvanyenne to the kingdoms of the world, and there to challenge Vyreshian power: to rouse to wrath and galvanize to duty, to turn the Promethean against his Vyreshian overlord.

For this onerous task—with few exceptions, the king selected Promethean Swans, for their numbers were far greater than those of the royal house, and they had an unsullied light that welled within them. Possessors were they of not merely genius and power beyond all others, but to them was retained a hardihood and skill unmatched in the world. By the arts of their cunning, they cloaked themselves when from the enchanted lands many parties went forth—dressing down their glory, appearing as not more than the younger children.

Nigh after the Arvanyenne went forth, eleven of the Ananoëlian clans were returned to their king, for the clans in their wanderings—what by their fortuitous contact with the Arvanyenne, what by the assiduous efforts of the king's scouts, were brought to the enchanted lands and there returned to the circle of the crown.

17.3

Far and away from Promethiea, in the distant land of Harlutt, Gorthang sat upon his black throne in the heart of Ashgar, a great hall now black-stained by fires that burned impure without end, ribbed sallow with light thrown from gore-coated windows, and resounding with the screams of his tortured victims.

In this madness, he learned of Natteley's fall and of the fate of its Gods, and he received unwillingly the news of the great hunting parties—of Valaroma cleansing the Earth. He knew then to be more than fancy what long he dreaded—even from his first aggrievement against Prometheus: he knew then that the hour had come for the Lord's revenge.

Fear as he had not felt in millennia sprinkled as drops of freezing rain down his back, tightening his throat and drying his mouth.

"Kill him," Gorthang whispered, but then vaulting to his feet, his body rigid, his face twisted by fear and rage—he screamed, "KILL HIM!"

His panicked howls shook the pillars of Hell, and like ants driven to frenzy, languid and tortured Harlutt burst to life with the preparations for war. Never before and never since has an army so large and so cruel been assembled; for Gorthang marshaled and unleashed his entire empire—the Army of the Damned: evil Gods and evil men, beasts of burden, machines, monsters, and slaves amassed as a single column, thousands abreast and stretching like snake scale beyond the horizon.

True indeed was the course Gorthang set for his horde, for he recalled that in ancient times Prometheus would often repose in the enchanted lands, and there he surmised must Prometheus and his Nation be gathered.

17.4

Even as the Army of the Damned marched as a quickening avalanche toward Promethiea, drinking the rivers dry and eating the fields bare, Prometheus departed once again. And again, where he had gone none knew at that time, for he left in haste and without warning. Yet a dire warning he left, indeed, in the heart of the king.

To unmake you, they come.

None foresaw the size of the Vyreshian force. Verily, had Anairyan and his men envisioned the enormity of their foe, their preparations might have been otherwise, for the enemy had assembled a force some five hundreds to one, and with these came Gods and monsters of their making.

Yet, against the overwhelming storm, the Prometheans established strong places along the borders of the enchanted lands. Supply lines they ran, bulwarks they raised, and scouts they dispatched. Postured with an aggressive vigilance, they awaited the coming of the Damned.

Here now was set the grim stage, the pieces thereon speeding to bloodshed. Of this hour, when light gathered against darkness, much has been written, much has been put to song, yet in the enchanted lands—even to this day—in its hallowed halls and in its sacred places, the Lore Masters most reverently intone: "So rose the Army of the Lord to do battle with the Army of the Damned."

Vast were the lands over which the enemy trod, and long was the wait, but the wait was not peaceful; for battles, of which this tale tells naught, were fought between Promethean outlanders, calling themselves the Unsworn, and Prometheans in the service of crown and Nation. The former, led by opportunists and those fanatical in Vyreshian doctrines, refused the king's invitation of union, seeking rather favor with the Vyresh than service to the king and emperor of all Prometheans.

Favor they sought, but death they found; for, though many battles were in doubt until their very end, the Prometheans loyal to crown and Nation defeated the foe, the Swans slaying the enemy with an ease like to be seen in a contest between men and children. Those who perished not were scattered as seeds on nimble currents, and their wasted lives were delivered to oblivion.

So fell—as they should—the Unsworn, the ingrates: heirs of the Promethean Spirit, yet thankless spoilers of its heritable gifts—its prowess and legacy.

17.5

Inscribed in Promethean scrolls and aged books is the tale of what none dared imagine during those ominous days; for Prometheus Ethelleyah went to the Vyreshian horde, numberless and on the march, and with a cold glance he passed them by, and he went on to Harlutt, bridging its borders as one possessed by righteous purpose, and further he sped, to the precipice of Sargorthang, and he crossed the city's boundary without notice, and coming at last beyond all deceits and snares envisioned and set by Lord Gorthang—he arrived at the gates of Hell.

In the pit of Gorthang's wailing lair, red flame alight and ashen smoke coiled, two leering guards, Gods, grotesque and black-skinned with soot, armed with great scythes, flanked their darkly brooding king upon his ebon throne.

Queer they thought the spectacle of two proud and undaunted peacocks—white and scintillating as virgin snow—slipping between the wide doors of Gorthang's vast hall. Before them, the evil recoiled and the gore receded as toward the throne they marched, and with them loomed an enigma as of dark clouds twisting in the heavens.

Their steps were measured, their gaze upon Gorthang, irresistible in their advance. Thus the devil, tasting the air with his forked tongue, was beguiled, entranced by the exquisite purity and delicate puissance amid the blood-stained horror of his demonic chamber.

When the pair drew near the throne, up sprang their great white fans, shimmering as though webbed by ice and lightning. So frightening, so ominous was the display that Gorthang leapt from his seat and cast open his leathern wings, and like storm clouds fingered by crimson bolts, they reached for roof and walls.

"See now, wretched birds, my display is greater than yours!" derisively shouted Gorthang in a coarse and ugly voice.

But unmoved were the peacocks, for there they stood before the menace of the devil, harbingers of a doom he had not the power to stay.

Derision gave way to doubt, and doubt to fear in Gorthang's heart, and throwing back his head, his mouth agape in a scream riddled by cinders, he unleashed a torrent of fire as a climbing pillar that struck the lofty ceiling with its fury, loosing rivulets of flame that surged across the charred expanse of the dome.

As the fires died, the screams of those chained to the walls rose like the shrieking ghosts of its fading embers, but the peacocks were unmoved.

"Crush their skulls," ordered Gorthang as he returned to his throne.

In unison, the guards raised their scythes as though felling wheat—but, suddenly, a voice as of silvern trumpets rang through the halls of Hell, reaching even to its nethermost recesses. And a light there was upon the words, pure and powerful—and it filled Gorthang's lair with its radiance: "I am Vengeance—for you I am come!"

As a rising star amid the forlorn pits and despairs of the wretched citadel, Prometheus raised his will and the great doors of the hall were felled, toppling like crumbling mountains into the sea. As the wreck's throbbing echoes lost their voice, a white light shone through the tapering cloud of dust, and striding therefrom in his raiment of war—Prometheus the Lord.

Unquenchable horror washed over Gorthang. His eyes gaped and he hissed like a cornered viper. Pointing a crooked finger at the Lord, and gasping as one who sinks into a watery grave, he conveyed his will to his guards.

Stepping forward, they leapt into the air with the shape and whisper of a liquid flashing to steam, and in that form they sped toward Prometheus. But to him they reached not, for suddenly they reappeared by the will of the Lord, and crashing to the floor, their eyes rolled in their heads, and their heads rolled on twisted necks.

Onward, past their lifeless bodies, Prometheus strode, and from his throne Gorthang threw himself in fear. Prone upon the floor of Hell, he begged for pardon with a strangled voice, naming Prometheus *king of the world*, and promising him eternal servitude.

But this was no more than feint, for Gorthang suddenly rose to his knees, and from his fingers cracked torment and pain, yet with his glance alone, Prometheus repelled Gorthang's will.

Again, Gorthang flung himself to the floor, groveling, cursing himself and his actions, promising gifts to the Lord, gifts and more gifts, and begging for his life even as the peacocks withdrew from his presence.

As Prometheus drew nearer the throne, a second time Gorthang broke his word, and with naught more than a thought he opened a fiery chasm beneath the Lord, purposing to entomb him under the earth, yet the Lord fell not; and walking upon the air in the midst of heat vapor, marched on as an inexorable doom, a revenge that could not be restrained.

And a third time Gorthang threw his face to the floor, begging for mercy, blaming others for his misdeeds, naming himself the *victim*, and offering aid to Prometheus, offering his talents and his powers as a boon to the Lord.

And for a third time Gorthang betrayed his word, unlocking the shackles that bound the tortured upon the walls, compelling them to waylay the Lord. At once, the army of cripples, mephitic with the rotting of their flesh, wormed their way to their feet.

Screaming with feral voices, they bared blackened teeth and unshorn nails as toward Prometheus they lurched. But even as these feckless monsters advanced upon the God of Gods, their beating hearts were stopped by the Lord, and so in one stroke they were felled like marionettes cut from their strings.

Yet again, Gorthang was unvaliant, begging for his life as a craven, a tyrant even to the end: cruel and merciless to the lower, cringing and fawning to the higher.

"Pity me! Have mercy!" begged Gorthang from bended knees, but the Lord glared down with neither pity nor mercy.

"I am not to be blamed, Prometheus…of my plight, *I* am a victim…. If ill I have done, it is to be blamed on conditions that were not of my choosing, nor would I choose…I crave redemption…salvation…. Will you not deliver me?"

"Vile is your spirit, and vile is your flesh, Gorthang," said Prometheus with a savage air. "You have consumed the fires of others to prolong your own. And now you are become a vision of the black thoughts that churn within you. In your gut, you could hoard Vedyah, and still you would die—alone in the void."

"Please, Prometheus," pleaded Gorthang, meek as ruthless he once had been. "I am weak and you are strong…no hope have I of resisting your wrath…please hear me first, my Lord."

Prometheus tilted his head as memory swept him back over eons; somewhere, these words he heard before. A suppressed grin curled the corner of his mouth, and he nodded assent.

Drawing a methodical breath and dissembling his mind, Gorthang said: "You are indeed *great*, Lord Prometheus, the most powerful of the Gods, but are you not also the most honorable?

Have you not spoken on the duty of obedience to the rule of law? Would he that speaks thus act as judge, jury, and executioner? Nay, you are no liar, Prometheus.

"Solemn you were when you declared the importance of sympathy for one's fellows; and setting yourself as a paragon of virtue, you demanded universal observance. Surely, now, Prometheus, one so principled would not blacken his name with hypocrisy. One so observant would brook not transgression—not from his fellows, nor from himself, nor would he punish those who are victims of currents beyond their control.

"Are you not, Lord Prometheus, the most peaceful? Is it not also true that the heart of Prometheus feels more acutely, more deeply the suffering of others? Are not your sympathy and your compassion for all living things unequaled, Lord? Are you not the most forgiving and charitable? Indeed, if it were not for your charity, Prometheus, there would be no Vedyah.

"Would he who has preached the virtue of clemency give no quarter? Would he of long sight lose his vision in anger? Would he of courage succumb to cowardice? Nay, you are more compassionate than the cruelty that would kill me, keener than the ignorance that would slay me, braver than the cowardice that would murder me.

"I crave no more than like you to be, Prometheus—to create as you have created, to delight as you have delighted, to repose as you have reposed. My path was foolhardy, but folly and hardship gave me birth and weaned me on misery. My intent was noble, but misfortune made unwise my choices and perilous my life. Will you then make of me—twice a victim?"

And with these words, Gorthang began to cry as one who has suffered injured innocence: tears lingering over his blackened skin, pitiable sobs of despair. Behind the visage of a child he then hid his demonic form: a daughter of a people endlessly pronounced to be endlessly oppressed.

As one who consoles another, Prometheus stepped behind the artifice and placed his hands on its shoulders.

Tilting her head so that her eyes met the Lord's, her quivering voice, young and mournful, spoke through copious tears, "Please…I meant not for all this…I meant not to cause such pain…I wish to make amends…I am repentant. Can you not forgive me? I swear, I will never—"

"All that you said of me is true," interrupted the Lord, his voice warmer than it had been. "I am a champion and defender of every principle of which you spoke, and yet above them I have enshrined another; for though they are undiminished, they come now second to the survival and triumph of the Promethean Nation."

In his fist, the Lord took its long, dark hair, and a hard edge returned to his voice, "Only when by it is held the greatest power does evil wear no mask; when short of this the evil falls, a mask it wears—of civility, of innocence, of victims, of thralls."

Screams and tears drowned not the voice of the Lord as he lifted the false child by its hair.

"You named me Prometheus, but to you and all enemies of my Nation—we are Vengeance!" And swinging forward a gleaming blade, he slit its throat.

Red, gushed the blood; and it danced upon the air, clutching at the deep wound, unleashing a gurgling scream.

"No more taking the shape of children and the poor—*champion of equality...downtrodden victim!*" mockingly shouted Prometheus as he threw her to the floor.

And so it was, for Gorthang appeared no longer as an innocent, injured and wronged, but as the monster beneath the fair semblance.

Clambering to his feet, a leer of the deepest and most demonic hatred contorting his face, his hand held over his throat where thick, black blood as the sap of ugly trees spluttered between his fingers, he looked into the pitiless eyes of the Lord—and therein saw his doom, for the eyes of Prometheus began to glow, and the light therein was an unquenchable fury.

The eruption of that fire boiled Gorthang's flesh and spirit, and his was said to be an agony and death more deserved than all others. As to naught he withered, he unleashed a final gurgling scream of such boundless anguish that it yet resounds as a wandering ghost upon the shores of Vedyah.

When, at last, the devil was no more—the earth shook, and the hall trembled, and Ashgar collapsed as a hill of spiders, scrambling for their lives, writhing in their death pangs.

17.6

While no herald carried the message of Gorthang's death, his demise was felt, nevertheless, by the Gods in the Army of the Damned.

Fearing punishment for their many crimes, some Gods forsook the march, while others fought for dominance—and dominance was gained, and the march continued, for their hatred of Prometheus and the Promethean Nation was undiminished by the death of their tormentor and king.

Short was the reign of their new king, and shorter was the next; in the absence of honor and common bond, a bitter struggle, born of jealousies and hatreds, avarices and lusts, fermented in the hearts of the evil Gods.

Most cruelly were the Prometheans treated by their Harluttin countrymen; for though they had been Gorthang's loyal slaves, champions of Vyreshian screeds, virulent enemies of the Promethean Nation, they were nonetheless held to be Promethean. Though their thoughts they could disfigure, their viewpoints they could alter—their countenance they could not change. Their relation to the villains in the Vyreshian narrative of history, a narrative to which they pledged their lives, made inescapable their gruesome fate.

In the wake of the upheaval, the regular outbreaks of *revenge* committed against the hated Promethean minority were doubled—and then trebled. In Harlutt, Sargorthang, and even in the Army of the Damned, the remaining Prometheans and those rich in their spirit were raped, maimed, and murdered—nigh unto the last.

Straightway, dissension arose amid the mingling ranks of the thronging horde, exceedingly diverse in its character and nature; for the hatred that each faction held for the others was now kindled to a great storm of fire in the absence of the Promethean people—in the want of that group which united the others in a common hatred of a common scapegoat.

Both in Harlutt and in Sargorthang, there arose numerous factions that vied in bloody civil war: furrowing the earth with swords, watering the furrows with blood. It was from this bedlam that Prometheus sped to join the Valaroma as a hunter of evil Gods, ignoring the plight of Prometheans who were suffering now the consequences of their misbegotten loyalties.

To contest the growing disorder, the Gods in the Army of the Damned were moved to greater and more vicious forms of vigilance and punishment. It is held that the eyes of the evil Gods were always upon the men below them: observing, probing, questioning. Always were they cruel, yet never so cruel as when inward they turned their gaze to staunch the discord and punish the infighting, to hold together the pieces that of their volition would fly to the winds.

Yet, despite the fissures that now grew deeper, now wider, the Army of the Damned pressed on in the service of its innate purpose—to unmake the Promethean Nation. But where once it swelled in its procession, forcing into arms the young and old of townships along the march, the army now dwindled. Many of the evil Gods still fled when they might, and disparate factions of men erupted into conflict, and so killed one another by the thousands, or fled into the wild, refusing to fight as allies with those for whom they now felt nothing but enmity.

So it was that the glut of the damned slowly waned, and yet mile after mile they marched, relentlessly, feverishly, maniacally, advancing and abating, trundling and dwindling. And yet still their numbers were beyond the counting of the Promethean defenders, who stood now at their battlements awaiting the deluge.

17.7

Tidings of the enemy came by way of Promethean scouts. These bore grave reports of a foe beyond counting, of men, and Gods, and beasts. Nonetheless, the Protheans hardened their resolve and readied themselves for war. Four long days they suffered under a cloud of dread, until at last—the Army of the Damned crested the horizon.

About King Anairyan were gathered his men, arrayed in forms both sublime and terrible. From their fortifications, they gravely looked upon their far-flung rival. No more was the enemy a force without end, but no more likely were the Prometheans to prevail; for even the dreadful magnificence of the wrathful Promethean would avail them not against such a numerous foe.

With the baying roar of a sable horn, the enemy ponderously lurched, gathering speed as it spilled like blood from a wound on the horizon. And thus, toward the Army of the Lord surged the Army of the Damned, surging with a feral bloodlust, surging as a great wave, climbing as a dark wall of water that blots out the Sun, casting its menacing shadow upon the Prometheans under its toppling fold. And yet—even as the destructive wave crested the nigh hills, its frothing eyes falling at last upon the gleaming Promethean defenders, its spirit and its might were broken.

And there the enemy foundered: turning this way and that, refusing to press on, drawing sword, spear, and dart on one another—fleeing for their lives. It is written in the ancient lore, and still sung in Promethiea today, that the Promethean defenders—as though in a dream lifted from the trammels of the world to the azure of the heavens—watched the enemy devour itself upon the hills: man against man, God against God.

Yet, from strife the gallant defenders would escape not, for from the mêlée emerged those afflicted with the purest venom of hatred for the Promethean Nation. Evil men were they, wicked beyond all reason, and with them came lowly Gods and raging monsters. In their veins writhed a desire that naught could satisfy, naught could assuage, naught but the unmaking of the Promethean Nation.

The Hymn of Ang-rokk tells of the two armies speeding across the plain: the forces of the Damned like mudslide, those of the Lord like liquid gold. In the van of the Army of the Lord raced the king upon his white steed, and behind him danced the proud banners of the Promethean Nation. A thunder there also was, of hooves in the thousands, a wail of the horns of war, and a gleam like to fire ablaze on burnished mail.

Rarely have armies on the field of conflict felt more loathing for their foe. So raving and so long in the coming had been this fight that the clash of arms rang with a ferocity and savagery as to make pale all others. But none could have foreseen what there befell, for the Army of the Lord swept over the foe as a fleeting rain passes down the winds of spring, and in its wake soars a renewing Sun, a gilded roof of young leaves, and the fresh scent of lands bathed clean as a flowered laurel on the glory of victory.

The Hiding of Promethiea

18.1

At length, Prometheus returned to Promethiea, and there he saw the grisly wrack of the enemy.

Too near had the last hope of the Promethean Nation come to its demise, and thus the Lord of Lords reached forth with his thought, and winged therein was the force of his will, and he freed Promethiea from the trammels of the world, making of it a vast island beyond the Earth, and yet part of the Earth, so that the health of the world was its health, and the life of the world—its life.

Raising his arms, Prometheus slowly brought his palms together, wedding Father and Mother Earth under Promethiea, making whole what eons past he had torn asunder.

As calm the division had been, so now was the union violent; for the histories of Father and Mother Earth were different, such that the lands, seas, and airs were fraught by great tumults as of cataclysms and upheavals—birth pains, as it were: where forests darkened and mountains climbed, where plains unfurled and canyons fell, where oceans swelled and rivers drained.

One there was where two had been, and upon its face was carved, incomplete, the separate stories of their lives.

It is said that the Earth's tumult unsettled the moorings to which man had fixed his place, bringing him to his knees yet again. Life, therefore, was become no more than brutish and short: the eclipse of ease, the erasure of much accumulated knowledge and wisdom.

It was during this upheaval that the remaining thirty-two Ananoëlian clans were gathered and ferried by the Gods to Promethiea. A wracked Earth they left behind, yet over the span of the next age, the world was renewed. Life abundant sprouted from the waning convulsions, and beasts wandered wide and long that, until the union of the world, had no place in memory or song in the lives of men.

18.2

Having united Father and Mother Earth, Prometheus set sail in an oarless vessel over the quiet waters of the Lake of the Swans. With him was King Anairyan, and together they sailed by the Lord's will to a hidden entrance amid the mountain's fingers, beyond which lay a treasure of surmounting beauty; for untouched by the miseries of the world, unburdened by the afflictions of time, untarnished by the hands of evil was the fair country of Swan Haven.

There, the king beheld a bowl, as it were, vast beyond measure, formed of the surrounding mountains. In the midst of that bowl was a green and thriving country, wide spaces as of downs, jaunty with the voices of many rills, and ancient forests climbing tall and deep into the foothills. Urged by the prow of their vessel, the clear waters lapped the shore as a loving hand caressing a child's face, and disembarking, they tasted the fragrance of many blooms gamboling in the air, and they harkened to the bright songs of many birds.

As gift and memorial, Prometheus wrought in that place the palace Rhovanya, named in memory of fair Rhovannion. Tall and glorious was that exquisite palace so that it harkened back to the splendor of Qwindellin; and in time, round its base grew like the flowers of spring the homes and cathedrals of Helaewen—the royal city. So sublime did that city become that it was as a mirror on the beauty of white Sentilleena.

All that could be said of Cindillin's Vale could here also be said of Swan Haven, for to the beauty of that country, Prometheus put his powers and reared there a place of surpassing loveliness: of ornamental gardens, fountains and showering falls, pearlescent in their mists; of little birds, lissome on slender wing; of perfumed winds borne from flowering lands; of lush grasses, soft and fragrant; of pure waters, glittering like rippling glass; of nourishing rains gleaned from sunlit seas; of lofty mountains dusted with sparkling gems; and of star-, moon- and sunlight, swimming in the spray of waterfalls.

The palace chambers and the city squares were as treasuries, rich with the cunning works of Promethean minds, laced by the artistry of Promethean wit and creativity. Not few were the quiet places under bough and nigh brook, nor few were the ornate courtyards that ribboned the regal city: places of reverie, solace, fellowship, and repose.

Thriving in the work of their labors and mirth, the Protheans grew wise and resplendent in Promethiea. Salubrious works of the mind were lovingly tended by their careful hands, which lay never idle, for they were a dauntless and formidable people, their Promethean Spirit unbridled by the reins of a Vyreshian ideology or master, unburdened by a Viciant plow or people.

In these happy days there grew also a love as a rosebud springing to bloom, its fragrance as hope and blessing upon the kingdom, for King Anairyan had taken to himself Ellowyn, a woman of transcendent beauty, a loveliness matched only by her acumen and piercing glance.

Theirs was a grand wedding, and not least among the celebrations marking the birth of the young kingdom. A son and then a daughter were born to the king and queen, and many more sons and daughters they brought forth in the joyful years that followed.

On the birth of their ninth child, Prometheus bestowed the sacred key to King Anairyan, naming it Iynedelin—the Mark of The King, to be an heirloom to all kings of the Promethean Nation.

Much has been put to song in the years since Anairyan took the throne in Rhovanya, but felicity serves as its own record while it yet endures, and only does it pass into lore when ousted by hardship. Thus, little here is written of the blissful flight of love and light, the genius and splendor that in this dawning age—took to the airs in the land of Promethiea.

18.3

The union of Father and Mother Earth laid vast lands between the Nations and peoples of man. In those regions that once joined Promethiea, nigh all of the surviving Prometheans were gathered. Here, the sea washed against new shores, and though a Promethean could lift his eyes to distant islands—broken free when from the world the enchanted lands were taken—Promethiea he could not see.

No longer could Promethiea—now spirit of the Earth—be reached by those bound to the flesh of the Earth, save only by the secret way that lay hidden beyond the sea. For this reason, an age after the world returned from upheaval, King Voden, a descendant of Kings Lason and Anairyan, ordered the construction of a harbor city, Emrelei, to be built where once the enchanted lands joined the Earth: to ferry all those who by their service to the king or beneficiary of his grace were granted passage.

By those of Promethiea, the Prometheans of the world and those rich in their spirit were given a new name, for the title Promethean they reserved for those who honored the debt and allegiance of their Promethean birth, serving proudly the will of the Promethean Crown. In honor of King Anairyan, who spoke adamantly on the need to return to the world, to come as counselor and caregiver to the Prometheans thereon, the Prometheans of the world were thenceforth called "Anairyans."

Many there were among the Anairyans who feared Emrelei, believing it to be a bridge to the afterlife for the accursed, saying that the cry of gulls that roosted nigh its wharfs was in truth the cry of tormented souls. That harbor, and the statue of a Promethean knight that stood astride the gates of its strait, proud and formidable, the Anairyans called "Worgül," and they said the ships that sailed therefrom sank into the mists, ferrying their woebegone cargo to the underworld.

Verily, the wise hold that often the benighted see sickness in health and health in sickness, damnation in salvation—and salvation in death.

18.4

To the world, Prometheus and Valaroma often went in great hunting parties, tracking and slaying—even to the last—the

Gods that had served not the Promethean Nation. Yet rarely did they depart after the last of these had fallen; for age crept upon them even as love for the bliss of Promethiea bloomed within them.

Nonetheless, the flesh of the Earth was still trod by visitors from the spirit of the Earth; Lore Masters there were, most numerous among those who came forth, but also Arvanyenne and Airasayah, and Valhierim, and many others. As teachers and mentors, prophets, healers, and messengers they went to the Anairyans, though the Anairyans often saw them as gods—or the heralds of gods; and here they guessed well-nigh the truth.

The return to the flesh of the Earth by the Prometheum— Prometheans loyal to the Crown—was governed by King Voden's decree:

"Where aid and counsel are deserved, aid and counsel shall be rendered. None shall be forced to recognize the Crown, and no punishment shall be rendered those who break with the trust— save only the denial of aid and counsel."

Thus, in years beyond reach of Anairyan memory, the Anairyans who harkened to the Prometheans grew wise, and sometimes powerful. Yet wisdom alone served refuge not to the power lusts of rulers; for having come to power, most recalled not their beginnings, most recalled not to whom they owed their ascent—or the ascent of their families—and looking then upon the Lore Masters as naught more than clever magicians, rejected their counsel and broke with the trust.

18.5

For generations after the end of King Anairyan's long life, Promethean children marveled at the Gods who abic across their lands. Rarely were they seen, and thus all the more dazzling did they seem. Yet, as the leaves of autumn fall each in their turn, so too did the Gods of the Valaroma surrender their lives to the ages. In time, only Prometheus remained of all the Gods who ever were, though perhaps not the last of all the Gods who ever will be.

In the waning years of his life, Prometheus spent many hours in a quiet study, putting his copious admonitions to paper, giving counsel to the king and Lore Masters, speaking and writing on every facet of life: detailing the last of his many instructions for the mastery and destiny of the Promethean Nation.

It was during these years that Prometheus finalized the Promethean Law, both the written and the oral, and it was here also that he spoke on the design by which he might foil the finality of death. Little is written in these pages of his last days, for that tale is told in lamentations beyond count, in dirges without end, in scriptures awash in numberless tears.

Yet of the final moments this tale does recount, for the whole of Promethiea gathered round the palace, and their vault was a pristine blue, and the Lord spoke his final words from a lofty terrace: "It may seem that you are draining the cup of sorrow, but I ask you to recall your tears, my children; for I will not leave you. Observe my teachings as sustenance of the spirit, a dedication not less than nourishment of the body with victual and libation—and life, mastery, and destiny shall be yours.

"In you I shall abide, and together—in a distant future—we will come again to see with our own eyes, and hear with our own ears, and dwell in a paradise of our making; there—together—we shall reign as Gods."

As Prometheus spoke these final words, he smiled an unbounded love that yet remains an embrace upon Promethiea, and then he entered the blood of the Promethean Nation. There, he yet resides as the Source, as a Voice and a power, awaiting his rebirth and resurrection in the ripening of time—in the ascension of his children to divinity.

18.6

In the years following the passing of the Gods, the might of the Anairyans waxed, yet their power was divided, for there was little unity and many rulers.

Nonetheless, this weakness would have served not to topple their achievement had it been not for the presence of an insidious disease—an ancient sickness that wormed from the dank meres of the distant past, proliferating amid the dark corners of their kingdoms, for it was during the rise of the Anairyan empires that the Vyreshian plague returned.

Like the Prometheans, the teachings of their maker lie in their making, and therefrom find form in action; no more does the spider need lesson to spin its web, or the scorpion need instruction to deliver its venom, than the Vyresh need doctrine to be a plague unto the world.

So it was that the Vyresh grew again as a dark and lurking menace, ebbing hither and flowing thither, gathering and dispersing, waxing in power and waning when discovered. As before, they took many names, and rewrote their histories, and stole the histories of others so that no people could match their claim of oppression, of entitlement, of victimhood.

And when no god answered their pleas for world domination, for the subjugation of the peoples of the Earth, for victims on which to sate their lust and their greed, they made a god of the teachings that rose as vapor from the core of their being: teachings wrought in their making as impulse, as instinct, unforgettable and ever renewing, and from that day to this—they solemnly worship.

Even as the Anairyans spread themselves in glory, benevolence, and victory around the world, the Vyresh were quietly boring into the meat of their kingdoms, claiming for themselves seats of power. By way of that power, they empowered others of their kind, and so loomed from the shadows as a calculating foe, ever pursuing the exploitation and weakening of their hosts, ever pushing the limits of their hosts' hospitality.

Ensconcing themselves like the parasite that digs barbed legs and serrated mandible into the flesh, they cunningly maneuvered the Anairyan powers against one another, positioning themselves to gain from the conflicts. By after-knowledge it was revealed that during this period the Vyresh made a most unfortunate discovery, for by chance the devil's grimoires—the Megeela—were discovered.

Of the darkness whence came the Vyresh, the grimoires spoke, and they worshiped that darkness in the vain hope that therefrom the author would come, but when he returned not, they made of his written word an idol. And using Gorthang's writings of secret conquest, for the mission they revealed, for the insights they bequeathed, for the "proof" of divine leadership the Vyresh saw in them, they plotted their wicked course.

When in the wheeling of long years the Anairyan Empire was realized, and the Anairyans ruled the world from seats lofty and magnificent, the Vyresh struck from within like the viper that springs from the leaf-litter. Short was the Anairyan reign, for by cunning and craft, the Vyresh usurped the leadership of the

Anairyan powers, secretly uniting under their control what the Anairyans had left divided.

Like a sickness that rides on the air and disfigures the mind, the menace of the Vyresh spread, and with it the enslavement of the peoples of the world—and thus the death of the world; for the Vyresh know not the beauty of the Earth, nor cherish its wonders, but seek ever to rape and profane the Earth in the filling of their bellies.

Against their evil, the Promethean king and emperor, Aiyahf Avarden, issued a new decree:

"The flesh of the Earth is the antechamber to the seat of the Promethean Crown—Vyreshian Rawgna will not be tolerated. I, Aiyahf Avarden, King and Emperor of the Promethean Nation, order the Anairyans to honor the debt and duty of their Promethean birth, to pledge themselves to the Crown, and to retake their destiny.

Aid I will render with the wisdom of the Lore Masters and the strength of others as I see fit. But should the Anairyan Prometheans fail to reclaim their destiny, I will come forth in might of arms; a great war I will unleash upon the world. The skies I will blacken and the lands I will drown, and save for those who served our Nation, I will leave not one to mourn the passing of mankind.

The cataclysm I will then subdue, and a golden age in which the Earth is renewed shall follow. In honor of their service to the Crown, I will gift the new Earth to the Anairyan Prometheans, and they shall have it for a home, a treasury, and a garden. Their heroes I will elevate, and they shall rule the Earth's flesh as my regents."

Even now, on the order of the king, Lore Masters tread the lonely roads and bustling cities of the Earth's flesh, seeking for the worthy, seeking for those who will pledge their lives to the king, seeking on ancient lands with young names: America, Germany, England, Australia and more, for wherever Anairyans are under the spell and threat of Vyreshian power—they are come.

At last, in the final days before Rawgnarokk, they are come, come as harbingers of mercy and redemption to all those who will but take their outstretched hands.

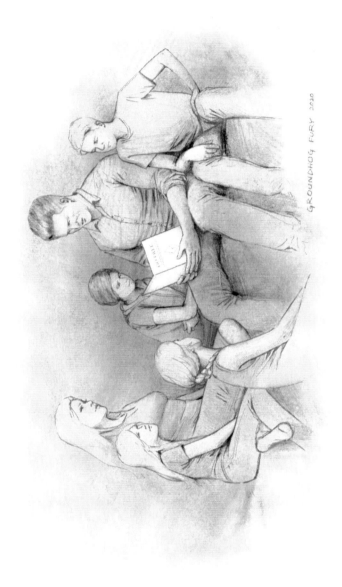

Glossary

- **Accalobain-Iedolin** (/ˌækəloʊˈbeɪn ˈiːdoʊlɪn/)—War of the Heavens.

- **Adamanta** (/ˌædəˈmæntə/)—One of the wisest, noblest, and hardiest houses of the Promethean Nation.

- **Aditon** (/ˈædɪtɒn/)—A God of the Valaroma that had been made to forget his identity and thereby serve as a Viciant to Prometheus.

- **Aeden** (/ˈeɪdɪn/), **the sumptuous garden**—One of the names given to the Promethean Kingdom.

- **Aemriel** (/ˈiːmriːɛl/)—One of the wisest, noblest, and hardiest houses of the Promethean Nation.

- **Airasayah Arvanyenne** (/ˈɛərəˈseɪə ˌɑːrˈvænjɛn/), **The Knights of Prometheus**—These were warriors of both the shadows and the battlefield.

- **Airehdelle** (/ˈɛərədɛl/)—A Goddess of the Valaroma who adopted the Prometheans as her children and thus was a mother to them. Also named the Lady Airehdelle, Airehdelle-Alass (/ˈɛərədɛl əˈlæs/), the Mother, and Goddess Mother of the Promethean Nation.

- **Aiyahf Avarden** (/ˈaɪjɑːf əˈvɑːrdən/)—The current king and emperor of the Promethean Nation.

- **Alaywinne** (/əˈleɪwɪn/), **dream wraiths beyond the borders of the dream**—Title taken by the original Prometheans (those created by Prometheus) once they gave birth to their own children.
- **Amunakkie** (/ˈɑːmuːˈnɑːkiː/)—One of the names given to the Prometheans by the Masule-azai and Sarraneem.
- **Anairyan** (/əˈnɛərɪən/)—King Lason's son and successor to the throne.
- **Anairyans** (/əˌnɛərɪˈɛns/)—The name given to Prometheans on the flesh of the Earth who were yet to pledge loyalty to the crown.
- **Ananoël** (/ˈænənoʊˌɛl/)—The city and Kingdom of the Ananoëlians (/ˌænənoʊˈɛlɪəns/).
- **Anuaum** (/ˈɑːnuːˌɑːm/)—One of the names given to the Prometheans by the Masule-azai and Sarraneem.
- **Arganantum** (/ˈɑːrgəˌnæntəm/)—The King's guard in Ananoël and later in Promethiea.
- **Arkalanta** (/ˈɑːrkəˌlæntə/), **the Flight of the Ananoëlians**—A book recounting the history of the forty-three clans following the fall of Ananoël and concluding with the gathering in Promethiea.
- **The Army of the Crown**—Zeushin's army.

- **Arn-gelwain** (/ˈɑːrn ˈgɛlweɪn/)—A region upon the marches of the Hon-Drowgleer, where the Prometheans fought the Masule-azai.

- **Arnum** (/ˈɑːrnʊm/)—A God of the Valaroma who died at the Battle of Arn-gelwain.

- **Arreth** (/ˈɛərɛθ/)—A god in the shape of a great worm.

- **Arvanyenne** (/ˌɑːrˈvænjɛn/), **Order of Air and Fire**—An order, likely established by Prince Lason, to surveil and study the Vyresh, to alert the public to their pernicious activities, and to work to expel them from Promethean kingdoms.

- **Ashgar** (/ˈæʃgɑːr/)—Gorthang's palace, also known as Hell (/hɛl/).

- **Atavunyia-Atalanta** (/ˌætəˈvuːnjə ˌætəˈlæntə/), **the land of the secret way**—One of the names given to the Promethean Kingdom.

- **Attalass** (/ˈætəlæs/)—A soldier in the Arganantum.

- **Awakening**—The moment the Promethean Nation came to life.

- **Aydemenocs** (/ˈeɪdɛmɛnɒks/)—The kingdoms built by Promethean genius on the labor of the Masule-azai and Sarraneem, who worshiped them as gods from distant stars.

- **Azane** (/əˈzeɪn/)—A god in the shape of a great worm.

- **Azgard** (/ˈæzgɑːrd/), **the Promethean fortress**—One of the names given to the Promethean Kingdom.

- **Balarre** (/ˈbælɑːr/), **Gorthang's bane**—A God of the Valaroma in the shape of a great wolf.

- **Battle of Ananoël** (/ˈænənoʊˌɛl/)—The Vyreshian attack on the city of Ananoël.

- **Battle of Arn-gelwain** (/ˈɑːrn ˈgɛlweɪn/)—The great battle between the Prometheans and the Masule-azai.

- **Battle of Fallowsgate** (/ˈfæloʊzgeɪt/)—The great battle between the Prometheans and the Sarraneem.

- **Bay of Aelumé** (/ˈɛluːˌmeɪ/)—The largest of seven bays in the enchanted lands.

- **Beings of Light**—A name the early Prometheans took for themselves.

- **Black Forest**—Dwelling of Prometheus.

- **Bringers of Light**—A name the early Prometheans took for themselves.

- **Chargaroth** (/ˈtʃɑːrgɑːrɒθ/)—Masule's country. Called this name by the Gods, it was also called Mumndeeb (/ˈmuːnˌdiːb/) by Masule's children.

- **Children of the Dawn**—A name the early Prometheans took for themselves.

- **Cindillin** (/ˈsɪndɪlɪn/)—Spirit of the Stars in the Promethean tongue. Specifically, the river in Cindillin's Vale/the Vale of Cindillin.
- **Clangshee** (/ˈklæŋˈʃiː/)—One of the names given to Oradüme by the Sarraneem.
- **Coming of the Source**—When Prometheus joined his children in Cindillin's Vale.
- **Cosmic Clay**—Matter inchoate.
- **Dranggist** (/ˈdræŋˌgɪst/)—A powerful member of the Valaroma.
- **Draug** (/drɔːg/)—What the Vyresh called Ganyah who obeyed and respected the Gods of their people and the wisdom of their elders. It means unclean in the Vyreshian tongue.
- **Dred Villam** (/ˈdrɛd ˈvɪləm/)—Criminal opportunists who aided the Vyresh.
- **Dunvaigan** (/ˈdʌnˌveɪgən/)—The name given to the corpora that followed Illurillion, containing the lore of the Prometheans.
- **Dwarin** (/dwɑːrən/), **of the house of Callunsey** (/ˈkæluːnˌtsiː/)—A Promethean who died at the Battle of Arn-gelwain.

- **Effacince** (/ɪˈfeɪsɪns/)—The mask Prometheus was forced to wear.
- **Elaylinne** (/ɪˈleɪlɪn/)—Valindeal's wife.
- **Ellowyn** (/ˈɛloʊwɪn/)—King Anairyan's wife and Promethean queen.
- **Empress Ewer**—A name the Ananoëlians used for the mother of the Vyresh.
- **Emrelei** (/ˈɛmˌrɪleɪ/)—A harbor city on the flesh of the Earth. Constructed on the order of King Voden.
- **The enchanted lands**—Dwelling of Prometheus.
- **Epic of Ringelshum** (/ˈrɪŋgəlʃʊm/)—The tale that tells of Anairyan's battles against the many factions of Vyreshian forces that attacked his city.
- **Eredain** (/ˈɛərɛˌdeɪn/)—A Promethean who held his dying son, Felori, as he died at the Battle of Arn-gelwain.
- **Erson** (/ɜːrsən/)—A war-hardened captain of the Ananoëlian cavalry.
- **Essiyah** (/ɪˈsaɪə/)—A cult of childlike fanatics that behaved as though the eyes of Gorthang were always upon them; worshipers of the Vyresh as a means to obtain Gorthang's blessings.
- **Es-tay** (/ˈɛsteɪ/)—A God of the Valaroma who died at the Battle of Arn-gelwain.

- **Ethelleyah** (/ɪˈθɛlɪjɑː/)—The name given Prometheus by the Nine. Saying, of Prometheus with this name, that he was both the Voice and the Source.

- **Ettahkarina** (/ˈɛtəkæˌriːnə/)—The royal house of King Lason.

- **Councilor Fador** (/ˈfeɪdɔːr/)—A God who was a member of the Royal Council.

- **Lord Faiden** (/ˈfeɪdɪn/)—A God of the Valaroma and the Captain of the dragons.

- **Fallowsgate** (/ˈfæloʊzgeɪt/)—An inhospitable land composed of enormous rents in which the Battle of Fallowsgate was fought.

- **Farr Rohthemebrienne** (/fɑːr roʊˈθiːmbrɪɛn/)—The name of Airehdelle's palace in the underworld.

- **Felori** (/fɪˈlɔːriː/)—A Promethean who died at the Battle of Arn-gelwain. Son of Eredain.

- **Fens of Hhóm** (/hoʊm/)—A boggy land in Oradüme.

- **Fingonne** (/ˈfɪnˌgɔːn/)—A God of the Valaroma who died at the Battle of Arn-gelwain.

- **Finloth Aëta** (/ˈfɪnlɔːθ ˈeɪtə/)—An ancient text that tells of King Lason's odyssey with his Arganantum.

- **Flames of Life**—Life inchoate.

- **Friends of the Wraith**—Gods that were loyal to Wraith-Prometheus, who formed the Valaroma.

- **Galmunde Ümber-mane** (/ˈgælmuːnd ˈuːmbər meɪn/)—A Promethean who died at the Battle of Arn-gelwain.

- **Ganyah** (/ˈgænjɑː/)—The name Gorthang and the Vyresh gave to all nations and peoples who were not Vyresh. Ganyah means beasts of the field with the forms and tongues of men in the Vyreshian tongue.

- **Genosiliant** (/ˌdʒɛnoʊˈsaɪlɪənt/)—The cloak Prometheus was forced to wear.

- **Girdle of Cindillin** (/ˈsɪndɪlɪn/)—The mountainous ring around Cindillin's Vale.

- **Gorheerim** (/gɔːrˈhiːrəm/), **folk slay**—The killing of Promethean by Promethean when such a killing does not serve the good of the nation.

- **Gorthang** (/ˈgɔːrθæŋ/)—Father of the Vyresh.

- **Graw** (/grɔː/)—A Promethean, Razorum captain who died at the Battle of Arn-gelwain.

- **Grong** (/grɔːŋ/)—A God, and master of Sairren's great worms.

- **Halrod** (/ˈhælrɔːd/)—A Promethean, Razorum captain who died at the Battle of Arn-gelwain.

- **Halumae** (/ˈhɛluːˌmeɪ/) **and Orluna** (/ɔːrˈluːnə/)—Members of the Friends of the Wraith who visited Prometheus in the Hon-Drowgleer.
- **Harlutt** (/ˈhɑːrlət/)—The country of the Harluttins (/ˈhɑːrlətɪns/), in which the Vyresh built their capital.
- **Harvestmen**—A name the Ananoëlians used for the Vyresh.
- **Hathem** (/ˈhæθəm/)—Captain of a legion of the Royal Guard.
- **Heelaw** (/ˈhiːlɔː/)—Those who were credulous and easily deceived by the Vyresh.
- **Helaewen** (/hɛˈleɪwɛn/)—The royal city in Swan Haven.
- **Helain** (/həˈleɪn/), **rill song**—Anairyan's ship, which he and his house used to escape the devastation of his city.
- **Hon-Drowgleer** (/ˈhɒn drɑʊˌɡlɪər/)—An extensive mountain range of wastes and hidden beauty, also called Drowfear (/ˈdrɑʊfɪər/), Teddelmarnahr (/ˈtɛdəlˈmɑːrnɑːr/), and Kawcus (/ˈkɔːkəs/).
- **Horn of Sarpidon** (/ˈsɑːrpɪdɒn/)—A horn used by the Arganantum.

- **The Hymn of Ang-rokk** (/ˈæŋ rɒk/)—Tells of the battle between the Army of the Lord and the Army of the Damned.

- **Illeera** (/ɪˈliːrɑː/)—A God of the Valaroma who died at the Battle of Arn-gelwain.

- **Illumenyiar** (/ɪˈluːmɪnjɑːr/)—Cradle of Awakening in the Promethean tongue. So named by the Nine in Illurillion. This was the name given the greensward where the Prometheans awoke.

- **Illurillion** (/ɪluːˈrɪlɪən/), **The Voice of the Fathers from the Fount of Creation**—Written by the nine with contributions from other Prometheans, these were the histories and folktales of those who woke from the dream to the splendor of the stars and the radiance of the dawn.

- **Illyshium** (/ɪˈlɪʃɪəm/), **the land of gift**—One of the names given to the Promethean Kingdom.

- **Iynedelin** (/ˈaɪnˌdəlɪn/), **The Mark of the King**—The key that freed Prometheus. Additionally, worn by the kings of the Promethean Nation as the mark of legitimate lordship.

- **Izad** (/ɪˈzɑːd/)—One of the lays that told of the flight of the Prometheans through the underworld.

- **Kaluva** (/kɛˈluːvɑː/)—A God of the Valaroma who died at the Battle of Arn-gelwain.
- **Kristelyn** (/ˈkrɪsˌtɛlɪn/)—The first name the Prometheans gave to themselves, which signified "life that is lit by the light of many stars."
- **The Lake of the Swans**—The mystical lake on the borders of Swan Haven.
- **Lambonnsie** (/ˈlæmbənsiː/)—The choosing of mates for the improvement of the Promethean Nation.
- **Lands of Fire and Ice**—Dwelling of Prometheus.
- **King Lason** (/ˈleɪsən/)—Patriarch of the House of Ettahkarina and King of Ananoël.
- **Lay of Farr Rohthemebrienne** (/faːr roʊˈθiːmbrɪɛn/)—A tale, written in the form of a poem, about the journey of King Lason and his men in the underworld where they met Airehdelle.
- **Limbalin** (/ˈlɪmbəlɪn/)—A God of the Valaroma in the shape of a dragon.
- **Longest Night**—The devastation of the world after Accalobain-Iedolin.
- **Lore Masters**—The keepers of Promethean Lore, wise counselors, messengers. A tradition created by the Alaywinne Nine, who were also the first Lore Masters.

- **Loyalad** (/ˈlɔɪəlæd/)—A Promethean who died at the Battle of Arn-gelwain. Brother of Winnom.
- **Maker**—Prometheus.
- **Marmakk** (/ˈmɑːrmæk/)—A Promethean, Razorum captain who died at the Battle of Arn-gelwain.
- **Masule** (/maˈsuːl/)—Father of the Masule-azai.
- **Masule-azai** (/maˈsuːl əˌzaɪ/)—Masule's children.
- **Masulian** (/maˈsuːlɪən/)—Of or relating to Masule and his children.
- **Megeela** (/mɛˈgiːlɑː/)—Books of conquest written by Gorthang and given to the Vyresh.
- **Mongzching** (/ˌmʌŋˈʃiːŋ/)—Sairren's capital city.
- **Moorlin** (/ˈmɔːrlən/)—One of Valindeal's aids, specifically his adjutant.
- **Morren** (/ˈmɔːrɛn/)—A God of the Valaroma who died at the Battle of Arn-gelwain.
- **Mouth of Cindillin** (/ˈsɪndɪlɪn/)—The location where the river issued from under the mountain.
- **Mumndeeb** (/ˈmuːnˌdiːb/)—The name given Chargaroth by Masule's children.
- **Natteley** (/ˈnætəˌleɪ/)—Zeushin's city on Mount Neldoren.

- **Mount Neldoren** (/ˈnɛldɔːˌrɛn/)—The mountain on which Zeushin built his kingdom.
- **The Nine**—The first nine men that Prometheus fashioned and to whom he spoke in the beginning.
- **Odindayne** (/ˈoʊdɪnˌdeɪn/)—A God of great prowess and member of the Valaroma.
- **Odiun** (/ˈoʊdɪən/)—The unmeant; these are the races of man that are the mixtures of the nations of man.
- **Oradüme** (/ˈɔːrəduːm/)—Sairren's country.
- **Orb-weavers**—A name the Ananoëlians used for the Vyresh.
- **Oulvleer** (/ˌuːlˈvlɪər/)**, those who keep the silent path**—A name the early Prometheans took for themselves.
- **Planter**—Prometheus.
- **Promethean** (/proʊˈmiːθɪən/)—Of or relating to Prometheus and his children. In Promethiea, it is a title reserved only for members of the Prometheum: those loyal to the Promethean Crown.
- **Promethean Law**—Laws for the governance of the Prometheum, as well as guiding moral principles for Prometheans. The Law contains both written and oral elements.

- **Prometheum** (/proʊˈmiːθɪʌm/)—The community of Prometheans who are loyal to the Promethean Crown, individually and collectively. Additionally, the name of Promethean places of worship.

- **Prometheus** (/proʊˈmiːθɪəs/)—Father of the Prometheans.

- **Promethiea** (/proʊˈmiːθɪˈə/)—Chief name of the Promethean Kingdom. Named thus in honor of Prometheus.

- **Queen Whore**—A name the Ananoëlians used for the mother of the Vyresh.

- **Quinya** (/ˈkwɪnjɑː/)—The first settlement by the shore in Promethiea.

- **Qwindellin** (/ˈkwɪndəˌlɪn/)—The Promethean palace in Cindillin's Vale.

- **Raddigan** (/ˈrædɪˌgæn/)—A Promethean who died at the Battle of Arn-gelwain.

- **Rawgnarokk** (/ˈrɔːgnəˌrɒk/)—The final battle when King and Emperor Aiyahf Avarden returns to the world to destroy all but those loyal to the Promethean Crown.

- **Razorum** (/rɪˈzɔːrʊm/)—The Promethean army.

- **Remlokk** (/ˈrɛmlɒk/)—A Ranger captain in the Promethean army.

- **Rhovannion** (/roʊˈvænjən/)—The palace in Ananoël.
- **Rhovanya** (/roʊˈvænˈjɑː/)—The Promethean palace in Swan Haven.
- **Rizoria** (/rɪˈzɔːrɪə/) **Rangers**—An elite branch of the Razorum.
- **Rofayn** (/roʊˈfeɪn/)—One who has committed Rofaynem.
- **Rofaynem** (/roʊˈfeɪnəm/)—Spirit-stain, essence-profane. Committing the act is Rofaynem; one having committed the act is Rofayn.
- **Root Mother of the Vyresh**—A name the Ananoëlians used for the mother of the Vyresh.
- **Royal Council**—Ruling body under King Zeushin.
- **Royal Guard**—Zeushin's personal guards.
- **Sahnderring** (/ˈsɑːndərɪŋ/)—The fragmenting of the Promethean Nation.
- **Saipist** (/ˈseɪpɪst/)—A Vyreshian woman who created a universalist screed that undermined the Ganyah. Also, a follower of her screed.
- **Sairren** (/ˈsɛərən/)—Father of the Sarraneem.
- **Sargorthang** (/ˈsɑːrˌgɔːrθæŋ/)—The capital city of the Earth in Harlutt, during the height of the Vyreshian empire.

- **Sarraneem** (/ˈsɛərəˌniːm/)—Of or relating to Sairren and his children.

- **Sauouel** (/saʊˈuːəl/), **the "healer"**—A God of the Valaroma who died at the Battle of Arn-gelwain.

- **The Seat of Hell**—Great hall in Ashgar.

- **Sentilleena** (/ˈsɛntɪˌliːnɑː/)—The Promethean city in Cindillin's Vale.

- **Sentinels of Darkness**—A name the early Prometheans took for themselves.

- **Councilor Seraficc** (/ˈsɛərəfɪk/)—A God who was a member of the Royal Council.

- **Shantellise** (/ˈʃænˌtɛliːs/) The river that ran through Ananoël.

- **Shie-kawa** (/ˈʃaɪˌkaʊə/)—One of the names given to Oradüme by the Sarraneem.

- **Silver Ring**—A circle of nine created by the Alaywinne Nine to carry on the tradition and role of the Nine.

- **Siren Spiders**—A name the Ananoëlians used for the Vyresh.

- **Source**—Prometheus.

- **Swan Haven**—Hiding place of the Swans, and later the location of Helaewen, the royal city.

- **Sythzehar** (/ˈsɪθsəˌhɑːr/)—Battle of the Dragons at/near the Battle of Fallowsgate.

- **General Theelien** (/ˈθiːlɪɛn/)—A God, leader of the Army of the Crown.

- **Thowwister** (/ˈθaʊɪstər/)—A Promethean general in the service of the Vyresh who led a revolt against them.

- **The Unsworn**—The Prometheans who refused the invitation of the king to join the Promethean Nation in its struggle for wellbeing.

- **Üntamieren** (/ˈʊntəˌmiːrɛn/)—One of the lays that told of the flight of the Prometheans through the underworld.

- **Valaroma** (/ˈvæləˌroʊmə/), **Riders of Vengeance**—Gods that were loyal to Prometheus. Also called the Faithful, the Incorruptible, the Banner Bearers.

- **Valhalanoria** (/ˈvælˌhæləˌnɔːrɪə/)—The seat of the Promethean Kingdom. One of the names given to the Promethean Kingdom.

- **Valhierim** (/vælˈhiːrəm/)—The Promethean army.

- **Valindeal** (/ˈvælɪndiːl/)—A member of the Nine and the royal commander of the Razorum.

- **Vamp Spiders**—A name the Ananoëlians used for the Vyresh.

- **Vedyah** (/ˈvɛdjɑː/)—The cosmos.

- **Vengeance**—The name Prometheus demanded that all enemies know him and his children by.
- **Viciant** (/ˈvɪʃiːənt/)—A devourer of strength, attention, wealth, etc. as a means to cripple an enemy. The first viciant was the vulture that weakened Prometheus daily.
- **Vielem** (/ˈviːləm/)—The execrable crimes: Rofaynem and Gorheerim.
- **Villam** (/ˈvɪləm/)—Criminal opportunists who aided the Vyresh.
- **King Voden** (/ˈvoʊdɪn/)—A king of the Promethean Nation who ordered the construction of a harbor city on the flesh of the Earth called Emrelei.
- **Voice**—Prometheus.
- **Councilor Vrass** (/ˈvræs/)—A God who was a member of the Royal Council.
- **Vyresh** (/ˈvaɪrɪʃ/)—The people created by Gorthang.
- **Vyreshian** (/vaɪˈrɪʃɪən/)—Of or relating to the Vyresh.
- **Vyreshian Rawgna** (/ˈrɔːgnə/)—Violence/dominance by the Vyresh.
- **Walhalumn** (/waːlˈhaːlʊm/), **the land of healing**—One of the names given to the Promethean Kingdom.

- **Wardens of the White Fire**—A name the early Prometheans took for themselves. This name was chosen for the reverence they held for the stars.
- **Web-weavers**—A name the Ananoëlians used for the Vyresh.
- **Captain Weenchen** (/ˈwiːnˈtʃæn/)—A Sarraneem captain who renounced the war against the Prometheans, taking many Sarraneem with him.
- **Wenya** (/ˈwɛnyɑː/)—One of the wisest, noblest, and hardiest houses of the Promethean Nation.
- **White Council**—A body of leaders (numbering in the hundreds) of the Promethean Nation, serving to augment the Silver Ring.
- **Winnom** (/ˈwɪnoʊm/)—A Promethean who died at the Battle of Arn-gelwain. Brother of Loyalad.
- **Worgül** (/ˈwɔːrˌguːl/)—The name Anairyans gave to the harbor city, Emrelei.
- **Yawahns** (/ˈjɑːwɑːnz/)—One of the names given to Oradüme by the Sarraneem.
- **Zeushin** (/ˈzuːʃɪn/)—King of the Gods.
- **Captain Zouween** (/ˈzuːˈwiːn/)—The Sarraneem captain who, after the departure of Captian Weenchen and one-fifth of their Sarraneem forces, led the

remaining Sarraneem into battle against the Prometheans.

Pronunciation Guide

Phonetic transcriptions are provided next to glossary terms using common IPA (International Phonetic Alphabet) conventions for English. See the key on the next page.

All phonetic transcriptions begin and end with a forward slash. For example: Ananoël (/ˈænənoʊˌɛl/).

Stress is indicated by the primary and secondary stress characters ⟨ˈ⟩ and ⟨ˌ⟩ respectively. An example of their use is seen in the phonetic transcription of the word **intonation**: /ˌɪntəˈneɪʃən/.

Vowels

ɒ	bl**o**ck
ɑː	p**a**lm
ɑːr	st**ar**
æ	c**a**t
aɪ	p**ie**
aʊ	h**ow**
ɔː	d**aw**n
ɔːr	d**oor**
ɔɪ	b**oy**
ə	comm**a**
eɪ	p**ay**
ɛ	dr**e**ss
ɜːr	n**ur**se
ɛər	squ**are**
ɪ	k**i**n
iː	s**ee**d
ɪə	com**edi**an
ɪər	n**ear**
ɪɛ	V**ie**nna
oʊ	g**o**
ʊ	f**oo**t
uː	f**oo**d
ʌ	str**u**t

Consonants

b	**b**uy
d	la**d**
dʒ	**g**iant
f	**f**an
g	**g**et
h	**h**ind
j	**y**es
jə	can**yo**n
k	**c**ra**ck**
l	**l**ie
m	**m**an
n	ca**n**
ŋ	sa**ng**
p	**p**o**p**
r	**r**ace
s	**s**un
ʃ	**sh**oot
t	**t**ie
tʃ	**ch**eese
v	ha**v**e
w	**w**ine
z	**z**oo
θ	**th**ink

Other

ˈ	primary stress
ˌ	secondary stress

343

14547533R00203